LITERATURE AND ...
THE CHICAGO PUBLIC LIBRARY
400 SOUTH STATE STREET
CHICAGO, ILLINOIS 60605

endangered species

a novel

endangered species

a novel

louis bayard

alyson books
los angeles | new york

ALL CHARACTERS IN THIS BOOK ARE FICTITIOUS. ANY RESEMBLANCE TO REAL INDIVIDUALS—EITHER LIVING OR DEAD—IS STRICTLY COINCIDENTAL.

© 2001 BY LOUIS BAYARD. ALL RIGHTS RESERVED

MANUFACTURED IN THE UNITED STATES OF AMERICA.

THIS TRADE PAPERBACK ORIGINAL IS PUBLISHED BY ALYSON PUBLICATIONS,
P.O. BOX 4371, LOS ANGELES, CA 90078-4371.
DISTRIBUTION IN THE UNITED KINGDOM BY TURNAROUND PUBLISHER SERVICES LTD.,
UNIT 3, OLYMPIA TRADING ESTATE, COBURG ROAD, WOOD GREEN,
LONDON N22 6TZ ENGLAND.

FIRST EDITION: APRIL 2001

01 02 03 04 05 a 10 9 8 7 6 5 4 3 2 1

ISBN 1-55583-641-0

COVER DESIGN BY MATT SAMS.

R0400768319

LITERATURE AND LANGUAGE DIVISION
THE CHICAGO PUBLIC LIBRARY
400 SOUTH STATE STREET
CHICAGO, ILLINOIS 60605

For Paul and Chris

LITERATURE AND LANGUAGE DIVISION
THE CHICAGO PUBLIC LIBRARY
400 SOUTH STATE STREET
CHICAGO, ILLINOIS 60605

Acknowledgments

For medical information, I am indebted to my brother, Dr. Paul Bayard, as well as to Dr. Jeff Ecker and Mary Kendall. I am equally indebted to Elizabeth Noble's book, *Having Your Baby by Donor Insemination.*

Jamie Davis helped me build an entire character from scratch. Dana West and the Rev. Jim Steen contributed useful details from their own lives. Jennifer Howard helped to rescue this manuscript at a crucial juncture, and Denny Drabelle has been an ongoing fund of wisdom and encouragement. Many thanks as well to my fine editor, Scott Brassart, and to Alyson's marketing whiz, Dan Cullinane.

I am most grateful for the inspiration of my father, Louis Bayard, and the keen critical intelligence of my mother, Ethel Bayard.

And as always, my partner, Don Montuori, has given me everything: eye, ear, heart. Acknowledgments don't begin to cover it.

Medium Virgin Mary

one

It's when you've been rejected by your third sperm bank that your life such as it is begs to be reconsidered.

So that's what I've been doing these last wet days of March, two weeks past my 34th birthday. Taking the scratchy woolen sock that is Nicholas and turning it inside out and shaking it clean. Mostly, though, I've been thinking about Atlantic herring. These are fish that travel in large schools and reproduce about as casually as I untangle phone cords. When they're ready, they just gather in the same vicinity and, on the count of three, they divest themselves of eggs and sperm. No courtship rituals. No ecstatic unions. No lace valances in the nursery. They scatter their seed, and they swim on. The rest of their lives stretches before them like a putting green. Maybe one night in 40 they wonder how their little soldiers have made out, but mostly they swim.

I think about the Atlantic herring because apparently I have been trying to become one. The latest letter seems to acknowledge this subtly: It refers to me as an "aspirant."

Dear Aspirant,

Thank you for your interest in Capitol Cryobank. At the present time, however, we find ourselves in a surplus situation, insofar as supply far exceeds current demand. Consequently, we are unable to consider even worthy candidates at this time.

You may be assured that we will keep your application on file and will contact you should any future need arise.

We thank you again for your interest....

All very businesslike. The vague reference to "worthy candidates," for instance, the unwavering politeness. I nearly choked the first time I read it. Maybe if they'd known how hard it was to find them in the first place, how I spent the better part of a day calling around to Ob-Gyn offices and fertility centers looking for names, names. The longer it went, the crazier I got.

"All I want to do is donate some sperm!" That's what I blurted to the receptionist in Gaithersburg. "The rest of it doesn't matter," I said. "Really. You wouldn't have to hear from me ever again."

"I'm sorry," the woman said. "As a rule, we import from California."

Which threw me, I admit. *California?*

"In addition to which," the woman said, "we cannot take these kinds of inquiries over the phone."

"Can I make an appointment with someone?"

"Well, you can, but not here."

"Why not?"

"Because our sperm comes from California."

I said, "Maybe if I *telephoned* you from California..."

"Now you're being silly," she said.

It was like that the whole afternoon. I couldn't shake the feeling that everyone I talked to, by prearranged agreement, was trying to *stop* me—stop me outright or just send me down unprofitable side routes.

"Now let me get this straight," said one woman. (They did all seem to be women.) "You want to donate, or you want to freeze your own?"

"I don't want to freeze anything," I said. "I just want to leave my sample and go home."

By 4:30 in the afternoon, I was sagging in my swivel chair, staring at the crumbling tile on the office ceiling and trying to decide if I could go on. I could. I make one more call, to a scratchy-voiced woman from the Franconia Family Complex, who gave my question about two seconds of thought and said, "Well, there is Capitol Cryobank out in Manassas."

At which point I was so tired I failed to detect the anomaly: *Capitol* Cryobank, located not in the monumental corridor of Washington, D.C., but in the suburban splatter of Manassas, Virginia, which made me wonder why it bothered to call itself "Capitol." What patriotic imperative—what call to arms—was this?

But that was the name I was given, so that's the name I went with. My desperation clearly got the better of me, caused me to become emotionally invested in what for all I know is a borderline Chapter 11 operation. The name alone should have warned me, and if not the name, the 12-page questionnaire they sent.

Understand, I didn't go down this path with any illusions. I expected questions. I recognized that the sperm highway needs toll-keepers. But these inquisitions! My job, my salary, hobbies, sports, sleeping rhythms, politics—every last offshoot of the family tree. I was asked the medical histories of women I've never met, women who came of age in mill towns and wore cloches and danced the lindy. How the fuck should I know?

But I soldiered on. I checked off all the medical conditions that could possibly apply (warts, moles, deviated septum), answered everything as best I could, stuffed the sheaf of paper into the pre-stamped envelope, dropped it in the mailbox the next morning, and waited patiently for the Call. And the Call turned out to be a form letter on pomegranate card stock.

Which, believe it or not, was a step up from the previous responses.

At least the first place I tried had a sweet-voiced young receptionist. "Reproductive Resources," she said, and as she spoke a picture emerged in my mind: an auburn-haired colleen with a big heart-shaped locket, freckles running across the bridge of her nose. She called me "Mr. Broome," which in the context I appreciated, and she didn't seem to mind all the questions. She was prodigiously patient.

"I'm curious about the afterward part," I said. "I mean, say there's a *child* that actually results from this. Would I ever know? Do they let you know?"

"No, sir. We would need to protect the privacy of the parents and, of course, the child, as I'm sure you understand."

"Oh, that's cool. That's, no, I just...OK, say the child grows up. Turns 18, 21—whatever the age is—and wants to get in touch. Can he do that? She. He, she."

"No, sir. We keep your medical information on file, naturally, but your name would not be attached to it."

"Oh."

"That's how we protect all the parties involved. Including *yourself,* Mr. Broome."

Such a lilt she imparted to my name. She gave it a coloratura bloom.

"No, that's fine," I said. "I'm perfectly comfortable with that."

"And are there any other questions you have at this time?" she asked.

I wanted to keep talking. I wanted to listen to her bell-chime voice for the rest of my life.

"No," I said. "I think that's about it."

"OK, Mr. Broome, my name is Tammy. If you have any questions in the future, please don't hesitate to call us."

That rejection arrived three weeks ago: a Xeroxed form letter that began, "I'm afraid we have some disappointing news...." I called about the possibility of appeal. I left a long and I think coherent message, specifically requesting Tammy. I said, "Tammy has already spent a great deal of time with me on the phone, and I would like to discuss with her whether these decisions are irrevocable or whether there are materials I could send in that would bolster my candidacy." I think I kept it under five minutes, but I suspect my message is now diagram C in the training-course syllabus: "Stalkers, Prevention and Handling of."

Tammy never did return my call, but that spark of human contact gave me the momentum to take on Fertility Emporium, an enterprise with no street address and endless tunnels of voice-mail options, mazes with no center. At each mailbox, the same ersatz female, speaking in the same computerized timbre, said: "The party you are seeking is not available. At the tone, please leave your name and number. When you have finished..."

Who *were* these parties? What species? I couldn't evoke a single freckled colleen from their ranks. All I could imagine, after days of message-leaving, was that they were operating a *virtual* sperm bank, and every morning I would hook up my dick to a modem and fire off a load of digitized seed and receive a two-line E-mail bulletin when contact was made.

In all, I left six messages with Fertility Emporium. To this day, not one call has been returned. For all I know, they're gathering my sperm as I sleep.

Sometime around Valentine's Day (and what a discouraging holiday that was) I had an epiphany: The direct engagement of sperm banks was a fool's game. Because—and don't we all know this?—proper channels are for suckers. Isn't it entirely possible that just beyond the line of everyday consciousness there's a vast black market of sperm, a byzantine underworld accessed by passwords and casually dropped names? "You don't know me, but my friend *Gameto* suggested I call...."

In quick succession, I telephoned five Ob-Gyn offices in the Bethesda area. As soon as a human got on the line, I made the usual discreet inquiries, and then the moment the wall reared up, I'd shift into conspiracy gear and collapse my voice into a faintly European register.

"So that's what you're *telling* me," I'd say, "on the record."

"Yes, sir."

"So maybe now we can talk about some other way."

Whereupon the receptionist—we'll typify her as a grandmotherly sort named Eileen—would say, "I'm sorry?"

"I mean, since we're both adults. All I'm saying is maybe you know someone who can refer me to someone...."

And Eileen would say, "Someone what?"

"Someone who—" Here's where my resolve would falter. "—who knows about some other way of doing it—not through channels."

Whereupon Eileen, watching the phone lines light up like Roman candles, would say, "Sir, if you or your wife need an appointment, I would be happy to set up a time."

The humiliation and, yes, the surrealism. *When did it become this hard to give away your sperm?* From all I've read—from all I've ever heard—college boys have been making quick bucks at this for years. Successive generations of young men, astonished at not having corsage money for their house-party dates, have hightailed it to the nearest clinic, shut themselves in a closet, and emerged 50 bucks richer a few yanks later. Isn't this how it's always worked?

I can't help thinking that if I were still in college, still an inchoate being, I would have a much better chance of being selected than I do now. It's *living* that has disqualified me. It's being alive at the front end of the 21st century...fatally compromising. The tollkeepers want none of me.

"I should have known better."

That's what I tell my friend Shannon. Shannon knows I need sympathy, so she provides it the way she knows how, which is to take me to a piano bar on Capitol Hill, across the street from a boarded-up lesbian bar, treat me to one round of my favorite drink (sidecar), and interrupt our conversation every time her cell phone rings.

"Shit!" Up comes the index finger. "OK, sorry, just...hold the thought, all right?" Out comes the little espionage phone from her black Fendi bag—she starts speaking before it even reaches her lips. "This is Shannon. Yeah. *Hi.*" Her eyes roll a little for my benefit. "No, I haven't heard back, but remember what I said? *The Times* is very low odds. Ten quintillion op-eds a day, so it's 10 quintillion to one. Right. *Right.*"

Shannon is wearing a bright red minidress with large brass buttons; it looks like the top half of a bandleader's uniform. More and more, she is dressing like a blond, though she has the darkest coloring I've ever seen on a blue-eyed woman.

"So I'll let you know as soon as I hear," Shannon says. "OK? And if it doesn't fly there, we try the *Post*, the *Journal*. But you gotta be patient on this, OK, Harold? OK. *All* right." The phone vanishes into the handbag. She takes a draft of air. "Fucking idiot."

She is sitting on a rattan throne next to a sagging rubber tree, and behind her a black woman in an enormous anthracite wig is playing "The Girl From Ipanema" on a baby grand. Shannon claims to hate the music here, but now and again you can see her lips moving, almost sulkily, to the words.

"*O*-K," she says, drawing herself back together. "You were saying..."

"That I'm a fucking idiot."

"Oh, right."

"Even trying to negotiate with these places, playing their ridiculous fucking games. Giving my family's medical histories to...to men in dingy lab coats. Men with phony stethoscopes."

She nods absently. "Tell me the name of that last place again."

"Capitol Cryobank."

"Hmm," she says.

"Does that inspire trust in you? Cry-o-bank. Is any trust inspired by this name?"

"Um." She frowns a little and eyes me over her vodka martini. "I don't know about trust. Maybe it inspires science fiction."

"Exactly. That's my *exact* point. Dime-store science fiction, which is what I'm talking about. I should have known."

She's squinting at me. It's an effort sometimes, figuring me out. *Do you understand*, she seems to be saying, *what an effort it is?*

"So when you first got in touch with them..." she says.

"Yes?"

"And you sent them your application..."

"Yes."

"You thought they were legitimate, but now you don't."

"No. The point is, this is clearly not a legitimate company—was never—and I didn't know enough then to know whether it was."

Shannon nods twice. She clicks her tongue against the roof of her mouth. "OK. Now how would you feel if they had *accepted* your application?" She has a slightly triumphant, professorial manner to her. She believes she has found the crux of everything.

But it's not the rejection, or it's not *just* the rejection. Although when I think about it, who knew this industry was so selective? Who would guess that aspiring mothers—*aspirants*—driven to this particular exigency could be so damn choosy? They must sort through the genomes like wallpaper patterns. *Well, sure, he's healthy and HIV-negative and college-educated, and there's not a single misdemeanor or felony arrest, but look over there, see—he finger-paints. And his grandmother had colon cancer and his great aunt had a hysterectomy when she was 67. And he's vulnerable to hay fever. We can do better....*

"They could do worse than me," I say.

"Of course they could," she says, nodding emphatically.

"For all they know—for all anyone knows—somebody's wife-beater genes are, you know, being implanted in wombs across America. Molestation genes. They let all that shit through, and then something unbelievably minor shows up and...and down comes the portcullis."

"What's a portcullis?"

"You know, that...grating thing."

"Oh."

"On the door of a castle."

"Right." Shannon tugs at the hem of her bandleader skirt, rubs her fingers together. "You know what I'm going to say," she says.

I honestly don't.

"How the world? Being the way it *is?*" she says.

"Yeah?"

"You're going to make me say it, aren't you?"

"Yeah."

"All right." She rehearses the words silently for a few seconds. "A gay man," she says. "A gay man is not going to be picked to spawn new generations. I mean, it's awful, but that's the world."

My left knee, out of nowhere, starts doing its agitato dance. The sidecar, balanced on my thigh, bounces along. "Actually," I say, "I didn't tell them that part."

"Which part?"

"The gay part."

There is a charged silence from the rattan throne, a sigh of apprehension. "Haaa-haanh," it sounds like.

I am looking away now, but I know what's happening: Her left eyebrow is trembling with irony; her lips are sphinctering together, to avoid all possibility of irony. I start talking into my drink. "There was a process to this, right? The first two times I just laid out the facts. I told them everything. Because maybe these are progressive kinds of places, with hip moms and dads, you know, twin Volvos and funky credit cards and random acts of kindness, you know? Come in, maybe, and look over the data and kind of like all the rest of the stuff, and maybe they're willing to overlook the one part."

"Uh-huh."

"So when I got turned down, I figured well, wrong, Nick. 'Cause parents aren't progressive about their own kids. So the *third* time around..."

"Uh-huh."

"That was the one thing I changed. By change I mean I didn't mention it. They asked: 'Have you had sexual encounters with men?' And I just left it blank. But everything else was right on."

"So just a little illegal," Shannon says.

"I don't know. I didn't think much about it."

Which is not really true. In fact, as soon as I found myself swerving, even by a small degree, from truth, a whole new realm of license opened up in my mind. I thought if I can change this one elemental part of me, why can't I create an entirely new Nicholas? Give myself a more attractive birthplace. (Screw Norfolk.) A Stanford education. A graduate degree in international finance.

And then start in on the whole Broome clan. That wacky bunch of nonagenarians! Feisty, cancer-free. Poets and silversmiths and squash champions. My sister: an archeologist, sieving Etruscan crockery out of Sicilian ruins. My brother: healing Kurdish lepers. My parents: eccentric venture capitalists riding the bull-market rodeo.

Oh, what I could have created! But I didn't. I ran straight up the high road. And not from principle but from paranoia, the kind only a technological ignoramus could entertain. I was convinced that Capitol Cryobank had computer applications that would sniff out deceit and flag even the subtlest forms of wish fulfillment. Maybe I gave them too much credit; almost certainly I did.

"You know what?" Shannon says. She's craning her neck, looking for our waitress, who was last seen about 20 minutes ago. "Even if you left it blank, it wouldn't matter because they probably assume no answer means guilt," she shrugs. "The only reason I mention it is ethically you're off the hook."

"I don't care about the ethics," I say. "It was an experiment. The first two were the control, right, and the third one was the variable."

"So..." She's turned herself around now. She's waving both hands at the waitress, like a gospel preacher. "So the experiment failed."

"Well, yeah. I mean, in the sense they blew me off. Yeah."

She turns back around. "No, no, no. Nicky, listen to me. It's a credit to you it failed! You don't want to be fathering those little evil *mall* kids...." She makes a small shudder for me. "All the shoes you would have to buy—the shoes *alone*, Nicky. Listen," she says. "Who gives a shit if they blew you off? It's, like, a badge of honor."

She doesn't get it. I haven't made it clear. It's not the rejection—really—it's just that I had this vision of how it would be. In this vision, I'm making the weekly trip to the Manassas, Virginia, headquarters of Capitol Cryobank. I leave early, a little after 7:00, to beat the traffic. Something baroque is playing on the classical music station. Sound walls—limestone and beige—line the highway, and peering over them are the emptied balconies of Arlington condos and brick ramblers, four decades old. I drive alongside the high-voltage fences of the Metro tracks, and my car easily outpaces the westbound Orange Line train chugging toward Vienna.

I see the familiar names, the Beltway outposts: Falls Church, Fairfax, Reston. I am going home—to where I grew up. Ravens on power lines. Oaks and sycamores and Virginia pine. Park-and-rides and half-built town homes with Arthurian names. Wal-Mart and Kohl's and the National Rifle Association.

Within 50 minutes, the outskirts of Manassas materialize. I ease off the highway, and two minutes later I'm turning into the Cryobank headquarters, in a small office park with pebbled sidewalks. I park my Toyota Camry in space number 23. I walk into the onyx building and give my name to the receptionist. The physician's assistant, an attractive young Asian woman with teardrop earrings, smiles as she bumps open an oak-paneled side door with her hip and motions me to follow. She leads me down a long hallway with shell-colored carpet. Formaldehyde tickles my nostrils. My ears pick out the diaphanous strains of Enya.

"The usual southern view," the woman says.

"Thank you," I say.

She hands me three medium-size glass vials, a box of Kleenex, and a back issue of *Pro Wrestling* magazine. "Will you be needing anything else, Mr. Broome?"

"Thank you, no."

She doesn't bother asking me the other things, the things you ask the first-timers: *Have you ejaculated within the last 48 hours? Have you engaged in any strenuous physical activity within the last eight hours?*

"All righty, then," she says. "I'll let you get to it."

The door closes behind her. I stand by the window, watching Jeeps and Mercury Villagers assemble in the parking lot below. I am thinking about fish. I am spooling out the life history of a male Atlantic herring: the shock of birth, the scaling of the food pyramid, the senseless locomotion of adolescence. I see his entire destiny, right up to the unforeseen moment when the female next door, answering signals he doesn't even recognize, lets loose with a platoon of eggs for his benediction.

Come on, kid, I'm whispering to the herring. *Do your stuff. Make your old man proud. Attaboy.*

My hand is playing with the zipper of my twill trousers, and Enya is cooing in my ear, and this is how life begins....

"The Arboretum sucks."

Shannon is back on the phone. Her legs are tucked beneath her, and her head is tossed to one side—she looks like a bobby-soxer, except for the *bandito* grin.

"Do you know where that is?" she's asking. "Have you been there? It's fucking northeast D.C. Now tell me—Nicky, the waitress, walking down the stairs—tell me how many—no, *run* and get her—reporters—vodka martini, two olives—are going to schlep out to the fucking arboretum?"

The waitress is wearing a field-hockey uniform and a large cloud of electric-blue hair. She writhes when I touch her shoulder. For a second I'm convinced she's going to scream.

I clear my throat. "Vodka martini, two olives. And a sidecar, please."

She gives me a brutish nod and charges down the staircase. The noise from her clogs lights sparks under her feet.

When I get back, Shannon is cooing into the phone. Such a professional seductress. She has extended one of her shapely legs; a red sling-back pump with a brass buckle dangles from her big toe.

"OK, honey, get back to me tomorrow, all right? 8:30-ish sound good? OK. *Bye* bye." She stares at the phone for a few moments. "That was Joel," she says.

"Ah."

She lunges for her handbag, pulls out a toothpick with a small green ruff at the end, drives it into the corners of her mouth. "Barf. What were we talking about?"

"Nothing."

"Oh, the...right." Her lips flare back from her teeth. The pick darts in, wiggles out. "So what does your sister say about all this?"

"Celia doesn't know."

Shannon's eyes are large interpretive blanks. *Huh. How interesting,* she seems to be saying. *How engrossing.*

"This is top secret," I say. "No one's supposed to know."

The waitress blows past us, blue hair rippling like a sapphire, the pleats of her tartan skirt emitting an audible hum. The glasses fly from her tray and make a concussive landing on the bamboo coffee table.

"I'm doing this on my own," I say.

Which is intended to close the matter, but the only thing that really closes it is Shannon's fatigue. The empathy is starting to wear on her.

"Don't let me go," she says, raising an index finger, "without telling you about the *U.S. News* guy."

"The one...his pubes are a different color than—"

"Oh, please! That's the least. The other night the condom starts to slip, like, halfway through. He says, 'Well, what do you want me to do?' And I say, 'Well, what do you *think* I want you to do?' And the rest of the night, not a word to me. Like a little child. Like it was my fault."

Many years ago Shannon and I almost consummated a brief love affair, and I sometimes think she tells me about her sexual exploits just to show me what I've missed. Oddly, it has the opposite effect: I feel as if I've been there the whole way, fanning my wings over the bed.

"And he makes yipping noises, like a Pekingese..."

When we totter out an hour later, Shannon has her hand attached to my arm. She does that now and again, and for the first time I am struck by the tenderness of it. Arousing, frankly. Here it is almost 10:30, and when was the last time—think hard, Nick—when was the last time you got laid?

We have stopped at the corner of 8th and D. The night actually got warmer while we were inside. It's barely spring, and the world is flirting with summer, and it makes you want to flirt back. I turn to look at Shannon, the way you look at someone after several hours of looking at them—as if their reality is in question. She is tugging with drunken ostentation on the gold braid of her bandleader's jacket.

"Refresh my memory," Shannon says.

"Yes."

"Why is this so important to you? No." She shakes something out of her brain. "Forget that one. What interests me is the deadline. Why does it have to happen now?" Both of her hands hoop around my elbow. "Tell Shanny Girl."

"You're in no condition to discuss this."

"Am too."

"You won't even remember."

"I will. Tell Shanny Girl. Big rush, what's the big rush?"

She's yanking on my arm, and my balance is already a little suspect, and I see the two of us coming undone, shattering, our limbs settling into a big jumble on the pavement. It would take us the whole night to reconstruct: femurs, tibias, patellas.

"I have a year," I say. "I have less than a year to conceive a child."

two

Two months before my grandmother died, we went to her hospital room in Staunton, Virginia, to celebrate her birthday. A nuclear unit: me and my parents and my brother and sister, dressed like we were going to church, crowding around her bed in the middle of April. It was quite warm outside, but nobody told the radiator, which spilled wave after wave of dry heat into the room. Gran didn't seem to mind: She was wearing one of those flimsy white hospital gowns. She was so tiny by then that the gown barely stayed on her—it kept sliding down to expose her collarbone, which looked massive against her shrunken flesh, like the collar of a space suit. A long catheter tube glowed with her urine, and through her porous orange hair I saw a single violet vein pulsing softly.

Because it was her birthday, there were balloons—large silver lozenges tied to the railing of her bed—and flowers: a big swarm of roses from Mom, already decomposing in the heat, another spray of roses from Gran's other daughter, who lived in Tucson and couldn't get away. My brother, Greg, had brought a bouquet of drooping tulips from a local florist. The florist had assured him the tulips would perk up as soon as they got inside, but they didn't.

Oh, and there were presents. Celia brought grape-cluster gold earrings, and I came with glycerine hand lotions because Gran had always been a world-champion moisturizer. I never really believed she would die until the moment in the hospital room when she removed one of the lotion bottles from the bag, held it in her hand, and returned it to the bag without a word.

She covered herself by saying she didn't want gifts lying around anyway because the hospital staff was sure to steal them. So Mom packed away the gifts, and the five Broomes sat staring at an old woman on a bed. It was almost a relief to hear the nurse's voice breaking in on the intercom every few minutes. "Can I help you?" she would ask. Each time she buzzed, she got a little more churlish. "Can I *help* you?" It took us half an hour to realize my father was leaning against the call button.

Gran still had a couple of months to go then, so she wasn't doing that thing that would so unnerve us later: staring up at the ceiling, as though any second the Virgin Mary might come crashing through. No, on this particular occasion, she carried the day. She had a single definite idea about each of us, and she pursued it relentlessly. She asked my mother about her volunteer work. She asked Greg over and over when he was going into private practice. She probed Celia about last night's dinner, even though Celia was barely eating then, let alone cooking. And eventually Gran's consciousness expanded just wide enough to include my father.

"Oliver," she said. "How's the congregation?"

"Not there." Dad leaned into her. "I'm not there anymore, remember."

"Nicky," she asked, "you seen any good movies lately?"

"Not lately, Gran. But as soon as you get out of here, OK? I'll take you to a matinee. Some nice shoot-'em-up, flying arms and blown-up heads."

She made a soft shooing motion with her hand. "Stop, Nicky."

"And then maybe a baseball game. Cal Ripken keeps asking when you're coming."

"That's nice," she said faintly. She pressed the button at her side, and the back half of her bed rose a few inches and levered her torso forward. "Celia," she said. "What's for dinner tonight?"

"I don't know, Gran. They're going to bring you something, aren't they?"

"I don't want it."

Five minutes later dinner came on a shiny metal cart. Fish cakes, mashed potatoes with no butter or gravy, mixed vegetables with no sauce. Gran started crying. Or crying as best she could. Her body was so desiccated by then, the only thing she could produce was the muscular spasm of crying—a dry heave.

"I want a hot dog," she said suddenly.

"I'll get it!" Celia cried. She was out the door before the rest of us could move. None of us could object: She had worn one of her wool suits from work. Every pore in her body was gasping for air.

"Celia's too thin," Gran said.

"Well, she's lost a lot of weight," Mom said. "We're very proud of her."

"Too much," Gran said. "Too thin."

Celia came back a half hour later with a foil-wrapped hot dog on a paper plate. Gran needed a few seconds just to get her jaw around the bun and a few more seconds to remember how to operate her mouth. She took a single cautious bite, and her eyes moistened and swelled. "S'good," she said.

About two thirds of the way through, she carefully laid the dog on the paper plate and raised her head. It was then I realized, in a quick stab of self-consciousness, that we were aligned shoulder to shoulder, a grim chorus line at the foot of Gran's bed: Mom and Dad in the center; Greg, the oldest, taking up the left flank; me, the youngest, on the right; and Celia between me and Mom. Without thinking, we had arranged ourselves for maximum viewing efficiency.

Gran's jaw was still moving in an echo from her last bite. Her eyes, a jellied gray, scanned the Broome wedge, and the color that had animated her just two seconds ago drained away. She opened her mouth, and a dry, hot whisper came out.

"Is this it?" she said.

Afterward there was some debate within our family about what Gran meant. No, that's not quite true. There was only a prevailing opinion, publicly uttered and endorsed, and a silent opinion, held by me and expressed only several months after Gran's death.

The majority opinion runs like this: Gran saw the five of us standing there like Death's welcome wagon and became suddenly, powerfully aware that she was going to die—sooner rather than later. "Is this it?" she asked, already knowing the answer.

It still tears Mom up, reliving that moment. She thinks she should have been steering her mother into that last, elusive Kubler-Ross stage, but she didn't know what to say. It was left to Dad, professionally trained consoler, to mumble the necessary comforts.

"Now, come on, Sylvia," he said. "Don't talk that way; you're too cussed to go anywhere."

Gran didn't answer. After a few labored squeezes, her breathing calmed, and her papery skin filled with air again. But she kept staring at us. She couldn't help herself.

And I remember thinking: *She's not afraid for herself. She's afraid for us.*

I tried to explain this to my brother and sister. I knew I couldn't explain it well, but I tried anyway. The occasion was our annual day-after–New Year's lunch, which, like many Broome family traditions, began in a casual manner and quickly ossified into an awkward and unavoidable ritual. It started five years ago when Celia and I were sitting in our parents' living room on New Year's morning, staring bleary-eyed at the TV, some float coming down the main street of Pasadena, horrible and blue and inflated, swaying to its own demonic vibe. We were talking about how much we hate parades, and how funny it was that we always watched them, and then Celia said she was coming into D.C. the next day, and why didn't we get together for lunch? And before I could answer, Greg's voice came flying toward us from some skyward region. Silent, room-haunting Greg, on the landing overhead, rubbing the bed creases out of his face.

"Me too," he said. "I had the same idea."

So the next day, at Celia's suggestion, we drove to an area of northwest

Washington that wasn't convenient for any of us, to a restaurant named after the duchess of Windsor, stocked from floor to ceiling with Wallis Simpson memorabilia—photographs and *Look* magazine covers and lemon-hued news clippings, one of which posed the question of whether Wallis was really a man. Greg and I had already been prepped for this question by Celia, who spent the whole car ride plying us with Windsor trivia. She was a Wallis lover from way back, and so she was all the more perplexed to get to the restaurant and find stainless-steel tubing and mirror paneling and cane-back chairs.

"I don't know," she kept saying. "I thought it'd be...I don't know...."

Who can say how we made the time pass? Some congenial subject must have presented itself. All I can remember is trying to flirt with the waiter and staring at the five heavily bankrolled ladies at the next table, with their custom-wrapped Nordstrom gifts and their silk jackets, all different shades of Jackie Kennedy pink.

The rest of that first annual lunch is a brown wash except for the way it ended. I remember I had just pushed my chair back from the table, and I was drawing myself up from my chair, feeling the protest in my knees, and from the periphery of my right eye, I saw Greg, still glued to his seat, frowning at his napkin.

"You know what?" he said.

I shook my head.

"We should do this every year," he said.

Celia and I inhaled at the same time.

"We could do that," I said.

"I mean, it's crazy," Greg told us. "We live a few miles apart, and we never see each other. Unless we're at Mom and Dad's, and we can't talk there, and anywhere else, there's someone *else*."

I looked at Celia, but she was rooting through her handbag.

"See, it's the ritual thing," Greg said. "I really think people need to create their own rituals."

Celia stopped fumbling, set her bag on the table and sank back into her chair. "Greet the New Year," she said, trying to warm to the idea. "A new restaurant each time."

"No," Greg said. "The same one."

"Really?" Celia asked. She'd already written the place off.

"Maybe the same table," Greg said. "If it's available."

So that's how it started. And that's why, when I wanted to tell my brother and sister what Gran was really telling us, this was the occasion I chose.

"Here's the deal," I said. "I think Gran was more or less at peace with the dying business. That wasn't her problem. It was her legacy. She looked at us, she realized, *Oh, my God, this is how I go on living and this is it? Five people.* She could've died 30 years ago and it would've been the same five. Nothing's changed, not a single new face. A dead end."

Celia didn't look like she was even following, so it was up to Greg to respond.

"Nick," he said, "you need to tell me where this is leading. Because maybe I'm dense or something."

I leaned forward until my chin almost touched the table. "OK," I said. "None of us is getting younger; that's obvious. And there's this *family* here, for better or worse, and it's us, and unless somebody has a child, we're going to go extinct."

And it was done—much more quickly than I would have thought possible—and I felt like I could lay my head on the table and go to sleep. But Greg was wide awake.

"Gee, I'm starting to feel a little cornered here, Nick."

"Why?"

"Because I look around and it looks like—tell me if I'm wrong—I'm the only one of us who's married."

"Or anything at all," Celia said, softly.

"Which means the burden here is on me and Sally. Is that your point, Nick?"

"No."

"Because it occurs to me that this is very easy for you as a...as a non-heterosexual person to tell us what we should do with our lives and—"

"No, you're right."

"It's very easy for you to say, 'Have children, make us all happy,' when you don't have the responsibility, the expense of actually doing it. I mean, it's—"

"No, wait. Stop." I put out my hand, like a cigar-store Indian. "I understand what you're saying—I'm not putting it on you. I wouldn't even bring it up if I wasn't going to, you know, back it up some way."

Then silence, half a minute of silence. Except not silent at all—full of static, *our* static, and the static of everyone else. Celia had her eyes almost completely closed, as though she were filtering us through a memory.

"What?" she asked, finally. "What are you going to do, Nick?"

"I'm going to have a child," I told them. "Soon. By this time next year, I will father a child."

And that's the last time I discussed the subject with them. For all I know, it's never reentered their heads. At the end of the year, I will come stumbling toward them with a swaddled infant in my arms, and they will say, "Remind me?"

So I am operating under a deadline that exists only in my mind. There's no one, really, to hold me accountable—except for science, which has now imposed a deadline of its own. I discover it while riding my search engine through the Internet. As sensual an experience as I get nowadays, plugging in the word *sperm* and weeding through the impotence cures and the scientific abstracts and the reproductive clinics in Tulsa and Billings and East Lansing, steering my way at last into the Great Source Waters.

Where else but California?

O, California! What a sperm bank is nurtured in your breast! It takes me half an hour just to negotiate its Web site, and I still can't find any phone numbers or application forms—a space only for E-mail inquiries. And then, after leaving a long and detailed message with my height, weight, occupation, annual salary, and SAT scores, what else is there to do but wander into the Fun Sperm Facts page and read the following injunction:

Although fertility does not automatically decline after the age of 34, scientists have found that men over that age are less likely to produce the consistently superior quality of sperm required for successful freezing and subsequent thawing.

So there it is, my little endgame. I have entered my final year of reproductive viability. In 12 months' time I will be beyond California's reach. I will be reduced to marketing schemes like the one Shannon proposes over the phone.

"You've been going about this all wrong," she says.

"Oh?"

"Think about it. What do sperm banks do for you anyway? They're middlemen. The thing to do is go into business for yourself. I mean, how hard can it be? Wake up, give it a couple of swipes, shoot those bad boys into a big porcelain bowl."

"Uh-huh."

"Which probably needs to be heated because don't they need warmth? And then every weekend you take this bowl to Eastern Market, which is what, two blocks away?"

"Right."

"You set up a little stand—don't worry, I'll make the sign: SPERM BY THE THOUSANDS. GET 'EM NOW. Of course, you'll need to do the research first, figure out what the market can bear."

"Yah-huh."

"Maybe you offer syringes if they're needed—*basters*."

I should remember never to call Shannon after she's just visited her father. A certain grim subversiveness clings to her for days afterward.

"Just promise me one thing," she says.

"What?"

"No matter how this donor business turns out, OK? No matter what happens, you're not going to ask me to do that gay-guy–straight-woman thing."

"What thing?"

"You know—that best-friend, platonic-parent thing."

"Platonic..."

"Oh, come on, Nicky. The 'straight men suck, so let's raise a baby together,' utopian alternative-family thing."

"I would never ask you to do anything utopian."

Really. It never occurred to me. Very early in our relationship, before I was out, Shannon had wondered out loud what it would be like to sleep with a gay man. "You know," she said, taking a man-size chunk out of her dinner roll, "I don't think I could fuck anyone who's imagining me with a penis."

In retrospect this seems to miss the mark. Why would I have imagined Shannon with a penis? As anything other than what she was? I've never told her this, but I actually cherish the memory of our intimacy. In some ways, making out with her gave me a clearer sense of my attractiveness than most of the sex I've had since. I'm like any man, I suppose: in need of unremitting proofs. And now I have one...from California, of all places! My sperm may be reaching the tether end of its vigor, but I'm a lead-pipe cinch in all the other donor categories.

Candidate must have graduated from a major four-year university. It's not on their suggested list, but I'm guessing that if UCLA makes the cut, so does the University of Virginia. English major. Junior varsity tennis. Managing editor of school paper. Senior thesis on Jacob Riis.

Candidate's height must be between 5 feet 11 and 6 feet 2. I top out at 6 feet 1, though I look bigger because of a certain inherited burliness. (The slight bowing of the shoulders is also inherited.)

Candidate's weight must be approximately proportionate to his height. I'm somewhere around 190 last I checked—but a big-boned 190. A healthy pair of buttocks and a modest thickening around the middle—unresponsive to jogging and swimming—but people tell me I carry my size well. Judging from my family history, I have about five years of metabolic grace left.

If adopted, candidates must have access to medical histories of biological family. No question of being adopted. The Broome features ripple through the generations. My father's squat potato nose finds its twin in mine. The family overbite turns up in varying degrees in all of us—Celia has a mostly invisible lower row of teeth. All of us struggle in our various ways with an acquired Midwestern fleshiness. Greg is only now starting to lose the battle, and it seems to come as some relief. Celia, by contrast, has taken up residence in the land of the skinny. You will have to kill her before she agrees to be fat again.

All things considered, then, I'm a reasonably healthy specimen of my age and culture. Nonsmoking, jazz-listening, white-meat–loving. I ride a hybrid bike down the Mount Vernon trail. I usher for financially unsound theaters. I drink sidecars, the occasional Manhattan. Now and again I go to church—maybe the only one in my family who still does, the Rev. Broome included. I work in the U.S. House of Representatives. I read Tolstoy. I love children.

At least I love to watch them. Some days, if the weather's nice, I take my lunch break on a small bench on the southwest side of the Capitol. Usually I take Tolstoy with me, but within minutes the book has fallen into my lap and I'm watching the long, slow pilgrimage of tourist children. Exhausted, most of them, worn out by the mid-spring heat and the wigged busts and the marble floors, their arms swinging like orangutans. Margarine-headed kids, wearing the faces of popular musicians on their backs, staring at squirrels, splashing each other with bottled water. Weeping in their mothers' arms. Boys with skirt-length T-shirts and jeans bunched around their ankles; and girls in denim jumpers, with thick, unfashionable glasses and smiles like wounds; and tiny things in baby strollers, waving their feet like conductors' batons. It's all unaccountably moving, like the parade of a distinct nation. And I look down at my book, and I flip back through the pages, back to where Natasha Rostov first bursts into the roomful of adults.

> *Escaping from her father, she ran to hide her flushed face in the lace of her mother's mantilla—not paying the least attention to her severe remark—and began to laugh. She laughed, and in fragmentary sentences tried to explain about a doll that she produced from the folds of her frock.*
>
> *"Do you see? My doll...Mimi...you see..."*

I want Natasha to burst in on the Broomes. I want her to be there for our next Christmas. I want her to see my father presiding over dinner like a camp commandant, shaking out his napkin and bowing his head so quickly you can't tell if he's saying grace or checking his fly. Last year he managed to combine the head drop with the gravy-boat reach, even as he launched the holiday rant.

"I don't suppose," he said in that deceptively casual manner of his—honed in vestry meetings—"I don't suppose anyone caught the little electronics display down the street."

It would have been hard to miss. My parents live off a narrow, two-lane road, once blanketed by forest but now giving way on all sides to suburban estates, massive edifices with copper awnings and finished basements and Olympic-size pools. The only relic from 20 years ago is a brick ranch house screened by hickory trees. You'd never notice the place normally, but every December the owners wreathe it in swags of colored light—chain after chain of light, running along the cornice, down the gutter spout, around the windows, whirling three times around the doorway and then making a breathless rush for the trees, raveling the branches, extending farther and farther until every tree is boiling with light and the entire landscape is blinking and glittering like a carnival Mass.

A spectacle by any year's standards, but last Christmas the owners outdid themselves. The first time I saw it, I was already past it. I had to slam on the brakes, shift the car into reverse, and edge slowly backward.

It was a nativity scene, set back five feet from the road's shoulder and braced against a wood pile. The holy family reposed on a deflated rubber pool. A log carrier, lined with grass clippings stood in for the manger, and two plasticine lambs stared indifferently to the east. Joseph stood straight and tall, with glazed pupil-less eyes, resting one hand on the brow of his son. Mary's head drooped slightly to one side—as though someone had just now crept over and reattached it—and in the center of her forehead sat a single cherry-red lightbulb, like a rani's jewel. Joseph's beard was entwined with blue electric bubbles, and the son of God was ribboned in white light, from the elliptical halo above his head to the last blockish toe.

It was hard to leave them. I pulled away slowly, and as the figures dwindled in the passenger-side mirror, they took on an ambulance glare.

"Electronic nativity scenes," said Dad, gazing into his middle distance. "Haven't we just about seen it all now? Makes you wish Christmas had never been born."

It's worth noting that my father grew up Lutheran and still bears the Lutheran hostility to holidays. This manifests itself in several ways, most notably in his refusal to begin decorating a tree until Christmas Eve. He says the church calendar recognizes only 12 days of Christmas, and the rest is Madison Avenue brainwashing.

"Which makes sense," he says, "because it's a pagan festival anyway, and who are the biggest pagans we've got? Corporations. So let 'em have Christmas. It was theirs in the first place."

The practical implications of this philosophy are that every December 24, Oliver and Emily Broome rouse themselves at 5:00 in the morning, haul a 12-foot Douglas fir from the backyard deck, jam it into its stand, correct and recorrect its axis, water it, and then, mindful of their neighbor's example, weave two sparse strands of white light through the branches. They drag four boxes of ornaments down from the attic, and my mother divides them into the ones that must be seen—heirlooms, children's grade-school projects—and the ones that can be safely hidden. My father hangs them accordingly, using the hooks saved from last year's tree, and then he crowns everything with the family angel, a slightly flattened creation of construction paper and glitter made by his son Nicholas 27 years ago. Depending on the angle of the top branch, this angel will either pitch forward or settle onto its back. Either way, it looks completely flightless.

The decorating is done before any of the Broome children come to help. We seem to prefer it that way, although my mother is usually a little breathless when we arrive—less, I think, from what she's done than from contemplating what still needs to happen. Last Christmas, though, I found her sitting rather quietly on the family-room ottoman, gazing at the tree she had just decorated.

"Next year," she said. "Smaller tree."

Carefully, I placed my overnight bag on the couch next to her. "Why don't you?" I agreed.

"One of those little three-foot things," she continued. "The kind you put on a table. Tie red bows around the branches." She looked at me now. "Maybe some of those gift-wrapped candies around the bottom."

"Or even a little felt tree skirt," I suggested. "Like in the Hammacher catalog."

Mom's head made a slow nodding motion—nodding through water. "Smaller tree," she said.

"Wait a minute!"

First Greg's voice, then his body, breaking into the space around us. He had walked over to the railing that separated the kitchen from the family room, and he was leaning over it now, and I realized then that I was the last to arrive. Celia was already in the kitchen, chopping up chestnuts for stuffing. Sally was wrapping presents on the living-room floor. The only one missing was Dad, who was probably in the basement working on his mission table, the one he'd been working on for four months.

"Is this a good idea?" Greg was asking.

"You're all grown now," my mother said. "Past grown."

"That doesn't mean it's not still important. Maybe it's, you know, *more* important. Maybe it's not even the *tree*, per se."

The rituals speech: I could hear it, all spooled up, ready to go.

"Well, it's up to Mom, isn't it?" I said. "Mom and Dad."

"I'll get here earlier," Greg said. "If that would make it easier. We can help you put it up, Sally and I can do the whole thing if you want."

My mother eased herself off the ottoman, paused to make sure of her footing, then began her measured shuffle to the kitchen. She spoke so softly as she passed, it sounded like an afterthought. "There's not much point anymore," she said.

And what was there to say? There *is* no point. Why can't we just admit it?

The sad thing is none of the Broomes even speaks of children anymore. We don't even know any. We sit together at family weddings—in places we've never been, like Carlsbad and Wheeling and Oak Park—and we watch tribes of kids, other people's kids, declaring war on their place settings, taking meaningless photographs with disposable table cameras. We see boys tripping over their trouser legs, girls lifting their party dresses like parachutes, and it's like a masked ball to which we haven't been invited.

The only children who even register on my parents' radar anymore are the neighbors' kids and only because they wander into the Broomes' backyard where they're not welcome. My mother is particularly vigilant about this. She has become one of those women I used to fear as a child, the kind we talked about in campfire whispers. *Old Lady Broome!* Once, after chasing away the young children of a successful Indian ophthalmologist, she received a personal visit from their father, demanding toleration for his kids. Oliver Broome's response was: "How would you like it if my wife came over and played in your yard?"

Which is quite an image to leave anyone with, let alone an ophthalmologist. Emily Broome doing cartwheels, backward somersaults, dangling facedown from the crossbar of a swing set. That may be the closest this family ever gets to a real child. It's a problem; it's maybe a crime. We are whistling ourselves out of the gene pool, and I'm fighting it; I'm fighting it the best I can. I'm subjecting myself to the indignities of the sperm market, I'm entertaining visions of porcelain bowls at Eastern Market. And I can't even tell my family I'm doing it because they would want me to stop. And I can't stop. I won't.

Now, don't misunderstand: There's no way in which the Broome genes are exceptional—by any standard. On paper, in living flesh. Trace the branches of our tree, and you'll find alcoholism, divorce, invalidism, bankruptcy, happiness...but no captains of industry, no artists, no tyrants. The only thing we have to offer, honestly, is *us*. We're who we are and not someone else. So why doesn't that count for more? Why hasn't it swayed the Broomes, for example? Why isn't anyone protesting?

That's the strange part. I will think back to some period in our family history, and I will reenact what we did and said, and it's incredible to me that none of us, in that short space of time, ever broke down. None of us ever said: *Enough. It has to change.*

And yet I couldn't even tell you what has to change. All I can do is map the coordinates. If, say, you'd come over to the house on the morning after Thanksgiving, you would have found the Rev. Oliver Broome on the backyard deck—the one place he's allowed to smoke—reading cancer cociety propaganda sent to him by an anonymous correspondent.

Emily Broome would have been on the cordless phone, the one she said she'd never use when her children gave it to her for her 63rd birthday. Talking to a young man named Hoy Phong, whom she met in the English as a Second Language class she teaches at the community center. Since then she has become a kind of unofficial social worker to him, tutoring him in reading, coaching him through job interviews, canvassing local employers on his behalf. When she talks to him, her voice assumes a low, blank, serene quality. She says his name over and over again, as though she were reading a first-grade primer. "Yes, Hoy. Hoy, that's not how you greet an employer. A potential employer, Hoy. Hoy, listen...."

And where were the rest of us? Gathered around the television, which had been muted because my father doesn't like noise in the house. There was a game on the screen: a pair of AFC teams none of us cared about. I was sitting on one end of the couch, two thirds of the way through a quote-acrostic puzzle. Celia sat on the other end, reading a back issue of *Cook's Illustrated.* Greg was on the living-room carpet, a headset clamped to his skull, listening to one of his abstruse modernist works—Bartok or Elliott Carter or somebody. His wife was flat on her back, in a T-shirt and exercise tights, performing a set of abdominal exercises: extending her legs straight up in the air and then letting them drop slowly to the ground, like a felled tree. Her thighs and hips had an unyielding engineered quality; I imagined them moving things: steel beams, drawbridges.

It was very quiet. If you'd closed your eyes, all you would have heard was the murmur of Hoy's name as my mother moved in and out of rooms, and the ticking of the clock on the kitchen wall. This had once been Gran's clock, and its progress has become erratic since it came to this house. It will go whole days without moving, then without warning kick back into life, with a series of fretful rasps. Even when it's working, you can hear the pendulum brush against the casing, and you can sense the imbalance that yields a slightly longer tick on the right side. It's like the winding down of a heart.

As I sat there listening, the ticking actually hardwired itself into my circuitry, and I realized how much I had come to dread these Thanksgivings. How *old* they had become, how old we had become *in* them. I sat there longing for Natasha to burst into the room—in a red fleece Winnie the Pooh sweatshirt, double-buckle jeans, saddle shoes. Carrying a ping-pong paddle or a fistful of dried flowers, a wedding bouquet, which she would give to me because I'm supposed to be the husband. "You have to, Uncle Nick! I won't marry anyone else."

A child. A child in our midst. Who would one day tell *her* child all about Thanksgiving at the Broomes. How awful it was. Boring, endless, and maybe a little nice too, now that she thinks about it. She will recount it so clearly that her child will be able to see exactly how we were, where we sat, what functions we performed.

You see, as much as I dread our Thanksgivings, the thing I dread most is losing them. I can't shake it, I see mortality everywhere: doorknobs, antimacassars. I'll look at my parents' family-room couch, which for the longest time my mother has been meaning to return because human-hair oils react with the anodized leather to produce large cinnamon-colored stains. You can see them from some distance: the stain where my father sits and, next to it and five inches below it, the stain where my mother sits. I stare at these stains and think: *If my parents died, this would be the only thing left of them—the only evidence they were ever in this room.*

Now, I can't say exactly how having children would improve the situation. My mother and father would still die, and so would I, and when that happens, the thought of who's left behind will probably cease to matter. But until then, it matters. It matters more than anything else—more than Tolstoy, more than life.

"You know," Shannon once told me, "this wouldn't be an issue for you if you were dating someone."

I think she said this in the kindest possible tone. I took it that way. And it's true that relationships have a way of pushing extraneous thoughts from the mind. When I dated that lawyer from the Resolution Trust Corporation, for example, we spent whole afternoons trying to determine if we trusted each other yet. With my last boyfriend—the Actor, as Celia refers to him—I needed two months' undivided concentration just to figure out we were dating and another two months to figure out we weren't. But even in my most obsessive moments, I don't think I've ever abandoned the thought of children. I remember coming home one night and finding the Actor in front of my bedroom mirror, performing some intricate maneuver with his hip, some bit of character business. (He was in a Tom Stoppard play at the time.) I figured he would give it a rest after a while, but he kept going. The same hip maneuver, again and again. Experimenting with different angles, trying it this way, that way, viewing it from every possible vantage point. And I remember thinking: *Not only does he have no time for me, he wouldn't have time for anybody else.* And it was then I realized I had been unconsciously vetting my boyfriends for their parental potential—which goes some way to explaining why I don't currently have a boyfriend.

Maybe that's for the best. I can't afford the distraction. I have a task now—a calling, as funny as that sounds—and it requires the kind of self-denial that I think I have been waiting a long time to practice. When I look back now at the semen I've expended over the last 15 years of my life, I wonder at the generative potential I've squandered. Oh, I wouldn't take it back, not a teaspoon, and it's not as though I've sworn off sex, not voluntarily, but I do feel a new kind of reverence stirring inside me. This must be the same feeling that the sex educators tried to instill in us in ninth grade: *Your body is something very special! Don't abuse it!* Completely meaningless when you're 14, but now for some reason I find myself reacting almost tenderly to things like skin and kneecaps and eyebrows.

And sperm. Sperm, most of all. I'm the class of masturbator who jacks off just to wake up some mornings. And lately, I've taken to staring at the issue, the pond of bleachy glue, opaque and strange...forever strange. I peer into it, and I can almost see my little Atlantic herrings, waiting to fan out. One of them could turn into a young boy. A young boy in a royal-blue down parka, unzipped, with the hood down, running toward me across a soccer field and endlessly dividing as he runs, so the whole field is aswarm with him, the same young boy in the same blue parka, stretching out his thousands of arms. Waiting to be lifted.

He always vanishes, of course, as soon as I open my eyes. And I'm washing my hands now, scouring them, the soap lather oozing through my fingers. I'm washing hard, but he doesn't wash off.

three

The call comes Tuesday morning, April 7, about 10 minutes before 9, just as I'm walking out the door. Even after coffee, I'm so groggy the phone sounds like the burglar alarm at a jewelry store.

"Mr. Broome?"

A man's voice: high-pitched, folksy.

"Yes?"

"This is Dr. Willinger from Reproductive Resources."

The name registers instantly; it's the circumstances that throw me. I never imagined it happening this way: on the threshold of my apartment, running late for work, wearing my Save the Children tie, carrying a satchel of bottled water and two frozen turkey sandwiches.

"You sent us an application," Dr. Willinger prompts.

"Right." I let the satchel drop. "You turned me down."

"Well..." A short gasping laugh. "That's right. Actually, we were calling to see if you were still interested in being a donor."

"Um." I edge back into the apartment. "I don't understand. Why am I being considered now?"

"To be honest, Mr. Broome, we do periodic reevaluations of past applicants. And in light of the fact that one of our growing client sectors is in the...the lesbian community, and since many of these clients have made specific requests for gay donors..."

"Ah."

"And since you were so candid as to indicate that on your application, we thought it might be worth a call to see if you were still interested."

I'm sitting on the edge of my sofa, staring out the front window of my apartment. I'm watching the wind shoulder through a ginkgo tree.

"Mr. Broome?"

"Right. No, I *am* interested. It's just I'm late for work."

"Oh, I'm sorry."

"No, that's...I don't know why I said that. I'm happy you called. I'm happy to be considered again."

"Well, that's good to hear, that's good to...let me see, we've got your paperwork, everything seems to be in order. I think the next step is just to have you come in and give us a sample."

"A sample."

"Now it looks like you have less flexibility on weekdays, so maybe we should schedule something for Saturday morning?"

So the next Saturday at 9:30 A.M., I am sitting in a slate-carpeted medical office behind a strip mall in Falls Church. The furniture is modular Bauhaus benches, and the only other person in the waiting area is a crop-haired 40-year-old woman in an apricot jumpsuit, skimming through *Us* magazine. The pages crinkle as she turns them, and that's the only sound in the room because the nurses and doctors' assistants are sealed off behind Plexiglas windows, bare except for two bank calendars and the magnetized decal of a high school wrestling team.

I haven't had any food or coffee—some vague notion of keeping my sample pure. It's warm and wet and gusty outside, so I've dressed like a flasher in a black belted raincoat over shorts and running shoes. I've got an umbrella in my lap, and I'm staring at its glen plaid pattern, trying to even out my brain waves.

"Mr. Broome?"

A frosted-blond woman, voluptuous in a black T-shirt and olive-drab trousers. Her waist juts forward, her feet turn out, and her eyes gleam through layers of kohl. She seems to be popping out at me from another dimension.

"We're ready for you now," she says.

I haul myself out of my chair and reach for my umbrella.

"You can leave that," she says, "if you like."

She holds the door open, and as I pass through, I hear her cooing in my ear: "Do you think you'll be needing any magazines today?"

"Um, what do you have?"

"Let's see...." She ticks them off like desserts. "Today we have *Hustler*, *Playboy*, a couple of *Oui*'s..."

"That's OK."

"*Screw*. Um, *Wench*. "

"No. Thanks, I'll just..." She looks at me expectantly. "I'll just wing it," I say.

"OK."

We walk down a long hallway lined with framed sonograms. The pictures have the glossy black finish of publicity photographs, and I half expect to see identifying tags under the fetuses. The longer I look at them, the more the astral shapes seem to unfold before me, like a narrative.

"Right in here, Mr. Broome."

Claudia gestures into a small examining room with a window that looks out onto the brick wall of a music store. Pasted at intervals across the window are tiny photo replicas of Big Ben, the Leaning Tower of Pisa, and the Eiffel Tower.

"Dr. Willinger will be right with you."

"I'm..."

Her head winds around, like a wading bird. "Yes?"

"Do I need to...?" I'm making a waving motion around my zipper.

"No," she says. "Not yet."

She closes the door behind her. I walk over to one of the two butterfly chairs by the window—it's slung so low to the ground that as I sit down it folds me in on myself. I'm struggling to get comfortable when I hear a shave-and-a-haircut knock, and without thinking, I rap out the two-bits coda on the floor. In comes Dr. Willinger.

His voice had led me to expect a smaller man, but he's six-four, easy, with big hands and shoulders and what could be a powerful abdomen or just a swell of fat under an ill-fitting lab coat. He's built for climbing onto roofs. He could be a contractor except for the tiny Mengele glasses and, most disorienting of all, a small golden hoop dangling from his left ear. When he smiles, you see the gap between his front teeth, wide enough to insert two quarters.

"Mr. Broome?"

"Yes."

"Nice to meet you."

A bone-chipping handshake. I almost think he's trying to pull me out of the chair, but then he lets go. He drops into the butterfly chair opposite me; his knees come almost to his chest.

"Well, now." He's paging through a legal-size manila folder. "I know you've read our literature, so you're probably familiar with how we operate." He pulls a felt marker from his shirt pocket, wriggles off the cap. "Maybe we can just discuss some of the key points here."

"OK, sure."

"I want to make certain, first of all, that you understand that the process of becoming a donor is a...a lengthy one. Assuming you pass the initial screening, you'll need to come back for additional sperm samples. We'll also require a full physical, and you'll need to meet with one of our genetic counselors to review your medical history. These are all standard procedures," he says, waving his hand dismissively.

"Uh-huh." I'm watching him very closely: the way he flaps his hand, for example, the trace element of femininity.

"Among the things we will be screening for: HIV, of course; STDs; hepatitis B and C; cytomegalovirus; um, cystic fibrosis. You're not..." He leafs through his file. "You don't have any Jewish ancestry?"

"No."

"French Canadian?"

"Um, no. Just English and a little German, I think."

"Then we won't bother with Tay-Sachs."

"OK, good."

"Now." He closes the folder and crosses his hands over it. I can see the wedding band cinching the skin of his ring finger. "Let's assume," he says, "that after three months of rigorous screening, you are accepted as a sperm donor with Reproductive Resources. Now what exactly does that mean?"

I start to formulate an answer—it's the B-plus student in me—but he's already moving on.

"More than anything else, it means dedication on your part. Because this is a weekly commitment that continues for six months."

"Right."

"And as part of that commitment, you are expected to ensure a healthy sample of sperm each time you donate. So what does that mean? It means avoiding any activity that would raise your scrotal temperature. Saunas. Hot Jacuzzis. Even a very hot shower can...can sometimes get things cooking."

"Uh-huh."

"And, as you know, we also require at least two days of abstinence prior to any donation."

Not a problem, I'm thinking. *My sex life is Trappist. The entire male population is colluding to keep my sperm counts high.*

"Now, of course, you *would* be reimbursed, Mr. Broome. Two hundred twenty-five dollars for each acceptable ejaculate."

"Uh-huh."

"Plus the satisfaction of knowing you're helping somebody who otherwise could not have a child, that's—"

"Right."

"That's priceless. No price tag there."

"Yes."

"At this point, do you have any questions, Mr. Broome?"

"Actually, I did have one. Question."

"Yes?"

I force myself to look out the window. "Is there any way I would *know?* I mean, supposing all this works out and a baby happens. Would I get told?"

"No, I'm..." I look back, and his gentle eyes are blinking, in rapid succession. "We have a strictly confidential process. Which is intended to protect the child and the child's parents and, quite frankly, you. We don't want you being sued for back child support, do we?"

A joke. Dr. Willinger has made a joke.

"You're right," I say. "We wouldn't want that."

"Now you can assume if you are selected that you are a highly fertile specimen, and, of course, that increases your chances of successfully reproducing, but beyond that..." His shoulders perform a slow upward press—a hydraulic shrug. "Beyond that, we can't guarantee or confirm anything."

"I understand."

I'm smiling, I'm nodding in deep affirmation. *I'm a team player, Dr. Willinger. Nick Broome is a team player.*

And it's then I notice the tiny gold fish hanging from a bracelet around his wrist—a Christ fish.

Dr. Willinger is a Christian. When he goes home to his wife today, in the car with the GOD KNOWS bumper sticker and the crucifix hanging from the rearview mirror, when he walks into their cul-de-sac home with the automatic garage-door opener and the Palladian windows and Pergo floors, he will drop his briefcase on the ground and kiss his wife, and he'll say: *Sorry, had to talk to a sodomite.*

"May I ask you something, Mr. Broome?"

"Of course." He's going to ask me if I've been saved.

"It's something we like to ask all our candidates: What got you interested, exactly, in becoming a sperm donor?"

To serve Christ? To glorify the Lord? Nothing's coming to mind. Amazing. Amazing how inarticulate you can be after you've already articulated everything.

I'm a moving target—that's the problem. I slough off theories like skin. Lately, for instance, I've become a believer in biological determinism. I believe that, by some quirk of inheritance, I am the Broome sibling destined to have children. What other destiny do I have? It can't be to read Tolstoy—there are only so many works. It can't be to spend the rest of my life working for an agriculture-obsessed member of Congress. It can't be to go on living in the same apartment building, three blocks from Eastern Market, with a landlord who forbids pets but offers me a bong hit every time I pass him in the courtyard. Destiny doesn't attach itself to any other area of my life. This is the only place left.

Well, anyway, that's how I see it. And it may be how Celia sees it too. Just the other night, she called and asked if I believed in karmic retribution.

"I'm not sure what that is," I said.

"OK, say you did something in a past life. You did something and it was wrong, and it threw the universe out of whack. A little. It disrupted the ethical balance."

"Yeah."

"So the idea is the universe has to realign itself by taking something back the next time around. You have to suffer a little before all the karma is back in equilibrium."

At first, I just assumed Celia had been taking another continuing ed course at the Smithsonian. But lately I've begun to wonder if maybe she and I are independently converging on the same idea. We both feel the inherent instability in the Broome family. We both, in some fashion, regret it. She identifies the problem as karma; I see a shuffle of the genetic deck. The end result is the same: Nick is the one who begets children in blue down parkas.

A woman named Arkeesha comes to take my blood sample. Arkeesha actually prays before she punctures me. "Jesus," she says, "help me stick straight and true." I think maybe she's praying because my veins aren't cooperating. (In the presence of needles, they tend to roll over on their sides like agitated sleepers.) But Arkeesha tells me she prays every single time. "I can't do anything on my own," she says. "The Holy Ghost has got to be working inside me."

And as she packs away the two red vials and the sphygmomanometer and hums a scrap of hymn and scratches herself under the sleeve of her green medical tunic, I think: *Another Christian. A sperm bank operated by Christians.*

So why are they helping lesbians reproduce? Why are they helping *me* reproduce?

In that very moment, I begin to doubt the whole enterprise. It could be the effect of starving myself all morning: I begin to think Reproductive Resources is a front organization for scientific zealots who are...*Just hold that bandage right there*...seeking to inoculate unsuspecting sperm donors with...*That wasn't so bad, was it?*...bacilli that attack the part of the hypothalamus that controls sexual orientation...*You sure got some rolling veins....*

The fear passes quickly enough. I think it's Dr. Willinger's voice. His hand rests lightly on my urine sample, a bright dehydrated yellow, and he says, "Let's review the procedures." And suddenly it's all right.

It's not a relaxing sound—nothing like my father's low liturgical tone, that deep plangent timbre that, when I was a child, sitting through the 9:00 Eucharist, had the same effect on me as a towel draped over a parrot's cage. Dr. Willinger's voice is high and reedy; you can almost see his vocal cords snagging and snarling. So why am I entranced? I watch his large vital hands, encased in latex gloves, gesturing and underscoring. Pointing. Pointing toward the sink.

"You'll need to wash your hands first," he says. "Please use the soap we've provided, and be sure to rinse your hands very thoroughly. That's important. And rinse with water only."

Dr. Willinger, what else would I rinse with? What else but water?

"I'm afraid we can't offer you any lubricants," he says. "They tend to have spermicides in them."

"No, that's fine."

His lips compress into a half-smile. He claps his hands together. "OK then! We'll leave you to it." He takes a couple of steps toward the door. "I don't know whether I mentioned the blinds. You can lower the blinds if you want."

"Oh, OK."

"If you want. It's not like you'll be disturbed."

And then he's gone. The door clicks gently behind him. I'm folded into a butterfly chair, my ankles pressed together and my knees splayed apart and my back to the brick wall of a music store. On top of the wash basin, three feet away, sits a short round flask, the size and shape of a grapefruit-juice glass, and wrapped around it is the label I filled out just 10 minutes ago.

NICHOLAS BROOME. 5/12, 11:03 A.M., 69 hours abstinence.

I pull myself out of the chair—it takes some doing, my knees won't unlock, my back has to unkink itself. I give the liquid soap dispenser two brisk pushes. The white solution coagulates in the palm of my hand. Gluey and opaque, very much like semen. I rub the soap between my fingers, along my palms, across lifelines and lovelines, tennis calluses, knuckles...and I can't shake the feeling: *I'm washing with semen.*

I twist the hot-water lever, and the water sluices over my hands in a white column. I rub, I rub—water *only*, Nick. The water gets hotter, raises steam off the white porcelain. I can see my skin chafing and contracting, and still I keep rubbing, until I can't stand it any longer, until the only thing I can do is pull my hands away.

I hold them in front of my face. They're pink from the heat, and already the skin is bunching into a topical relief map. *Sperm can't be too hot!* I start flapping them, grabbing at every last current of air. The throbbing ebbs, the layer of moisture lifts. My hands slow to stillness and, after a minute, they drop to my side.

It's time.

The examining table rises at a slight angle, like a poolside lounger. I set the flask on an adjoining console, I ease myself onto the table, listening to the scrunch of the protective paper. But the table isn't long enough to hold me; I have to rest my head against the stucco wall. Slowly, slowly, I draw down the zipper of my black twill shorts. I push my fingers under the white band of underclothing, and a few seconds later, I'm pulling clear. My penis lies sleeping in my hand—so peaceful I hate to wake it.

And this room seems calculated not to wake it. No music from the intercom. No violet scrims on the overhead lights. Just cream-colored walls and salt-and-pepper floor tile and a gray wash of rain-soaked sun angling off the music store. Why didn't I take the magazines? I might have been able to work with the magazines.

I start the motion: a slow, interrogative back and forth. And after a while, the muscle memory takes over, and I feel myself growing detached from the process—a turbine in a great valved apparatus, churning out seed, filling the human granary.

But then I realize the granary isn't filling. *The granary isn't...filling....*

I stare at my penis. It makes a Senor Wences frown. *No go,* it says. *Think of something else.*

And I can't. Not a blessed thing.

Who would have thought? All the anxiety that I used to associate with sexual partners...it's here! Lying next to me in the bed, the most demanding lover in the world. *I can't wait forever, you know.*

My eyes scatter across every surface in the room, looking for points of attachment. The wash basin. The supply cabinet. The stack of gauze. The paper-towel dispenser.

And then I look at the window sill. The monuments. Eiffel Tower, Big Ben, the Leaning Tower of Pisa.

Of course! Phallic reinforcement.

Except they're not working, Dr. Willinger. The monuments of Europe are not working. The back of my head scrapes against the stucco, the suspension bridge of my neck tenses, and everything else tenses too: feet, hips, wrists, everything but my penis, groggy and querulous, as rubbery as overworked pastry. I'm calling to it, silently, like a coxswain. *Stroke! Stroke!* I'm dragging it down the long green river to Pisa. *Stroke! Stroke!*

My lungs draw deeper drafts. My heart roars like a coal furnace. A tingle of sweat curls past my ear. Everything is converging toward this single act from which everything else begins. I'm hovering over myself, barking commands through a megaphone. *Your last shot, Nick! Don't fuck it up.*

And that finishes it: the image of me watching me. I stop stroking. My hand drops away.

It's not fair. That's what I want to tell them. I'm not in college anymore. It doesn't spring up anymore, not on its own; it needs wooing. I'm 34, nearly past my genetic viability. I need a better environment, I need *accommodations.* People with wheelchairs get ramps—what do I get? Where are the underwear catalogs, the Tarzan movies? The rodeo calendar?

My mind whirls on its axis, riffling through faces and bodies, sliding them across my viewfinder. Nothing. Nothing.

OK, now is the time to remain calm. Now is the time to remind yourself of certain truths. First, there are no demanding lovers lying next to you in bed. Second, no one is keeping time. Third, no one is standing outside the door listening.

And, of course, as soon as I've uttered number 3, my mind becomes an accomplice to the thought, and from the whirligig of images in my head, one breaks free, adheres. It is the image of Dr. Willinger standing just outside the door, checking his watch, making encryptions on the upper right-hand corner of his clipboard.

I close my eyes, and I try to drive the image away. But a subversive voice winds itself around my inner ear and purrs: *Invite him in.*

And I know then it's the only polite thing to do. *Come in, Dr. Willinger.*

The door opens practically on its own, soundlessly. All I see at first is a single hand with a large gold band on the ring finger. The rest of him comes later: the hillock of abdomen, a little firmer than I recall it, guiding him toward the wan squares of light on the floor. He's even bigger than I remember—his shoulders strain through the polyester weave of his lab coat. The clipboard is tucked under his arm, and his hands are shoved into his pockets. He's jingling his car keys, nonchalant and powerful.

He's not looking at me, but he's following my progress. He knows I will get there. There's no need for him to turn until the time is at hand.

And now, quick as a hiccup, all the anxiety is gone. All the blood is pumping into my Tower of Pisa.

Dr. Willinger turns, like someone on a rotating floor. His lips part to reveal the gap in his front teeth, through which his tongue slides back and forth. His mild hazel eyes warm and deepen. He is pleased. He is fascinated with my progress.

I grab for the flask on the console. I see Dr. Willinger's arm rise toward his face. The sleeve of his lab coat falls back, and there it is, the fish locket, and Dr. Willinger presses it to his mouth, kisses it with a gentle ecstatic pulse. And he is kissing me at the same time, just below my Adam's apple, anointing my carotid artery with his tongue.

He is saying: *Congratulations, Nick.*

And I'm saying...I'm saying...

And we're both looking at each other when it comes. We're smiling, and all around us schools of Atlantic herring are jettisoning eggs and sperm, and the whole room is full of creation, and children are screaming for the pleasure of it, and toy wagons are scooting around the examining table, and Dr. Willinger is undoing the top button of his shirt,and the music store next door is playing a mazurka so loudly that the window cracks into tiny fissures, and the children's voices are chiming along with the music, their hands are beating time on Big Ben, and the whole world is dancing mazurkas of my composing.

four

Over the next several days, the patch of skin where Arkeesha drew blood changes color. It passes from dusty rose to jade and emerald before settling into a malarial yellow, which gathers into port-colored blotches.

It expands too, my little bruise, from a thumbprint to a pond, spreads from the crook of my arm to the delta of veins in my wrist. It's currently about four inches in diameter. Now and then, my mind flashes back to the conspiracy theories that came over me in the examining room, and there are times when it does seem possible, slightly possible, that Jesus pushed the needle awry. But I can't take the idea too seriously because the arm doesn't hurt, and nothing else does either. I feel, for the first time in months, a flush of health. I take up running again, in earnest. Monday, Wednesday, and Friday, I leave my office building during lunch and jog down the Mall, past all the Smithsonian appendages, past the Washington Monument, the reflecting pool, the military memorials, all the way to Abraham Lincoln, melancholy baby, brightening a little each time I approach. I dance up the marble steps. *Mr. President, it's me, Nick Broome!*

At moments like this, I can almost believe that instead of drawing my blood, Arkeesha inoculated me with faith. What else explains this slow IV drip of euphoria? It's Arkeesha! She looms particularly large in my mind because by quirk of fate I run into her during one of my jogs—*literally* run into her. I am stopped on the west side of 14th Street, waiting for the light to change, and alongside me is a short, powerfully built woman in pink tennis shoes and surgical scrubs, and when the traffic pauses I bolt to the right, and she steps to the left, and by the time I have caught her arm and helped her regain her balance, I know who she is.

"Arkeesha."

Her face lights up with something that may be recognition. "Well, hi!" she says.

We stare at each other for a few seconds and then, by silent agreement, step back onto the curb.

"How are you?" I ask.

She says: "Blessed."

And, under normal circumstances, that response would throw me, I would have no answer for it. But today I understand her point exactly.

"I don't know if you remember," I say. "Reproductive Resources."

"Sure, sure! How's it going?"

"Well, great, actually, I'm...I'm waiting to hear back, you know, from my tests. The samples and the blood work." Instinctively, I wrap my bruised right arm behind my back. "I'm sort of nervous about it."

"Well," Arkeesha says, "if God wills it, it will be."

Her eyes close. Her head strains upward and her lips fall back from her teeth. I realize then that her serenity has made a kind of wall between us. I get the same feeling when I walk past my landlord and his friends in the courtyard—all of them wearing Hawaiian shirts and smoking pot.

"So I'm going away this weekend," I tell Arkeesha.

"That right?"

"Rehoboth Beach, actually. Over in Delaware?" Chattering, chattering. "It's my father's birthday—70th birthday—that's why we're all going. To celebrate. My parents, my sister, my brother, and his wife.

We're renting a house right off the beach."

"Well!"

"The only reason I bring it up, I wasn't sure...I was wondering if they might call this weekend."

"They might," Arkeesha says.

"They said they might be done in a week, and since I was there *last* Saturday, I thought maybe *this* Saturday..."

"Who can say?" Arkeesha says.

The WALK sign is flashing again. A bog of tourists is oozing past us.

"So I figured it might make sense to check my messages just in case. Because I'll be staying there Monday too."

"Sure," Arkeesha says. And then she considers it some more. "Or even call them yourself if you don't hear from them."

"Really?"

"That's what I'd do."

What amazes me is she doesn't seem to care how long I keep her. She never looks away, not once, even though she must have places to go, bruises to create on the other side of 14th Street.

It is this abiding quality that I try to carry with me to Rehoboth—but it blows off somewhere on the third day. I'm standing by the Atlantic Ocean; rain is lashing the water; and I'm remembering how, in my mind, this was going to be an absolutely still day, a frozen mid-spring moment, the clouds holding far off, the waves shuddering at the noise they make. A boat would have been cruising parallel to the shore—advertising for one of the local crab shacks—and close behind it a school of dolphins, just a row of fins at first, ominous until the grinning heads burst through the surface. My eyes would have stayed with them for a few minutes and then shifted farther to sea, past the scalloped lines of waves to the kiwi-colored horizon, where schools of Atlantic herring would have been swirling in columns of seed.

But that's not how it's turned out. We've gotten rain instead—endless siphons of rain. When we arrived early Saturday morning, the clouds were already massing in large sodden blankets on the western rim of Silver Lake. Such was the power of Arkeesha's faith injection that I saw the clouds as pregnant. Everything was pregnant. Hydrangea and lavender and bamboo. Seagulls with chocolate-dipped heads. A colony of monk parakeets screeching on top of a utility pole. People too: Jersey guys flashing gold; children building huge toothed forts in the sand; a group of Mennonites, sweaty and stiff in handmade bonnets, eating griddle cakes and clutching bags from Bargain Hut. The whole world was layered with life.

But now the rain is merging imperceptibly with the sky and the sand, and every outline has disappeared except for the hard black poles of the piers, climbing like ladders.

The house we have rented is not a good place to be marooned. The only board game is a 20-year-old edition of Masterpiece with half the paintings gone. The only music is Johnny Mathis and Patti Page. The art! A gallery of taxidermic birds—ravens, ospreys, screech owls—so understuffed that, even in death, they appear to be starving. Celia finally had to take down the grim black tern that hung over the fireplace mantel: It was breaking her heart.

I don't want to go back there. But the rain is dragging its fingers down my umbrella, and if I stay any longer, my skin will congeal, and my bones will turn to aspic. And so I go back. And when I step through the doorway of our rental house, everyone looks up at me with a ragged, forlorn hope. Am I bringing them food? Has the rain stopped?

But all they have to do is look at me, and the hope drains from their faces, and once again I see what happens to us when we're together too long: Our bones grow hollow.

A child would change all this.

My mother is knitting a raglan sleeve. Only in the last year has she taken up knitting, and she works about as slowly as my father does with his carpentry. As far as I can tell, she has been working this sleeve since Labor Day. "Do you want any cake?" she asks.

Probably she's being funny. The refrigerator broke down yesterday. We didn't realize it until late in the evening, and by then it was too late to save my father's birthday cake: a mocha ice cream creation my mother bought at the Tysons Corner Carvel. Greg and Sally volunteered to find a replacement, but since most of the stores were closed, all they brought home was an Entenmann's crumb cake. At 10:45, with my father openly yawning, we gathered around an aluminum tray of strudel topping. My mother inserted two lit matches—she'd forgotten the candles—and we sang "Happy Birthday," and Mom tried to cut portions with a butter knife but gave up after a few minutes. We ended up just reaching into the box and grabbing chunks of yellow cake.

Normally, that would have qualified as the low point of our stay, but today we woke up to more rain—barrel after barrel of rain. And so everything seems like a low point now.

"Nick," my mother says. "If you want to go out somewhere and do your own thing, that's perfectly fine."

"My own thing?"

"You know, local establishments."

By which she means gay bars. Emily Broome, bless her, vice president of the local PFLAG chapter. Wants to know every time I come over if I'm bringing someone. Saves me her back issues of *The Advocate.* Carries around little cards to reprimand homophobes.

"OK, I'll see how I feel," I say.

The last time I went to one of the Rehoboth nightspots, I made the mistake of going alone, three hours before nightfall, when everything was a little too lucid: the Chinese lanterns hanging from the overhead trellis, the stain on the bartender's pants. The only man who even eyed me twice was militantly bald, in a flowered shirt—Michel Foucault, vacationing in Tahiti. I left half an hour later, alone, and there was a parking ticket waiting for me on my car, tucked inside a yellow envelope like a telethon pledge.

I'm not eager to go back, and even if I were, I have my phone vigil to keep. Every hour on the hour, I check my messages (with the exception of Sunday: I figure Dr. Willinger won't call on a holy day). Whatever I'm doing—playing cards, making sandwiches, going mad—I stop doing, and I walk into the back bedroom, the one I share with Celia, and I dial my voice mail service and I wait for the woman's voice to say: "There are...*no* messages in your mailbox." And even after

I've heard her say it, I linger for a second or two in case she comes back. This has not yet happened. So far I have called 15 times and received exactly one message—from Shannon, who wants to tell me about the Mormon lawyer she met in her Pilates class. "He's very tall, he's taking me to a Frederick Keys game, you're not home yet. When are you coming home?"

I honestly don't know. It's 3:30 on Monday afternoon, and we're technically supposed to leave after 6, but the rain is still thrumming on our little A-frame, and I have come to believe it will never stop and the rest of our lives will look just like this: decorative flotsam, shellacked wood sculpture, hungry birds.

"Does anyone want to play cards?"

It's Sally: sitting on the sofa, skinny as an ermine in her oversize T-shirt and gym shorts. She's just showered after taking a very wet jog, and her face looks pink and fiercely scrubbed, as though someone's gone at her with a pumice stone. Her formidable microtoothed smile is blazing.

"What about hearts?" she suggests. "Everyone knows hearts, right?"

Sally has been part of this family for six years, and she's still waiting for something to happen. It touches me. I don't know how to disabuse her; I don't know if I should.

"Go ahead," Greg says. "Start without me." A Walkman is clamped to his head. He's hunched over a tiny magnetized chessboard, playing both sides because none of us can keep up with him.

"What about it, Emily?"

My mother draws her crochet hook toward her. "I don't mind," she says.

"Oliver?"

"Oh," he says.

We all turn to him, by common consent. He's sitting at the kitchen table, with a block of ash wood in his lap. He retrieved it last week from one of the neighbors' garbage cans, and for most of the day he has been whittling it with a Swiss Army knife. Through the legs of his chair, you can see the small mound of shavings. The wood has been hacked from all angles and is taking on the appearance of a starfish or a sea urchin.

"Cards," he says.

"Cards," Sally says, almost to herself. "We need cards."

But no one is exactly sure where the cards are. Celia was playing solitaire, Nick and Emily did a little gin rummy, maybe that was *another* deck of cards....

"No, wait," Sally says. "They're on the sun porch."

And she's already up, her veined brown legs skimming across the floor, hurling herself at the screen door.

We're getting to her. I make a mental note to myself. *We're finally getting to her.*

"I had a very unusual experience the other day," says my mother, lifting her head. "Did I tell you about this?"

"No, I don't think so."

"I was shopping at Nordstrom. Don't ask me why, the markup is incredible, but there I was, trying on sweaters. I must have tried on three sweaters. Didn't like a-one of them. I put them back, I started to leave...and I looked back, and what did I see but this man? Following me."

"Uh-oh," says Celia, politely.

"And he had a store ID, so I knew he had to work there. So all I could think was I was still wearing one of the sweaters. But I wasn't."

"Uh-huh," I say.

"And what threw me was he was smiling. Grinning from ear to ear. So I said, 'I'm sorry, is there a problem?' And he said, 'I just want you to know. I have been working in this store for five years, and I have seen a lot of people try on sweaters, and you are the first person who folded them back exactly the way they were folded before.'"

"That can't be true!" Sally's back from the porch, a deck of cards crushed in her palm. "I always fold the sweaters."

"Well, he said people *try*, but they don't really do it. 'But you,' he said. 'You did it perfectly.'" My mother looks down at her raglan sleeve. Another draw of the yarn. "I made his day, apparently. I think it was the happiest he's been his whole life."

"He was pretty easy," Celia says. She's sitting on the twig rocker, next to the shell-encrusted coffee table. "I think he was too easy. What do you think, Dad?"

My father's Swiss Army knife is making a slow lazy circle just above the table. A martial art in miniature.

"However you can get it," he says. "Whatever it takes."

"Oh!" Celia rocks forward in her chair. "Dad, I forgot to tell you, on the way here? Nicky and I were coming down 404, and we stopped at this roadside stand? And right in front, there was this row of ceramic statues, little statuettes, you know, elves and...and bluebirds...."

"Cactuses," I prompt.

"*Cactuses*, and right in the middle, OK, was this *grove* of Virgin Marys. At least a dozen of them. Ceramic Virgin Marys."

"Different sizes," I say.

"Right, different sizes, that's important. So we looked at one of the price tags, and this is what it said." She waits, calculating her effect. "*Medium Virgin Mary, $18.95.*"

No one says a word. Sally stands by the porch door, flexing the deck of cards in her hand. Greg bends over his chessboard, sniffing out a rook. My father spins his block of wood.

"So it was a little expensive," my mother suggests.

"No!" Celia shakes her head. "See, what's funny is you think of olive oil. You think, virgin, extra virgin."

Silence.

Celia's voice is starting to rasp. "Extra-Virgin Mary...."

"Or Groucho Marx." That's *my* voice cutting in. "Remember? Doris Day or somebody. He knew her before she was a virgin...."

And now my father, for the first time in hours, reenters our atmosphere. His eyes engage mine in a spirit of collegial inquiry. "Did Groucho Marx say that?"

"Um."

"I thought it was Oscar Levant."

"It sounds more like Oscar Levant," my mother says.

Dad straightens his back. He's on a symposium panel. "And I'm not sure it was Doris Day. Although it might have been."

I look at Celia, and she's tacking on, God save her.

"But the *point*," she's saying, "is you have those neighbors. The ones with the nativity scene. You could buy it for them. Medium Virgin Mary, they could put it in their yard next Christmas."

"Their yard." And with that my father's gone again. The symposium is over.

"Oh, we have lots of neighbors," says my mother.

"I'm talking about a particular neighbor," Celia says. "One particular neighbor."

"Well, why would we give those people a statue? We don't know them."

"Give up!" Greg is roaring to us from deep inside his headphones. "Give up!"

But Celia won't. "OK," she says. "Here's the thing. It's not whether you know these people. That's not relevant. What's relevant is that this statue, this *particular* statue—Medium Virgin Mary—would, by its nature, be in keeping with the nativity scene in their front yard. Which is the only point that is being made here."

And my mother just keeps drawing the yarn. "If you want to give them the statue," she says, "you can give them the statue."

Suddenly, I'm on my feet. A minute ago, I wouldn't have had the energy, but now I'm brushing past my mother, past Celia (who *has* given up now: rocked to a halt, drawn her knees into her chest), past Sally, past Greg. I'm speaking as I go.

"I need to check my messages."

And by the time I'm finished saying it, I'm already halfway to the back bedroom. I close the door behind me. I seat myself on the leftmost side of the sofa bed. I stare at the one-room schoolhouse that's imprinted on all the cushions. I reach for the handset, punch in the numbers. I listen to the welcoming timbre of the voice mail woman. I wait one second. Two. Three.

And then, like a chord of memory: "You have *one* message."

Listen. I press the key. *Let me listen.*

I hear: "Mr. Broome."

The voice. Unmistakable. I bend over the handset, cradle it against my belly.

"This is Dr. Willinger from Reproductive Resources. Please call us when you get a chance. We'd like to go over your test results."

I look at my watch: five minutes to 4. There's time. There's plenty of time. And I have already committed the number to memory. It's burrowed so deep it's like a prime number.

Dial slowly now. No mistakes. Try not to think of Dr. Willinger's wording. *Go over. Go over...*

"Reproductive Resources."

"Yeah!" I look up suddenly. "This is Nicholas Broome, returning Dr. Willinger's call."

"Hold on, please."

My eyes dance across the room, settle finally on a strange crooked heap in the corner—a mass of feathers, dove-gray shading into tar. From the jumble, a beak materializes, and from there a head, and from there a single black eye, bottomless.

It's the black tern. The one Celia took down from the fireplace. She must have tossed it in the bedroom corner; she must have thought no one would have to look at it again.

"Mr. Broome!"

I'm looking so intently at the bird that the voice doesn't quite register at first. It rolls around the rim of my ear like a basketball.

"How are you?" asks Dr. Willinger.

"Fine! I'm calling you back." I shake my head. "From the beach."

"Oh, the beach," he says.

"It's warm here."

"I'll bet."

"Although it's raining now."

"Raining."

Close your eyes. Wait. Wait.

"Well," says Dr. Willinger, suddenly breezy, "I'm sure you want to hear how your tests turned out."

In my mind's eye, I see the large hands flipping open the legal-size manila folder, thumbing through the sheaf of papers, tracing the columns of numbers.

"OK," he says. "The blood work was fine."

"Good."

"The only problem was the sperm sample itself."

My eyes close so tightly I can hear the sound of my lids welding to my face. "The sperm?"

"Let me explain, Mr. Broome. To *qualify*, at least 50% of your sperm must be motile."

"Motile?"

"By which we mean capable of movement. You can probably guess that the ability to move is a good quality for sperm to have."

"Uh-huh."

"They have to be able to swim, don't they?"

"Uh-huh."

"And, unfortunately, your sample did not meet the 50% threshold."

Breathe. Breathe. "So..." The words are so deep in my throat, I have to muscle them back up. "What you're telling me. I don't know what you're...no, you're telling me I'm sterile."

"Oh, no, no, no. Not at all, Mr. Broome. It's a common condition, and you're still quite capable of having children. It's just that at Reproductive Resources, we have to limit ourselves to the *most* fertile specimens. I'm sure you understand, we want our clients to have the best up-front odds for reproduction."

My eyes are open now. "Maybe I could get more motile," I say. "With time."

"Usually not, I'm afraid. Fertility tends to decline with age. But once again, Mr. Broome, you are still fully capable of fathering a child. Nothing I've said changes that."

And now the black tern is looking at me as closely as I'm looking at him. He is cocking his head, trying to get me in his sights. One of his skinny talons has unfurled.

I say, "I'm a Christian."

"I don't understand."

"I go to church. Once a month. All the sacraments, the full Episcopalian mass."

"That's not—"

"My father's a minister," I say, a little more loudly. "He completely approves of what I'm doing. There's no question of religious incompatibility here. Quite the opposite."

"Mr. Broome, I have to tell you—"

"Ask Arkeesha. We talked the other day. We *talked*."

"Mr. Broome—"

"*Nicholas*!" My mother. Calling to me from the living room. "We need you!" she cries.

And Dr. Willinger's voice, that instrument of seduction, has become a businessman's drone. I can barely hear it now. "...no religious affiliation, and these issues have no impact on our selection process, which is entirely in accordance with..."

And I find myself actually looking to the black tern for comfort. Because even in his broken condition, he looks receptive.

"No one can remember the bridge thing!" my mother is yelling. "The scoring business."

"...understand your disappointment. We wish you the very best in future endeavors...."

Dr. Willinger's voice vanishes. The only thing I hear now is rain, pelting the roof and the windows and the hydrangea bushes. The tern closes its eye.

"I'll be right there," I say.

Natasha

five

It's the tail. I've been reading up on the subject. A single flagellum, several micrometers long, motoring the sperm cell through the prostate and seminal vesicles, through the Cowper's glands and urethral duct. The tail, propelling everything else forward.

But this makes me ponder something: What about the sperm that don't have tails? What compensating functions have *they* developed? Joke telling? Something less hopeful? I'm reminded of my high school gym class: me and the other weaklings, sitting behind the batting cage, raging at the athlete gods. We were bitter, of course: We lacked motility. And so now my sperm pay me the perverse compliment of imitating me. They sit in the bleachers while more muscular specimens execute perfect spirals, punch fastballs into deep right field. And it's no easier to accept this now than when I was 14. I chafe. I chafe. The only thing that makes it even bearable is the fact that no one else knows. No one except Dr. Willinger, who has surely forgotten all about me. And Shannon, of course. There is always Shannon. As soon as I get back from the beach, I blurt the news to her, and she, in the name of friendship, tries to convince me that my problem is everything except what it actually is. For a short period, she is convinced it's generational.

"Think about it, Nick. If you'd been born 40 years earlier, you wouldn't have *thought* of coming out when you were, how old were you?"

"24."

"Please. You would have been pressured into marrying some poor dupe—*me* probably. Three kids, you're 40, you fall in love with our son's scoutmaster, art teacher, I don't know. Get some cabin on the West Virginia line, see the kids every Christmas."

"Sounds kind of brutal."

"Oh, trauma, of course. Trauma for days. But you'd have the kids, free and clear."

I'm not convinced. Even if I were married, I would still have dog-paddling sperm, so how much more breeding could I have done in the days of Eisenhower? I don't mention this to Shannon because she's already moving on to her next theory.

"You know what your real problem is? You are too hung up on the biological thing."

"The biological thing?"

"The gene thing. You need to ask yourself: Why is it so important to pass on your genes? What does it matter? We're all dust anyway."

And then I remember: Shannon has just been to visit her mother. After the last visit, she talked very seriously about tubal ligation.

"Listen to me," she says. "Do you know how many people are in this world?"

"I don't know. Trillions?"

"And growing! In 40 years, the world's population will be double what it is today."

"How do you know this?"

"One of my clients," she says. "International Commission to Ban Birth. Their motto is NO MORE NEW BABIES UNTIL EVERY LIVING CHILD HAS A HOME."

"Oh."

"Tell me something, Nick. How are you helping the world by bringing more bodies into it? People are starving, where are they starving?"

"Uganda?"

"At *least.* We can't even feed the people we have, why add more?"

I'm never sure what to say when poverty and hunger are used against me. The only response I can think to make is: "Why are you yelling at me? I'm completely celibate."

Or at least I *was* celibate. I will be once again. In between, there is a remission. It lasts 15 minutes and is triggered by a man I pass on the way home from work. He is 40 possibly, in a threadbare undershirt and green soccer shorts, resting one of his feet on a high wrought-iron gate so I can catch a good glimpse of the back of his thigh. An absurd position. I think: *This man is trying to be seductive.* My dick doesn't grasp the humor. My dick's response is irony-free. Three minutes later, I am lying on a bare mattress in an unfurnished apartment with parquet floors. We are circled the entire time by a pair of shih tzus who keep darting toward the mattress, then darting away again. I half expect them to climb on with us, but they're too busy watching, and when the whole sorry business is over, I have the strongest urge to go over it with them, point out some of the nuances they may have missed.

I don't say good-bye. I don't check to make sure I have everything. It's only when I reach my apartment that I realize my belt is still unbuckled, and my undershirt is missing. I close the door behind me, throw down my bag, collapse on the sofa. After a few minutes, I get up and cross the room, reach for Tolstoy on the top shelf of the bookcase. The pages fall away like wheat; the passage stands revealed:

> *Natasha's face, which had been so radiantly happy all that saint's day, suddenly changed: Her eyes became fixed, and then a shiver passed down her broad neck and the corners of her mouth drooped.*
>
> *"Sonya! What is it?...What is the matter?...Oo...Oo...Oo...!"*

And I realize then: *She's getting away from me.* Every time I forget my mission, every time I sleep with a man in green soccer shorts, Natasha slips further and further away. And unless I get myself back on track, she will *not* come bursting into the Broomes' Christmases, she will *not* be part of our birthday celebrations. The Broomes will bob and sink, like a cloud drowning in a lake.

The phone rings.

"Oh, you're home," my mother says.

Always, this astonishment when I pick up my phone—and a faint overlay of rue. I think she'd rather talk to my voice mail.

"Now I know you're busy," she says, "but I'm just calling to ask a little favor."

"Sure, Mom."

"It's about Hoy Phong. You remember Hoy."

"Of course."

"Actually, it's good news, because Hoy's best friend has this cousin who works in a convenience store, and this store needs a stock boy—entry-level kind of position—and so Hoy applied, and they offered him the job, which I couldn't be happier about. But the *amazing* part is this store is right around the corner."

"From where?"

"From you!"

"You're kidding, what's the name?"

"Um...I know this sounds awful, but it's a Jewish kind of name. You know, Kleinberg or Weinberg or something."

"So you want me to stop by and check on him?"

"Well, I don't want him to think I'm spying. Maybe you could just stop by sometime on your way home from work or something. But give it a few days, because it's not a big deal or anything. I just wanted to see how he's doing."

"OK."

"Only because it's the first real job he's had since, you know, prison."

Has any felon ever had a more devoted champion than my mother? She spends three hours every Thursday afternoon tutoring Hoy Phong in English, math, and American history; reviewing classified ads; helping him fill out job applications. And that doesn't include the hours she puts in on the phone, the dark nights of Hoy's soul: busted marriage plans, accidental run-ins with old drug connections. It's a half-time job, really, and whenever I call my mother, chances are good she's on the other line with Hoy, and chances are even better she'll ask me to call back.

"Honey, I can't talk. He just got through his last rehab class, and it's a mixed feeling...."

I've never actually met Hoy, although I have seen a picture of him—a soft-focus portrait of a small, fine-boned man standing with my mother in a rose garden near Ballston. There's about a foot of space between them, and Emily Broome is looking down at her hands, and Hoy is gazing directly into her face, nakedly adoring. They look embarrassed, as though they've been caught smooching, and Hoy's spiky black hair shoots for the sky like a gusher of oil.

My mother keeps this photograph in a gilt frame on the wine table in her living room, and whenever I see it there, I realize that in another world this same table would be swarming with photographs of children, round pink heads thrust into the viewfinder. In this world, Emily Broome would be knitting scarves, baking oatmeal cookies, slipping crisply folded dollar bills into her grandkids' pockets. Instead, she is penning references. She is consulting with parole officers and engaging in on-the-job surveillance. This is what we have reduced her to: a promiscuous philanthropy.

I tell her I'll look in on Hoy next week.

"Now don't look like you're looking," she says. "Don't *look*."

Later that night Shannon and I are sitting in a coffee lounge with saggy-bottomed burnt-orange sofa beds, draped in shawls. One of those places where you feel like you're spending the night in somebody's parents' basement, and all the people around you are having their own private slumber party—playing chess, banging out novels on laptops, reading Blake poems, doing everything but drinking coffee. Shannon and I are the only ones drinking anything, and it's iced Raspberry Zinger.

"You know what your problem is?" Shannon says suddenly.

"What?"

"You're a wimp."

Is there a vein of tenderness in her voice? I'm struggling to find the tenderness.

"Think about it," she says. "You've been going through sperm banks, which are what? Corporate interests that have no stake in helping you realize your goal. They could give a shit. Am I right?"

I shrug.

"So what does that mean?" she asks. "It means, if you'll excuse the expression, taking this into your own hands. You want to father a child, you're going to have to start getting a little proactive."

She spends the next few seconds smearing her straw with plum-colored lipstick. "Your real problem is you don't know any goddamned lesbians."

"That's not true," I say. "I know two."

Quickly, I tabulate them in my mind. Charlotte, the aerobic boxing teacher at my gym. Nancy, or maybe Pamela, Celia's friend, the silk-screen artist who used to belong to a Carmelite order...

"No, three," I say. "I think our new legislative assistant might be."

"Please, legislative assistant, do you know how pathetic you sound?"

"I knew more in college," I insist. "I lost touch."

"Jesus, what is it with you people? Don't you even go to the same meetings?"

"I don't go to meetings." I mean it to sound defiant, but it comes out wistful, and I hate myself for the softening it produces in Shannon's tone.

"The only reason I bring it up," she says, "is there must be zillions of lesbians out there looking for someone to father their child. I mean, they can drink all the hibiscus tea in the world, they can do Wiccan chants till they're blue in the face, they still need the guy stuff." She leans toward me across the ceramic coffee table. Her eyes flare open like a wolf's eyes. "*You've* got the guy stuff."

"It doesn't move."

"Nick." She drops her head back until she is staring at the ceiling. "How many—out of all the zillions, trillions of sperm—how many do you need to do the job? *One*, right? Last I checked it was one. Now I think you can handle that."

This touches me, I have to say. I'm not galvanized exactly, but I am warmed. For the first time it seems somebody is actively wishing me well. So how can I not wish myself well? A good question because I have been struggling with a cold for several days, and eventually it gets deep enough into my chest to warrant a sick day, and so I spend most of Thursday on my couch, watching those mysterious television programs that play themselves out every day without my knowing. It's hard work. By 4:00 in the afternoon, I'm so doped up on talk shows and antihistamines, I have to go for a walk.

I don't have any clear purpose in mind; I'm just wandering in the general direction of an iodine strip of cloud. And when I pass the playground, I almost don't stop because it's not on my itinerary and because I've passed this place dozens of times before—one of those urban Catholic schools where the students wear pleated green-tartan skirts and pants and look nothing like the kids who used to sing with Bing Crosby. Most of them have already gone for the day, but a few are still clustered in the center of the blacktop, wriggling through a massive orange-and-blue interactive complex. Playgrounds have changed! When I was a kid, our school blacktop housed a single swing set, a set of monkey bars, and a single netless basketball hoop. Now the blacktops have condominiums: mazes of interlocking cages and landings and grids, firefighter's poles, tic-tac-toe abacuses, slides, and chutes—a riot of squiggles and corkscrews and hairpin curves.

God bless 'em, though, there's still a swing set, and two kids are still swinging on it. A pair of girls, sisters maybe, pointing their saddle shoes to the sky and screaming all the way to the nearest satellite. "Hi!" they're screaming.

Not "hi," I soon realize. "High!" And the sound they make is their engine, propelling them upward, and their arc is so absorbing I barely notice the short, wide-waisted woman in the unbuttoned raincoat, standing between them and leaning into them as they pitch forward. A silent woman, proprietary, unruffled, ready for anything.

And as I watch her, an image of my father comes to me in a rush of memory, like a current running just beneath my skin. I remember him standing in this same position, behind the candy-cane swing set in our backyard, pressing his hands into the small of my back. I always wanted to go higher, too. I wanted to keep swinging until I whirled in a perfect circle, until the swing ran out of chain and left me dangling like a parachutist. But something in me always pulled back.

Hard to believe it was really my father there. Hard to imagine him standing like that for 30 minutes, a full hour. But he was there the day I made a compact with death: hurled myself from the swing and got nothing but a sprained knee for it. Dad was right on top of me. Grabbed me around the waist, hustled me into the house. "Incoming wounded!" he called.

And when I think about it, this was when he was most intimately and demonstratively happening to me—most clearly my father. In moments like this I was fashioned. What a mistake, then, to think that casting my sperm on the waters would be the same as creating a child. I must have known I was wrong. I must have seen that filling vials for Dr. Willinger was just a preparatory exercise for the work of fathering a child, knowingly, with another human being. *This* is the mission that gathers inside me. When this long long year has finally popped its spring, I will go to my family and the news will *not* be "I have fathered a child" but rather "I have just begun to father a child." And my brother, my sister, anyone who has ever doubted me, will know that I am serious, that I welcome the consequences. Colic, tantrums, semi-liquid solids, chipped teeth, locked doors, pubic hair, mortarboards, second mortgages...bring 'em on!

I am no longer an Atlantic herring. I have rejoined the mammals, and I am seeking another mammal the only way I know how. I am placing an ad.

> *PARENTING PARTNER SOUGHT. GWM, 34, 6'2", 190lbs., br/br, HIV neg, seeks GWF/GBF/GLF/GAF, prof, nonsmoker, for joint-parenting arrangement. Artificial insemination preferred.*

Applicant must be willing to share birthing adventure + custody of resulting child from birth to adulthood. Joint residency not necessary. Discretion and confidentiality assured.

So strange to see it laid out like this, reduced to market terms. This is how people sell their old skis, isn't it? Get rid of their Acuras, their high school trombones. Start book clubs. And when I scan the ad, I notice that other than requesting a lesbian, I have been quite vague about whom I'm seeking. Perhaps that's for the best. I think my problems have always come from envisioning things too clearly. Capitol Cryobank, for instance. Love.

My ad will appear in tomorrow's *City Paper*, in the "None of the Above" section. Respondents (18 and above) will have to dial a 1-900 number and leave a message that costs $1.49 a minute. They will find the ad floating in a great ocean of yearning: slaves, dominatrixes, square dancers, back rubbers. It will be sandwiched between ads for escort services, phone-sex lines, breast and penis augmentation. I'm amazed by how much this embarrasses me. A new puritanism hardens my jaw. I envision the moment when my son/daughter asks how he/she came to be, and already I'm censoring the account, devising some plausible reason for knowing the mother, a random encounter in a lane of sycamores. And yes, it will be a lie, but it will be the first lie I ever tell my child. And the last one, I swear to you, the last lie.

The night before my ad runs, I get a call from my father. He says, "I want to know who's been sending me these letters."

"Which ones?"

"The antismoking propaganda. You've seen 'em, I know you've seen 'em. Little ransom notes, cut-up newspapers and magazines. 'Smoking Kills.' 'Next Cigarette Will Be Your Last.' Terrible melodramatic stuff."

"Um, I can't really think of anyone. I thought it was maybe your—what was her name, Doris?—your old secretary."

"Well, that was a theory," my father says. "But I can't think it's anyone who really knows me. You know, the last one said, 'Think of Your Grandchildren.'"

"Oh."

"Which makes me think they don't know me."

"Probably not," I say.

My father is always the one I want to tell. He's the one I picture dangling from a sisal bridge, over a piranha-choked river. I want to tell him help is on the way. Within two years' time, Takoma Park will inherit its newest nontraditional family: a boy with your overbite, a girl with your large, staring, gray eyes. Your future, Dad.

"There must be a list somewhere," my father is saying. "Some list that gives you the names of smokers, where they live. Something any nutcase can get ahold of."

"Maybe it's just someone who wants you to live longer," I say.

"Like *that's* some kind of favor."

six

The day after the ad runs, I get four separate responses—seven if you count hang-ups. The first is probably the most surprising, if only because it's from a man.

> *Yeah, about your ad, OK? My girlfriend wants to fuck you. She wants me to fuck you while she watches, and then she wants us to fuck her at the same time, and we'll all be too busy fucking to care about anything. I like it rough. Do you like it rough?*

The blubbery, monotonous voice almost makes me stop right there. *Lie down with dogs*, I think. *Put your ad next to spankers and wife swappers.* So I call up the image of Natasha, and just having her there behind my eyes lets me move on to the second response, which also comes from a man.

> *Brother, you're burning in hell. Can you smell it? The flames are hot and fierce....*

And that makes me wonder if my ad is too cryptically written. Have I pushed it over the heads of my true audience? GWF, GBF, GHF...do people know these are not Myers-Briggs rankings?

A lesbian. I'm looking for a lesbian.

And on the very next response, I get one, although it's hard to be sure because the message is so brief.

Hi. (Long pause) *God.* (Click)

Who can explain it? I find this encouraging. It seems to me this woman has a need almost as great as mine, so great she is unable to communicate it. And this means—doesn't it?—that I am no longer alone. Out in the ether is a tiny hand groping for mine.

And then, as a confirmation of this very point, comes the voice of Ruth. A voice of discipline and subtle cultivation. A voice of no clear age or race, defined only by its wisdom.

> *Good afternoon. I'm calling because I was very intrigued by your ad. I don't know exactly how these processes work; I'm not a veteran of these processes. I thought the best approach might be to get together sometime—for coffee perhaps. And then we could discuss it and see where we both arrive. Now, I'm home during the day and most evenings, so you can call me at your convenience. And let's see, the only other thing you'll need from me is my phone number....*

I love everything: the dignity of her attack, the measured tramp of her sentences. That "see where we arrive"...it has the force of something inalienable. Of course. You leave somewhere, and you arrive somewhere else, and you hope where you arrive is better than where you left. Ruth understands this!

I even like the name. I say it a few times to myself: "Ruth. Ruth." It makes an elegant, classical sound; it gathers brackets of silence around it. I imagine myself calling to her, walking into her kitchen, or shouting up a staircase, or knocking on a bedroom door. "Ruth! Hey, Ruth! Do you know where she left her markers?"

Ruth leaves her message a little after 3:00 on Friday afternoon, and I play it back about two hours later, over my office telephone, and then I have to wait another hour before I can leave the office. It's 6:30 by the time I get home, and when I dial Ruth's number, I'm half-convinced I've waited too long. Someone else has found her in the interim, someone with a better offer.

"Hello."

It's the greeting that stops me cold. Not the voice so much—it's the same voice—but the laminate of suspicion.

"Hi, Ruth?"

"Yes?"

But my mind is saying: *Not Ruth. Ruth wouldn't greet strangers this way.*

"This is Nick Broome. You answered my ad in the *City Paper*?"

"The ad," she says, blankly.

"For the...it was about a possible coparenting arrangement."

"Arrangement."

Not your Ruth, my brain is hollering. *Not your Ruth.*

"Yeah," I say, "I was wondering if you wanted to get together sometime, as you mentioned, to see where we arrive...."

There's a long pause now, and for about half of that pause I'm convinced I have the wrong number. And I'm trying to figure out how deeply I've incriminated myself, how much I have divulged to this woman, when Ruth suddenly breaks back in.

"All right, I have a question for you, Mr. GWM nonsmoker. Are you a lover of foreign principalities?"

"Foreign..."

"Don't play that game with me. I'm speaking of places like Monaco. Luxembourg."

"No, I'm pretty much American."

"Hah!" A scorning laugh. "Nice try. The Americans have all gone to Cuba and Puerto Rico. *Malta.*"

"No one told me," I say.

"Maybe you have a girlfriend in Russia. Do you have a girlfriend in Russia?"

"No."

Only a minute into our conversation, and I feel like we're in it for the duration of our lives.

"Rick, would you like to see a movie with me?"

"Actually, it's...I'm sorry, it's Nick."

"Then why did you call yourself Rick?"

"I didn't, I think you may have....Which movie were you thinking of, exactly?"

"Union Station has six or eight showing."

"Hmm."

"And I'm a lady at a certain time in life, Rick. Who needs to ask a gentleman if he will see a movie with her at Union Station. Which is only appropriate because in these days of the Holocaust, one must go underground, one must carry on beneath the jungle floor."

I've always felt schizophrenics aren't really superior to the rest of us, even if they act that way. But in Ruth's case, I admit I'm a little awed by her poetry. Our conversation lasts all of two minutes, and I feel myself being elasticized by her, even as my mind tiptoes out the room.

"Well, listen," I say. "This has been a nice chat? And I'm just...I'm going to talk to some of my other callers and then kind of close that loop later. So I'm grateful for the response and, as I said, there'll be, there'll be decisions made."

"Rick," she says. "Am I free?"

"Are you free?"

"Am I *free?*"

I think it over. "You're free," I say.

"Thank you. Good night, Rick."

After Ruth, I don't get another message for two days. Oh, no, I take it back. There is a return visitor, calling in the early hours of Sunday morning.

...and then we're gonna make a little doggy sandwich out of you, and you're gonna fuck her, and I'm gonna fuck you. My girlfriend likes it up the ass, which I'm betting you do too, you little motherfucking meat eater.

The sad part is I listen to the whole message. Who knows why? Something parsimonious in me says get your money's worth. What a mistake. When it's finished, I am completely, permanently drained of desire. I will never have a hard-on again. Not if a squadron of Brendan Fraser came parachuting onto my roof.

And then 24 hours of silence. A strange, rootless day, not because I'm waiting by the phone exactly, but because everything seems to be hanging in abeyance. I go grocery shopping and I'm unable to buy anything, unable to think about eating past lunch. I go for a run down the Mall, and in my mind I'm already running home, from the moment I leave my door.

Celia calls to ask if I want to see a movie, and my friend George calls because he needs an eighth for a dinner party. George is very keen on symmetry, and so are his guests: No one ever disarranges a place setting or raises his voice or veers too far from the topic of bathroom renovation. Introducing the notion of children would be the most subversive act imaginable. I remember once broaching the subject of gay adoptions to George; I thought his hair would fly even farther from his scalp than it already does.

"But...I don't...isn't that the best part of being gay?" The terror was constricting his trachea. "We don't have to. I mean, no one expects us to."

Clearly, George would be in no mood to hear about my *City Paper* adventure, and so I pass on the dinner party. But I don't want to stay home either, so I wander the streets for an hour, staring into people's windows. I see living rooms with a harlot-pink glow. I see photographs of jazz musicians, built-in bookcases. Now and again, I catch glimpses of the owners, backlit by candles and accent lights. I am trying, I think, to become one of the people who would answer my ad.

I fall asleep early, a little after 10, on my living-room couch. As a rule,

I try not to do this, because if I lean my face against the couch too long, the ugly raised-plaid pattern gets stamped onto my face. I stare at my honeycombed cheeks in the mirror and wonder when I'm going to get a job that allows me a nicer couch, and everything spirals down from there.

I'm not sure what my face looks like the next morning because I am woken unexpectedly, a little before 6, by a tom-tom beat on my door. It's my landlord. He's leaning his pink, fleshy, goateed self against the door-jamb (any later in the day, he would look amorous) and pointing a bare lightbulb at me. His eyes are glittery.

"Nick! I've got it."

"What?"

"Um, you needed a bulb," he says. "You needed me to change a bulb."

Even now—6:00 in the morning—I can see the vapor trail of weed coiling from his sinus cavities, the descending cloud of unconsciousness. It's touching the first few times you see it.

"No," I say. "I need a new kitchen faucet and someone to spray for roaches, but not a bulb. Usually I handle that."

His hand makes a fist around the bulb, and then he flings it over his shoulder, like a grenade. It shatters against the fire extinguisher and settles into an opaque ruin on the far side of the landing.

"Well, fuck," he says brightly. "Have a good night."

So the first act of my new day is to get out a whisk broom and dustpan, and as I kneel in the hallway gathering the filaments and shards, I think, suddenly, mysteriously, of Hoy Phong. This is what he does now, right? He corrects accidents. Bottles of salad dressing knocked loose...

And then I remember I still haven't checked on him. So this becomes my Sunday-morning mission. I get to the convenience store a little after 9—the front counter is empty and so are the long, cramped aisles. The shopkeeper is in back: a young, spectacled Asian man, second generation, fully assimilated. He says, "Two mornings in a row, Hoy didn't show up; he didn't call. So he doesn't work for us anymore."

And for some reason, I nod foolishly. As though I fully expected this to happen. *Of course. Of course.*

Later that day, I phone my mother, and in the middle of a long, unfocused conversation, I say, "Oh, hey, I haven't seen Hoy yet. At the store."

She says, "Really? Did you try in the mornings?"

"Yeah. A couple of different mornings and evenings and then this morning, so I don't know. Maybe he keeps weird hours."

"Huh." A long pause. "I'll have to ask him."

And when it's done, I feel even worse than when I started. I'm sorry about Hoy. I'm sorry about my landlord, my couch, my ad. My ad, most of all. Of all the missteps, this feels like the largest, the most flamboyant.

Late that afternoon, I walk through the springy mud of Marion Park. I walk down numbered streets, lettered streets. I wave to people I don't know. I see a mockingbird perched on a front railing, taunting a tortoiseshell cat. It's nearly 5 by the time I get home, and as I climb the stairs to my apartment, I tell myself I will have a beer, I will let the rest of the day fade to black.

Instead, I check the messages.

And a good thing too, because there's a new caller. A fluting, girlish voice.

> *Um, hi, this is Daphne? I'm responding to your ad in the* City Paper. *I just saw it, in case you're wondering why I've taken so long to call, but I was reading it and...cool! This is great, because I've been thinking about that kind of possibility in my own life and, frankly, the medical establishment has not been what it could be in supporting that. So, yeah! Take it into our own hands, that sounds like the best way to me. So what do you need to know? I'm a hair past 40, just a hair, and I don't drink or take drugs, never have. And I'd be really curious to meet and see if there's, you know, something we can go with here. I'm, no, I have to say I'm really nervous making this call because, I don't know, it's all about the unknown, isn't it? But I guess you're nervous too, so, hey, we're even! Anyway, give me a call and let's talk, OK? Oh! Here's where you can reach me....*

I have to play the message back three times just to get the phone number, because each time I listen, I fall into a reverie, and the digits just blow through me. As I dial the number, I feel a wave of energy passing through me, and when Daphne picks up the phone, I plunge right in. "This is Nick Broome," I say. "You called me about my ad." And I'm thrilled at the way my voice sounds.

"Oh, right, hi!" she says. "How are you?"

It's a very businesslike exchange, very cordial. We go through our calendars. We establish that we won't be able to meet until Thursday night. "Thursdays are good days," Daphne says. "I was born on a Thursday." We set a time—7:30—and a place, and we say good-bye. A minimum of fuss. Probably the most efficient human transaction I have ever undertaken, and maybe because it happens so quickly, it's still glistening with promise by the time Thursday rolls around. The moment I wake up, I can feel it. Daphne. The future. Opening.

But it doesn't last. That night, a few minutes after 7, I'm heading toward my front door, checking for my keys, trying to remember where I parked the car, and I realize suddenly I don't want to find my car, don't want to find my keys, don't want to leave the room.

How strange that in my search for solace I should phone Shannon. That's a little like applying a tick to a mosquito bite.

"Hi, it's me," I say.

"I'm disgusting," Shannon says. "Ask me what I'm doing."

"What?"

"I'm holding a handful of my own fat."

I need solace. *I* need solace.

"Ask me what it looks like," she says.

"What?"

"It's white and veiny and *fat*."

"You're...I'm sure you're exaggerating."

"I look like an alien. Just before they get the autopsies. You know, when they're lying there and they're all doughy and...doughy."

I want my solace.

"I'm having dinner tonight," I tell her. "With a potential mother."

"Oh, really?"

"Her name is Daphne, and she seems very nice. I mean, the initial signs are all kind of promising, but now I'm wondering if maybe this is too soon; maybe I haven't had time to think it through. But then again, you know, I've had all the time in the world—my whole *life*, really."

"Well, whatever," she says. "You know, fine."

And here's the thing. Normally, I could deal with "fine." Normally, I could find something in it to answer. But now I'm silly and panicked, and so I say, "*Fine*? That's all you...*fine*?"

So she gives the topic a little more thought.

"Don't let her stiff you for the whole bill," she says.

It's her feet I notice first. No, that's not quite right, I notice the bottom of her legs. Coral leggings: a loose, cottony-woolly fabric that wrinkles just above her boot line. She's sitting, per our arrangement, at the back corner table of a restaurant just south of the Cathedral. It's the kind of restaurant that jumps like a game token across the map of Europe: Provençal curtains, checkered Tuscan tablecloths, windows painted with Tyrolean tableaus, food that gives off Bavarian fumes. But as I walk over to her, all I see are the coral leggings.

Our child. Coral leggings.

She says, "You must be Nick." She stands—half-stands, half-crouches. Her hand is small, veined, and plump. She has a thatching of gray hair, dark eyes, small luminous teeth. And smile lines—I would never think to call them that, but she smiles a lot, and when she does, a delta of lines fans out from her mouth and her eyes and her slightly flattened nose.

"Sit down," she says. "You're making me nervous."

Luckily for me, she's the one who starts talking. Before the waiter has even arrived, she draws a long, slow breath and starts in. She tells me right off that she's a professional mediator and facilitator. Even if she hadn't told me, I might have guessed because she talks about naming her feelings and capturing ground. She says processes can be powerful. She says, "What I *hear* you saying," and I haven't said a thing yet.

"Where are you from?" I ask her finally.

"Well, I moved here from Dayton 10 years ago, and now it looks like I'm heading back. You're wondering why. It's mostly because all my D.C. friends have moved, and I never got around to replacing them. I can't replace people. Maybe you're the same way...."

It comes in a white-capped stream: relatives, jobs, hobbies, free-floating opinions. Her trip to Burma. Her favorite poem: "God's Grandeur" by Gerald Manley Hopkins. Her chief quirk: She can't wear shoes for months after she's bought them, has to keep them in their original boxes. We're well into the appetizers before the sound dies away, and it's here, feeling almost terrified by the prospect of silence, that I ask her the question Dr. Willinger asked me.

"Why do you want a child?" I ask.

Truth to say, there isn't a single answer to that, or if there is, it keeps dividing on itself. She wants a kid because she's a kid too. She wants a kid to honor the mother she could be, to honor the mother her mother *was.*

"You see, my mother passed away," she says. "Two years ago. Ovarian cancer."

"Oh!" I say. "Just like my great aunt."

Daphne keeps going. "Let me just share that my last relationship was with a woman. But before that, I dated a man for, like, six years—but not in a very sexual way. It was like a lesbian relationship with a man."

"Uh-huh."

"So that's why this way seems OK to me. I mean, not being in the same room doesn't seem like such a big deal."

Our salads have just been carted away, and this is the first time either of us has brought up the biological mechanics. God knows we should have been prepared for the subject, but I think it embarrasses us. It's as though a condom has dropped onto one of the salad forks.

"Well, I know you've read the ad," I tell her. "So I'm assuming you're OK with stuff. The joint-custody thing."

"Is fine," she answers. "As long as, I mean, Dayton and everything."

"Right."

"Because I'm kind of locked in there mentally."

"Sure."

"But that's not *far*," she says, and then the smile lines really get going. They fly from here to Ohio.

"Not far at all," I agree. "You could...one-hour flight. Frequent-flyer miles...."

"Right," she says, wheezing. "After awhile, they'd be *paying* us to fly."

"Right."

And here is where it breaks. I can't say what does it exactly. Maybe it's the fantasy of being paid to go to Dayton. Once we've taken that little ramp to unreality, there's no going back, and before we know it, a bubble of unreality has settled over us, and every gesture we make, everything that goes into or comes out of our mouths, sends the bubble higher. We have nothing left after awhile but the bubble.

So, before the meal is even halfway over, we understand. It's not going to work. And it should sadden us, I suppose, but somehow—this is the strange part—it relaxes us. Enough that Daphne permits herself a second glass of chardonnay, and I get playful with my food, twirling my fork through the little nest of sautéed cabbage on my plate.

And, relieved now from the strain of impregnating her, I realize I kind of like Daphne. I like her V-shaped smile and the soft Anjou outline of her body. And when the meal is over, I realize I'm not quite ready to leave, and so I order a scotch and start talking. And as I talk, I recognize how skillfully Daphne is drawing me out: giving eye contact, asking open-ended questions. "Let's break this down," she says, and it's with a dry, static shock that I realize I'm being facilitated.

What a good feeling it is too. It should happen to everyone. Seated in our little Provençal cottage with sauerkraut fumes, I'm so relaxed I tell her something I've never told anyone.

"OK," I say, "this happened my senior year in college. Midafternoon. I was lying on the dorm-room couch. I was going in and out, and at some point, I just went *out*. My eyes closed, and it was like my brain was being pried open because I *saw* him. Five or six, I guess, running across this very muddy field. Wearing a royal-blue down parka, unzipped, with the hood down. His face was exploding, he was so happy. He had his arms stretched out, and he was waiting to be picked up—it was going to happen any second now. His feet were going to leave the ground. He was going to go *flying*."

I stop there. I reassemble myself.

"I woke up before he could get to me. My eyes just kind of...jerked open. I remember thinking someone was blowing on them."

"Why do you think you still remember it?" Daphne asks me.

"Oh, I don't know. I suppose it made me realize stuff."

"Like what?"

"Well, like I was gay, for starters."

"How did you know that?"

"Well, because I was...I was telling him good-bye."

Daphne leans toward me across the table. Her pink kitten's face is cupped in her hands, held in relief like a cameo. "Have you seen him since?" she asks.

"No," I say. "I mean, yes. When I see him now, I don't—I'm *remembering* him. It's not happening."

"Maybe he was you. Did he look like you?"

"He did probably. It wasn't me."

"Maybe you'll see him again," she says.

"Maybe."

As soon as the bill arrives, I remember what Shannon said: "Don't let her stiff you." And so to spite her, I decide to pick up the check. This will be my large-hearted gesture. But Daphne is already prying open her wallet. "What do you think?" she asks. "Split it down the middle?"

"Oh, no, I had the scotch."

"My entrée was more. I think it works out."

So we go dutch. We leave a moderately generous tip, say good-bye to the headwaiter, stroll out to the street...and the whole time, I'm filtering our movements through the future, giving us an elegiac weight.

"Well," says Daphne.

For the first time, I am looking at her on a vertical plane, and I'm realizing how short she is, barely reaching my collarbone. And my heart breaks, just like that. A clean fracture.

"Let me know how things turn out," she's saying.

"I will. Let me know how Dayton goes."

"I will."

An awkward interval then: I'm extending a stiff Episcopalian hand, and she's thrusting out both her arms. We compromise. I take one of her hands; she wraps herself around one side of my waist; we stand there, like a pair of tango dancers.

"OK," she says.

"OK, bye."

It's raining by the time I reach Rock Creek Parkway. Barely raining. Not enough even to alert the wipers but enough to screen the forest on each side of the road. I like watching the beads of water accumulate. I feel huddled, as though I were peering through the entrance of a grotto thousands of years ago.

I will close out my "None of the Above" account. I know that now. Letting it continue would be a disservice to Daphne, to the two hours we spent together. It's not the end of the world. I can still meet my year-end deadline.

There's time. There's all the time in the world.

But when I get back to my apartment, the heaviness is still there, in the air, the furniture, the area rugs, making the bedclothes droop, dragging dust from the blinds. So to make it go away, I pick up the phone. Of course I do. And I dial my voice mail box, and I wait to be told I have no messages, except I have a message. Not my obscene caller either, but a woman. A woman I have never heard before, with a high, slightly metallic voice and a burbling undercurrent of laughter. She says:

> *Hey, what's with all the initials? GWF, GBF. Say them out loud sometime; they sound like animal noises. Gwuff! Guhboof! Gaaaf!*

And for a few seconds the line swells, crackles, with barnyard noises—a traffic jam of animals.

> *Well, I'm not any of those animals. I'm a swiff. For the, for the*

acronym-deprived, that would be single white heterosexual female, and I'm guessing you're in your late 20s or early 30s because if you were any older, you'd have all these swiff friends— same age—right outside your window, screaming: "Baby, I need baby!"

But I'm early 30s myself, and I'm already comfortable with the idea, and I'm sick of waiting for men to get comfortable with it—straight men, I mean—and so I welcome the chance to meet a, a gwimm and talk about babies.

I sit on my ugly raised-plaid couch, and the voice steals through me, from my ankles to my follicles.

I work very instinctually with stuff like this. So if you call, I will tell you within two seconds whether it's gonna work. And if not, fine, we get on with our lives, no harm done. And if it's yes? Well, that's up to you, Mr. Gwimm, isn't it? So here's my number. I dare you.

She goes silent for a few seconds, as though she's in the process of hanging up, but then the voice comes back.

Oh, and you'll want my name. It's Nattie.

seven

It takes about 10 minutes. Ten minutes of eating eggs in a family restaurant off Route 50 to know she's the one.

And there I was thinking it would take weeks and weeks of inching along, squinting, testing every water, and it's over before I've finished my breakfast. Nattie must understand how these things work. It was her idea to meet here. She couldn't have known though that I worked in a place just like it when I was a teenager—the same wood-paneled smoking section, nearly twice as big as the nonsmoking section, the same meat-fed agricultural couples. I respect it. I respect Nattie for choosing it. But what really turns the tide in her favor is the guppy story.

"OK," she says, scooping heaps of oatmeal from a tall bowl. "My brother and I, when we were kids, were not allowed to have pets because my mother didn't think animals should be enslaved. We couldn't go to circuses or have a dog or a cat, but we could have *guppies* because they were still in their natural environment or something. So one day we're at school, and my mother gets this brilliant idea. It's such a beautiful day, wouldn't it be great to take the fish outside to get some air? And this is what she does. Ha! She takes our guppies, the whole tank, she *pours* them into the nearest birdbath. A birdbath, Nick. Within minutes: *Awk! Awk!*" Nattie arches her wings back, shapes her hands into claws. "Miles away, every direction, bird after bird. Swooping down."

"Oh, wow."

"Most of the guppies were eaten immediately, and my mom was too distraught to save the rest. Which is too bad because the ones that survived got fried by the sun. *Fried.* And who's the one who finds the bodies? Nattie! Good ol' Nattie! Nine years old, back from school, finds her guppies swirling in the water, Nick. The only animals I was ever allowed to have. Charred. Looking at me, it's like they're speaking, they're saying: 'Your mother!' " A new voice, reedy, warbling through water. " 'Your mother *keeeled* us!' "

As far as I can tell, there's nothing Nattie can't laugh holes into. Missing the junior prom. Eating tofu burgers on Thanksgiving because her mother was having an attack of Buddhism. Or the time her mother talked her into freeing a tank of butterflies before her fifth-grade class could dissect them. Poor little brainwashed Nattie, carrying the tank into the school courtyard, prying off the cover. "Fly!" she told them. "Be free!"

Just last month, Nattie got her leather jacket trapped inside a newspaper vending machine. Couldn't open the machine because she didn't have another quarter. Couldn't leave the jacket because it cost her $500. Who should come to her assistance? Craig from down the hall. Craig, who slept with her once and never called again and now stood over her laughing. "Nattie," he'd said, "you are the only person in the world this would happen to."

"But he's right," she admits. "I *am* the only one. Ha! Ha!"

She really laughs this way: quick, loud spasms, as though she's reaching into her stomach cavity and squeezing her diaphragm. Her teeth weld together, and a glistening froth comes sliding through the crevices. She's gargling with laughter.

I like that. I like her appetite too. I like the way she engages her whole body in what she's telling. I even like the baggy puce tracksuit she's wearing, the one with tiny zippers everywhere—zippers at the collar, the sleeves, zippers at the ankles and hips. Her hair pokes through the flaps of a CBS News cap, and somewhere in the middle of eating her oatmeal, she whips the cap off, and her blondeness blazes out at me: shoulder-length, inner-driven, a geothermal force.

My Denver omelet tastes like the sum total of all the ham and onions and green peppers that were ever cooked in a cast-iron pan. I'm eating like a killer whale. There aren't enough omelets in the world to satisfy me. And everyone around me is feasting too. Luxuriant golden folds of egg; long, winding bacon trails; pancakes staggering beneath peaks of sautéed apples.

"So tell me about yourself, Nick," she says.

And suddenly I'm at a loss. I can't see any way in which my life plays out as entertainingly as hers. I talk about having the worst batting average on my Little League team. I talk about starting my own newspaper when I was 10. Family trips: sitting in the rear seat of a Buick station wagon, the seat that faced backward, and following our progress on the map, calling out each town, each interchange, as we passed it, until I had alienated everyone in the car.

I talk about throwing myself from the swing when I was little, and how I have the same urge when I'm sitting on ski lifts.

I talk about the Actor. Scenes from a long-running psychodrama: Nick and the Actor crawling across the floor of the Green Lantern; the Actor flirting with five women at Nick's office Christmas party, and later turning up completely naked outside Nick's apartment door; Nick standing in the rain, in the wings, on the opposite side of the room, trying to remember why he's there, what he's supposed to be doing.

"Oh, wait," she says. "I dated an actor. Did you have to talk about his Craft?"

"Yeah, that was the whole first month."

"Wow, it sucks, doesn't it?"

"I don't know, it seemed OK at the time. It seemed easier."

"Than what?"

"Talking about myself, I guess."

"Well," she says, "you're not going to get out of it now. You have to tell me about your family."

"Oh. Right."

"We can take the crass question first," Nattie says. "Are they healthy?"

"Yeah, no medical problems. My father's kind of depressed these days, but we think it's a function of being retired."

"What did he do?"

"Minister," I say. "Episcopalian."

"Aha! Minister's kid, say no more. What about your mom?"

"Um, she stayed at home when we were growing up, and now it's mostly volunteer work."

"Very nice. Altruism. Love it."

"And my brother is a doctor for a low-income clinic. Not far from where you live. Columbia Heights."

"I love it!" Nattie says. "I can feel it, all my selfish genes, they're...they're being erased as we speak. Ha!"

She opens her palm and extends it in a kind of stop-motion advance, as though she's pressing against an invisible wall, and at last I understand: I'm supposed to high-five her. And when our hands finally meet, it's more of a middle-five; there's no slapping sound, just the laying on of skin. We linger for a few seconds.

"Big hand," Nattie says. And I blush like a leaf.

"You know," I say, "one of the, the unusual things about my family is we're all still in the same geographical area roughly, which used to trouble me, only because I think if we were a healthy family, we'd feel, what, empowered to go to the far ends of the globe. But when I think about it, I have all these *caregivers* in place, right? This network of caregivers..."

"Nick," she says.

"Yes?"

"Here's what I think we should do."

"OK."

"I think we should shake hands."

Shake hands.

"And go home," she says. "I think we should plan to talk every night this week. By phone, at a prearranged time."

Prearranged time.

"And I think we should talk for as long as we need to talk. And then we should get together again this weekend and see if we're comfortable, if we're ready to go ahead. And if we are, if we're both ready, then OK! We go. We make it formal."

And just then, a hank of hair comes tumbling off her head, forms a curtain across one side of her face. On the other side, a single blue-gray eye blinks twice in quick succession. Her lips come unglued, a feeler smile peeps out, and her jaw—freckled, strong—executes a clockwise roll. She's pretty. Pretty like her name.

"What's Nattie short for?" I ask. I feel the stakes suddenly escalating around me.

"It's my grandmother's name," she says. "Natalie. But you can't call me that because I've been Nattie since I was an egg. Ha!"

Natalie. I say the name to myself. *Natalie. Close enough.*

Her hand is moving again, reaching across the table for my hand. She's trying to cover it, but my hands are too big, remember? And the damp, nutty feel of her skin keeps me from thinking all the things I would otherwise be thinking. How she wore a sweatsuit to our first meeting. How she pushes her cuticles down. How we've known each other for 30 minutes. All I'm thinking is nice. *Nice.*

She gives my hand a last bit of pressure and slowly releases. Then she paws through her handbag.

"Do you like it here?" she asks.

"Yeah."

"It's nice, isn't it?"

"Very nice."

"A good value, I think."

"Very good value."

She's standing now, and in her warm-up suit, she is a great piece of fruit; she is a costumed storybook character; she is the personification of puce. She's all color, and the only texture comes from her hair, which she has once again tucked behind both ears, and from her skin, streaked with proto-freckles.

The mother of my child.

"We have to pay at the counter," she says.

"OK, good, I'll just leave the tip here."

"OK, and Nick?"

"Yeah?"

"Let's not wait too long," she says. "Let's talk again tonight."

I always turn out the lights when I call Nattie. I sit on my ugly raised-plaid sofa, pressed against it like a test pilot impaled by G-forces. After a few minutes, though, I get restless, so I go to the window, and I scissor open the blinds and peer through. And then I stroll into the kitchenette and scrape crumbs off the counter. And before long, I'm heading to the bedroom: circling the bed and then stretching myself across it until I'm lying parallel to the headboard. Inevitably, sex comes to mind. The more I talk with Nattie, the more my best celibate intentions give way, and for a few seconds I forget about having children, and the only thing I want, really, is to have a man next to me. It was in this bed that the Actor and I thrashed away the night—he never did get a permanent apartment of his own—and the next morning I would always find tiny grapelike bruises in odd little corners of my body, and I would try to remember what I'd collided with. The bedpost? His forehead?

Nattie's the one who talks—about work, mostly. She's an assignment editor for one of the local TV stations, and her boss's favorite phrase is "Nattie, you fucking idiot," which is why Nattie now refers to herself as "Fuckiot." She talks about falling in love with her 10th-grade English teacher because of his hair and neckties. She talks about driving somebody's Volkswagen into a creek and eating crickets in Thailand and having a rat run across her face in Costa Rica and...everything, anything. By nature, by deepest instinct, she's an entertainer, and whenever she senses me drifting, her voice grows taut with the effort of distracting me.

Every now and then I suspect her of making things up just to get my attention, like when she tells me she was a lesbian for two weeks.

"No, really," she says. "My brother was dating this woman in San Antonio, right after college. Gorgeous woman, half-Latina, and every time I saw her, she just gave me this little *tingle.* Serious kind of crush. I thought, *Wow, I could be a lesbian, at least for a couple of weeks,* and I told my brother, and this is so funny, he said, 'You just don't feel like being straight today. Like I don't feel like being stoned today, it's the same thing.' Ha! Ha!"

"Are they still together?" I ask.

"Oh, no, she left. Broke his heart. Hey, he lives here now!"

"Really?"

"He's a bartender over at Union Station. You may have seen him."

"Oh, that little-"

"Right! The raised platform thing. He's gorgeous, Nick. My same perfect WASP nose and, you know, when he wears blue or green clothing, he's a model. Just like me!" And she must feel my attention wandering, because she suddenly does a riff from the guppy story. "*Keeled* us!" she screams. "Your mother *keeled* us!"

It's Friday night. There's a tiny thumbnail of moon I can just see from my kitchen window if I crane my neck. The window is open, and through the screen comes a murmur of air, a smell of eggs and salt and bird shit and clover. Summer, with its own special gravity, attaching flea-weights to my eyelids, making my socks slide down my ankles.

Nattie's on the other end of the phone. She's telling me how her stepfather used to make her live in the basement. "This little prison, right? I'm in prison because my stepfather hates me." My head is dropping backward...back...back. Moonlight is flaring across the ceiling, illuminating the long hairline fracture around the overhead light. I'm seeing the Actor, rising up on his knees, his flat chest, his ropy shoulders.

"Nick?" she says.

My eyes peel open.

"Are you ready to go?" she asks.

My head jolts forward. I'm looking around now—just to be sure it's me she's talking to. "You mean *go* go?"

"Go go," she says.

And it's strange. If she had asked me 10 minutes into our first meal, I wouldn't have hesitated. I would have said, "Let's do it." But now my head is flooded with extraneous images: the Actor, Nattie's brother, Hoy Phong. I'm thinking of everything except having a baby.

I say, "Yeah, I'm ready."

"You sure?"

"I'm sure."

"OK. I'm ready too. Let's meet tomorrow, OK?"

There's a Greek restaurant on Capitol Hill that becomes our regular spot. At least two times a week we meet there to reconnoiter, and each time we are ushered upstairs by a man with gray corkscrew curls and melted-down skin and coal-pellet eyes that grudgingly dampen with sentiment. "If you would please," he says, bowing his head, and the words seem to filter through to the end of his gesturing fingertips. We sit at our upstairs table—the same table every time—a window seat overlooking Pennsylvania Avenue. We make a show of looking at the menus, although we usually order chicken souvlaki. And before we even start eating, Nattie feeds me some morsel of flattery, coos it across the table. "You're so strong-looking, Nick. Are all the Broomes so beefy? Oh, I hope the kid gets your eyes." And we talk about our days at work, except Nattie's always has more drama, and we each have a glass and a half of merlot, and occasionally Nattie swallows a very small pill ("vighty-min supplement," she says). Dinner is over by 8:30 or 9. Suffused by sulfites, we pick our way carefully down the stairs. The man who showed us to our table has his hands pressed against his chest; a grandmother-of-the-bride smile parts his features. "Goo'night," he says, and we nod to him and push the door open, and a wave of grassy, incensed air splashes our faces, and young men in unknotted ties stride past us, and I try to catch the eye of every single passing man, and Nattie doesn't care because she's still talking. She's famous for talking. A couple of years ago, she was jabbering away to a friend in a Barcelona bar, and the man next to her leaned over and said something in Spanish, which her friend translated as: "A closed mouth gathers no flies." Nattie loved that.

One night she surprises me by bringing a contract to dinner. "Read it and weep," she says, and onto the table she slaps two sheets of parchment, banded by a fine, slanting script in evenly leaded lines. I angle the paper toward the window.

Agreement made on this 20th day of June between Nicholas Broome and Natalie Bryant, hereafter referred to as First Party and Second Party.

"That's good," I say. "That sounds legit."

"Of course it's legit. What do you think I am?"

The parties herewith enter into a joint-parenting arrangement for the sole purpose of producing a child.

First Party agrees to provide sperm. Second Party agrees to provide womb. Medical expenses not currently covered by Second Party's health insurance will be split 50-50 by both parties.

The two parties agree to:

1) Place kid first.
2) Not give a shit what their families think. About anything.

Agreement will be in force for a period of one year from date of signature. If, at said time, fertilization has not occurred, parties may continue, renegotiate, or terminate arrangement, howsoever they are inclined.

"See your name?" Nattie says.

I follow my finger to the bottom of the second page, and there, fixed in a sudden outpouring of calligraphy: Nicholas Broome, Natalie Bryant. And, just above the names, two horizontal slashes, where my pen hovers, like a record stylus.

"I don't know," I say. "Is this...I don't think this would be court-of-law admissible or anything. Not being a lawyer."

"Nick," she says. "It's for *us*, that's all. It's a trust document."

Slowly, wonderingly, I trace my vertical cursive, watching the swags and loops and ties bleed from the pen. And when Nattie hands me the second copy, my eyes seek out *her* autograph, the scrum of letters tumbling over each other in their dash to the right margin. Only a few emerge intact: a pair of *T*'s in her first name, the capital *B* of her last name, and a final *T,* exhausted, trailing off into silence.

"OK!" Nattie says. She leaves one copy with me, gathers the other, aligns the sheets with a couple of brisk raps against the table, folds them in half, and returns them to her handbag. And as she's doing this, my eyes range across her, collecting impressions. A cross-hatching of blue ink on her cream blouse, just over her right breast; a swatch of rust about six inches below; a speck of food, a white cheesy fragment, on her right cheek—the whole teetering disequilibrium of Nattie.

What have I done?

She excuses herself to go to the bathroom, and the soft slab of her buttock wafts past my face, and I realize how much she moves me, how much her body moves me. I never did get a good fix on it during our first meeting. It takes work clothes to bring it out: the narrow shoulders; the small, apostrophe-shaped breasts; the columnar hips; legs that end before they quite begin. The kind of sturdy, blockish woman's body that in an earlier time would have gratefully packed itself into a shirtwaist dress. And yet she has tiny white Japanese feet, and her nose is, as advertised, a flying buttress, smoothed by centuries of genetic engineering. Marbled blue-green-gray eyes, a mouth that sinks slightly at the ends. *What kind of child,* I ask myself, *comes from this face? From this body?*

Later that evening, Nattie says, "Tell me how you're feeling."

“Good,” I say. “I feel good.”

“Because my next ovulation is two weeks away.”

The tabulations begin from that moment. Before we even leave the table, the compressor in my head is firing off dates. Fertilization in early July. Amniocentesis in November. Second trimester ends in January. Onset of labor pains projected for mid-April. Child born 13 to 14 hours later. Two days later, child begins to discriminate odors. Following July: child distinguishes color and form. Following April: wordlike sounds. October: meaningful language. Ten to 14 years later: secondary sexual characteristics...

At some point the compressor whirs to a stop. It’s the morning after our dinner. I’m standing in the middle of Providence Park, a large treeless expanse teeming with soccer players. I see young boys in sparkling mesh jerseys and white trunks, barely as tall as the ball that caroms off their knees, chasing each other with a mindless, puppyish blood lust. And watching them, I wish suddenly I had one of them to root for. I wish I were standing on the sideline, calling his name, holding his orange section, his cup of Gatorade. I wish Nattie were standing next to me doing the very same thing.

And then the frame expands, and Dr. Willinger is standing next to us, and his high, folksy pharmacist’s voice is droning in my ear: “...limit ourselves to the most fertile specimens...sure you understand...best upfront odds for reproduction...fertility tends to decline with age.”

I call Nattie early the next morning. “I need to tell you something,” I say.

“What?”

“If it’s a problem, I’ll understand.”

“What is it?”

“Um.” My voice climbs back in my throat. “OK, there’s this deal with my sperm, see? The motility count, *my* motility count, last it was checked, was under 50 percent. Which doesn’t mean I’m sterile. It only means they don’t all move well. They’re not always good swimmers.”

“I’m not either,” Nattie says.

"So I thought you should know that. In case it's a deal breaker or something."

And as soon as I've raised the specter, it seems to vanish of its own accord. And still it leaves a residue, which has something to do with the relief I would feel if this deal got broken.

"Nick."

"Yeah."

"Is that it?"

"Yeah."

"I mean, that's all you wanted to tell me."

"Yeah."

"Jesus Christ!" A squawk, a titter. The public Nattie emerges. "Nick, do you know, I mean, are you familiar with the science on this subject? Because if you're reading the same things I'm reading, the sperm is the least of it. These days all you need is one healthy guy: one guy with a tail. They find him, they inject him straight into the egg."

"Really."

"Oh, yeah. They've got the male part licked." She pauses. "That sounds funny. You know what I mean."

I do know. It's exactly what Shannon said: *It only takes one, Nick. I think you can handle it.*

And she was right. I can handle it.

For the next week, Nattie and I talk almost exclusively by E-mail. We fire off messages two, three times a day. We respond the moment we receive. I could almost believe we have known each other for years. I discuss with her things I couldn't discuss with anyone else. Prostaglandins, for instance: the things in raw sperm that cause irritation and cramping in the uterus.

> *They're not a problem in normal sexual intercourse,* I write her, *because the woman produces cervical lubricants that filter out the bad stuff. But if it's donor sperm, they recommend doing it in a doctor's office so you can get the sperm WASHED first. But maybe we could take care of it in the kitchen sink with a little lemon Joy.*

And Nattie gets back to me in 10 minutes.

No, I think what they're talking about, honey, is when you inject it right into the uterus. Which I would not do because you increase your chances of infection and embolisms and scary shit. (Can I say shit *on a government line?) I think we can stick with the vaginal pool for now.*

Remind me to tell you about my mother and her tipped uterus.

When it comes to discussing the mechanics, this is as far as she likes to go. Now and again we'll be talking on the phone, and I'll find myself scorched with curiosity, wanting to know how everything happens before it happens. But Nattie is almost superstitiously vague.

"We'll get there when we get there," she says.

And I press her, gently, then less gently, and she says: "Well, OK, we've decided on your place. Because it's roomier."

"Right."

"Quieter."

"Right."

"So what more do you need to know, Nick? You do your bit. You give it to me, I do my bit."

"Yeah, OK, then how you...I mean, is it like turkey basters?"

"Turkey basters!" A gust of carbonated laughter. "You really think I'm a lesbian, don't you?"

"No."

"First of all," she says, "turkey basters are much bigger than you really need. You're not *that* much of a gusher, are you, Nick?"

"No."

"Because that would be scary. In addition to which, those things can injure your cervix, if you don't handle 'em right, which is bad."

I agree with her. That's bad. And I'm smiling because she's given me a little of what I asked for and because when I think about it, Nattie will get around to discussing most anything, given half a chance. The only subject that really shuts her down is family, specifically, the idea of alerting our families to what we are doing. She always sounds surprised when I raise the possibility, and maybe I'm surprised too, because, like Nattie, I was getting turned on by our freelance status. I figured having a child this way was sexy and countercultural. But then I began to feel the fragility of our position. Haven't we always said we want our families to be part of our child's life? How can we expect that if we only notify them after the fact?

But it's a delicate business. If I tell her I'd like to meet her mother, Nattie solders her lips together, and her voice disappears into a canyon. "Well, sure, she's in Dallas. You want to fly to Dallas?" If I mention her brother, there's a complete change of expression. "Oh, you *will* meet him! I want you to meet him!" And that's where it rests. It's as though she's already played the meeting in her mind, and it was good, so why bother doing it again?

Truthfully, I can't say it would be any easier broaching the subject with the Broomes. I wouldn't know where to begin. One night, we come out of our Greek restaurant and collide with Celia's friend Richard and for a few passing moments, I think: *Now? Introduce it now?* only because the encounter feels so blatantly engineered. But then I remember that every encounter with Richard feels that way. Even more so tonight because he's with a group of his peers, and they are all, to a boy, wearing scuffless work boots and flannel shirts, cuffed halfway up their biceps, and heavy black unibrow glasses that would have gotten them beaten up in fifth grade. If they had brought their dogs, it would be the world's largest assembly of German shepherds.

"You should give your sister a call," Richard tells me in that deep, mysteriously womanly voice. "She'd love to hear from you."

And I would love to tell him that I talk to Celia at least once a week, that I see her at least twice a month. That I know her better than he ever will or could. That I regret that Celia even for a second entertained the belief that he and I would make a good couple. But at moments like this, my mother's example takes hold, and I become the minister's wife.

"Oh, thanks for mentioning it," I say. "I'll be sure to do that."

And the next morning, I do call her at work, and it makes me sulky to realize I am, after all, following Richard's suggestion. Celia picks up her phone with a rush of exhaled air, as though she's just gotten a rubdown.

"Did Richard tell you?" I ask.

"What?"

Only two seconds into our conversation, and I feel her pushing something between us: a sound wall, a Plexiglas shield.

"I saw him last night," I say.

"Um, I haven't really...he's been in a meeting all morning."

"Did he tell you who I was with?"

"No," she says. "I mean, he didn't tell me he saw you, so he didn't tell me who you were with."

She doesn't want to know. That's so clear. She's disappearing behind her Plexiglas shield.

"I was having dinner with a friend of mine," I say. "I was thinking I'd like you to meet her sometime."

"OK."

"I'm curious to know what you think of her."

"That's fine," she says.

"So I'll let you know," I say, finally. "We'll set up a time."

And that's when she tells me about the fortune-teller.

Her name is Mrs. Abbruzzi, and she has a canary-yellow sign and a cane with a flask of whiskey in it and a tiny accordion-doored room where she reads tarot cards. And for reasons too deep to understand, my sister went to this woman for a personal consultation, and Mrs. Abbruzzi told her she would never be happy because someone had placed a curse on her early in life. And Celia is not a credulous person, but this particular theory could explain a great deal of things. "Aaron, for example," she says. "It could explain why the whole Aaron thing dragged on for so long. There's some, I don't know, there's karmic retribution at work."

And once again I curse myself for even inadvertently placing her in Aaron's way. It only happened because I invited her to a music-industry reception in the Rayburn Building. I remember she was four weeks into her target weight and still a little surprised to be drawing a man's eye. I left her for maybe two minutes to talk to a Gannett reporter, and that's when Aaron moved in. Kinky hair and caterpillar lips and a sharpster gleam: one of the purer forms of sociopath. Celia was never the same again. To this day, the mention of his name raises a collective hackle in the Broome family.

"So Mrs. Abbruzzi was telling me I need to placate this spirit," Celia says, "with an offering."

"An offering."

"An appeasement offering. It works out to 93 bucks, but the denominations are very important. You know, the numerology. Very important. One 20 and three 10s and..."

And then she starts crying. All told, I spend about half an hour with her. I remind her about that woman on the news who got scammed in much the same way: instructed to bring money to a bridge somewhere and drop it over the side, little realizing there was an accomplice waiting below to grab it. This particular scam had been running for several years, and no one was any happier for handing over their money.

And when it's all over, and I've assured Celia that her life is going to turn around any minute, and Celia has promised not to drop cash off bridges, I've forgotten why I called her in the first place. Too bad, really. It would have been nice to talk things over with somebody, and my good friend Shannon has officially declared herself off-limits: "Nick, I really don't have the stomach for the details. Let me know when it happens." Celia's the only other person I could raise this subject with. It's true, in my more sedated moments, I'm tempted to call Greg, only because I feel the need for a medical perspective. But then the memory of Greg's righteousness rushes back, and I hear him thundering over the phone line. "Nick, there's research! Children conceived with unwashed sperm are at higher risk of Bell's palsy."

So I end up back where I started: me and Nattie on one side, the rest of the world on the other. And most of the time that's enough. Most of the time, I'm happy to have her in my corner. It's just that the corner feels crowded sometimes, and the crowd is all Nattie. She's a populace. I don't feel it keenly except when I'm with her, staring across a table strewn with phyllo dough and realizing that one of the collars on her denim shirt has been twisted so hard by a dryer that the tip is pointing straight for her ear, and the shirt itself is missing its second button, and there's a faded smear of lipstick on her teeth. And normally these little synaptic fizzles wouldn't bother me, except they veer so sharply from the orderliness of her handbag, the superhuman completeness of her electronic Rolodex. Here is a woman who keeps the cleanest desk on the Eastern seaboard and can't remember from minute to minute where she's supposed to be. A woman who compulsively brushes crumbs off a restaurant table and forgets there's someone on the other side of the table.

Sometimes you can actually trace her brain waves via E-mail. The screen flattens them into a readout.

Whee! I just got a new ovulation test kit. Over the counter at CVS.
Is this a great country? I thought it would be...............

...............a big rubber finger!

But it's a urine test. Aren't you missing me? I would be
missing me
if I were you.

Ha. Ha.

Ha.

It's all there: the quarter-note rests, the shuddering stops. And this is the woman with whom I'm pooling my venture capital, the cofounder of my low-tech start-up. It's enough to set off every trip wire in my head. *Too fast. We're going too fast.*

And then Nattie will say something like "Did I ever tell you how I almost killed an endangered stick insect?" And I'm her prisoner. I would *become* an endangered stick insect if that's what it took.

She enters my head at unsuspected times. I'll be jogging down the Mall, past the empty carousel that on weekends boils over with children, and I'll realize I need a dose of Nattie. Or it'll hit me at work, eating a home-made sandwich or listening to my boss record a sound bite for the radio stations: a swelling of feeling and then a hollowness, almost indistinguishable from hunger. One night, it strikes just as I'm getting into bed. I'm actually pulling the sheets over me, reaching for the lamp, and instead of turning off the lamp, I find myself picking up the phone, punching her number, listening for the pigeonlike whir of her phone line, wondering if I'm going to wake her. But I've never woken her. I don't think I ever will.

"Nicky!" she says. "Oh, I'm sad. I know you can't tell."

"Why are you sad?"

"I just talked to my brother. Honest to God, he's so miserable, he doesn't even know it. Nick."

"Yeah?"

"We're doing the right thing, aren't we?"

My head sinks into the cavity of my pillow. I feel myself inching across a moonscape. "Why do you ask?"

"Oh, you know," she says, and her voice fills with breeze. "The world is terrible, and life is hard. The usual stuff. I mean, why bring a child into this? What right do we have?"

My father would know what to say at a time like this. He would just start talking autonomically, and maybe he wouldn't really say very much—maybe it would all be spurious comfort—but whoever was on the other end would feel better. They would be grateful.

But I'm lucky: Nattie doesn't need any of that. She recovers all on her own. She forgets the question as soon as she's raised it.

"On the ovulation front," she says.

"Yes?"

"According to my glucose readings, it should be happening sometime this weekend. Probably Saturday."

"OK."

"You know what that means, don't you?"

"What?"

She pauses then, and the silence stretches out. I can't decide if she's bothered that I don't know or if she's hoping I'll tell her. And when she comes back on the line, her voice has curled back on itself. She sounds amazingly like Celia, calling to me through the Plexiglas shield.

"Fourth of July," she says.

eight

When I was a teenager, the only time my family ever came into D.C. was on Independence Day. Some latent strain of patriotism made us drive the Buick up Shirley Highway to the Pentagon, deposit it in one of the parking savannas, board the Metro to the Smithsonian Castle, follow the sunglasses and blankets and picnic baskets onto the Mall. The sun would just be starting its slow descent behind the Washington Monument, and the Capitol would be gorging with pink. And the National Symphony Orchestra would be tuning itself, a sound like a hundred sea birds, and my father would be humming something from Sousa, who once lived a few blocks from the Mall, and we would find some square of turf that no one else wanted—a loveless tract, well to the south—and unpack plastic compartments of barbecued chicken and potato salad, spongy dinner rolls from the bakery near my father's church, and my mother's caramel brownies, which disappeared before dessert had formally begun.

I loved everything about these outings: the reveries of people collapsed on grass, the cannons sealing off the final bars of the "1812 Overture." Everything but the fireworks. I would sit on the blanket, watching the tall white wick of the Monument spit wheels of colored light, and I would work strenuously to feel something. Everyone around me was going, "Ooh, ooh," and it seemed to me the parents were simulating excitement for the benefit of their children, and the children were doing the same for their parents, and I figured no one would notice if I wasn't watching. When the last great shower of noise and light came, I was usually sleeping by my mother's knee, my fingers sticky with caramel.

Many years later, I came to associate the disillusionment of fireworks with the sensation of bad sex. Which may explain why I tend to be out of town when the Fourth of July comes around. The last time I was here, America had just won the Persian Gulf war. Tanks were preening down Pennsylvania Avenue, and women were groaning over ammunition belts, and I felt like I'd gone home with the loudest, chestiest guy in the bar and watched him fuck himself.

This year, thanks to Nattie's menstrual cycle, I'll be sticking around. And what do I have to look forward to? More bad sex. Even that is a little presumptuous. We're looking at *non*-sex, aren't we? And the real question is why I should be so anxious about it. Why do I feel that great labors are in store, that inordinate quantities of sperm will be demanded? I maintain a waking amnesia about my penis. I barely touch it even to urinate. Weeks into summer and I've converted myself into an ice palace, a nunnery. Nattie, by contrast, is all phallic determination, charging into my apartment a little before 8 P.M. on the Fourth of July. She's dragging a zip-top tote bag sprayed with rose blossoms and buds, and as she gives the apartment a quick scan and turns her wrist to get the latest watch reading, she has the brisk efficiency of a sex worker. She starts to unload the bag's contents onto the couch, and I'm waiting for a credit-card impresser to come tumbling out.

"Oh, hey," she says. "On the way in this guy in the courtyard offered me a bong hit."

"That's my landlord."

"Huh." She spends a few seconds absorbing it. "He's probably not very good on repairs."

"I'm told you can let the rent slide, though."

From where I'm standing, I can't see the contents of her bag, so Nattie raises the items one by one to the light. The first is a Ziploc jumbo storage bag housing a gray, cigar-shaped silhouette. It looks like something recovered from a car bombing, and it takes me a few seconds to recognize it as a syringe, shorn of its needle.

"Much better than a turkey baster," she says.

"Certainly," I say. The shudder ends about halfway up my neck.

"Let's looky-see what else we've got." Her voice is pitched to an abnormally high level of cheer. "Cervical sponge? Check. Cervical cap? Check. Thermometer..."

"Oh, I've got one of those," I say. She looks up at me, puzzled. "I mean, if you need it."

"Well, thanks, honey, I should probably stick with the one I've been using. You know, the basal body temperature does this fascinating little spike thing just before you're ready to, to...hey, is this going to work for you?" She hoists a squat-stemmed wine glass, almost small enough for cordials.

"Work for...?"

"Depositing."

"Um, sure. You don't have to, I mean, I've got wine glasses, too."

"Oh, whatever." She shrugs lightly. "I broke the other three in the set, so I thought what the hey."

"No, that's fine."

"Or you can just squirt it right in the cervical cap, if you want."

"No, glass is fine."

"OK, what else?" Her head disappears behind the couch. Her arms rise disembodied on either side, lofting new objects. "Glucose tester. Plastic baggies. Nightgown. Needlepoint pillow."

"Pillow."

"Oh, right, that's for, for supporting the hips during....oh, and a couple of incense candles—very mild ones, hope you're not allergic."

"No."

"You're sure?"

"Oh, yeah, I like incense." My mouth opens into a cretinous grin. "I've always said incense is...is..."

"And looky what Dr. Jack ordered for us!"

Two tiny airline flasks of bourbon sit like perfume samples in the palm of her hand.

"I'll probably take mine before," she says. "You might want yours—"

"After. Yeah."

"But make sure to clean out your wine glass first. Ha!" Her head jerks back as though it's been lassoed. For a few moments she looks almost winded. "I think, Nick, I think we're almost..." With a sudden burst of violence, she plunges her arm deep into the bag. The canvas groans and bruises as her hand spiders across the bottom. "Oh, yeah!" And now her arm reemerges with a strange violet garter attached. She extends it toward me, rotating the axes of her wrists so the garter reveals stratum upon stratum of imitation silk, rippling shades of purple.

"I stole it from a Mexican restaurant," she says. "See, it's got the rubber band still on the back."

"What's it for?"

She raises an admonitory finger, takes four or five burglar steps around the couch, snakes her fingers under the lampshade. A few seconds of fumbling, and then a jet of color rockets across the ceiling. A big bang of photons—not purples but pinks: underbelly of cloud, skin rubbed with ice, orthodontic retainers...

Nattie stares upward, hands planted on her hips. "Beats a silver ball, don't it?"

"Very nice."

"Oh, wait!" she says. "One more thing." And this time, instead of rooting through the bag, she simply flips it over: A small plastic casing drops clear. She gathers it in her hands, puffs a cloud of air over it, then yells "Catch!" and flings it across the couch.

It's a CD holder, transected by a shivering fault line. I turn it over, stare at the waxen Aryan features. "Peggy Lee?"

"Pe-*ggee*!" she cries. "My girl Peggy."

She must see the question forming on my lips, because she says, "Don't you think she's sexy? God, when I listen to her, it sounds like she's just been fucked. Like right there in the recording booth. I thought it might help you get in the mood."

I close my inner eye. I try to imagine fucking Peggy Lee in a recording studio. I try to imagine *I'm* Peggy Lee getting fucked in a recording studio. The man fucking Peggy Lee is fucking me—in a recording studio.

"Or maybe you'd prefer something on TV?" Nattie suggests.

"No, I don't think so."

"Channel 26 is showing the NSO concert. The fireworks'll start any minute."

"No!" My voice rattles across the room. "The music is fine."

"I'm only thinking of *you.* Because girls don't have to be in the mood."

"That's OK. I'll get there."

Nattie nods, rubs her hands together, releases a long satiated breath. "Well, OK." And for want of anything else to do, she starts taking in the apartment. The ashen, purple-inflected industrial carpet sweeping toward the plastered wall. The potted ficus tree, now in the twilight of its career, sloughing off a new leaf each week. The round, bare-legged dining table, water stains under a Nixon-era wood veneer. The painting of Lucky, long-dead Broome family pooch, placed over the imitation hearth. The gas jet in the fireplace, inoperable for two years.

And the couch, of course. Its faded harlequin coquetry: always and forever.

"Nice place," says Nattie, wheeling like a periscope.

"Thanks."

Maybe she imagined it more glamorous or more federal—shawls, cushions, ottomans—some place that didn't have Lucky's mournful beagle face staring back at her. But when she turns back to me, her eyes have faded into blue talcum slates, and I realize she's not thinking about where she is or where she came from. She has a task, and when she speaks again, her voice cuts through everything that is not this task.

"Let's go, Nick. The time is *now*." And then she's mysteriously mollified. "I mean, whenever. It doesn't have to be now. We have a few hours, right? Whenever you want to do it."

"I think maybe we should just do it. Get it done."

"OK." Her head is rocked by my good sense: front, back, front, back. "I didn't bring any lubricant for you."

"No, I know. It's bad for the little guys."

Over our heads the water pipes groan. From the apartment below, a crackle of human laughter disperses. Five blocks away, thousands of people sit on the Mall's parched summer grass, listening to "The Stars and Stripes Forever."

"Well, I guess I'll get going then," I say. "OK," I say. And I lean into the column of air that surrounds me, push it open like a heavy glass door, and take a couple of long, surprisingly definite steps toward the bathroom—I feel like I'm leaping across building struts.

Nattie says, "Come here."

I turn around, and she has her arms stretched out. "Come to Mama," she says.

But she comes to me instead. She wraps her arms around me, whispers in my ear. "It's going to be great."

"I know."

"No, really. It's going to be great."

And then she hands me the wine glass.

The bathroom door doesn't quite close behind me. It never has, and normally I wouldn't care, but tonight I have company. Tonight, I want the door shut. So I start hurling myself at the door—*all* of myself—shoulders, hands, hips, feet. And after 20 seconds, the door scrapes and sighs, slides halfway into its frame. I step back, panting. My hair is bleeding sweat, and a question is shivering through me. What if the door doesn't open again? What then?

A wine glass of sperm, looped inside a line of unlaundered bath towels, is lowered from a third-story bathroom window into the hands of a slightly heavyset blond woman. Neighbors stare through their blinds; cops converge from nowhere, slapping billy clubs in their palms....

"Come on, Nick!" Nattie's voice pierces the bathroom door. "Shake a stick. Ha!"

I turn around, and I'm already at the sink—where I'm supposed to be. I flip the old-fashioned, daisy-handled spigot, and a slim column of water whistles out. My hands lace together into a cat's cradle at the bottom of the stream. Slowly, slowly, a vein of warmth pulses through. The water simmers and whitens, and my hands luxuriate in the heat, and it's about half a minute before I remember how near I came to second-degree burns in Dr. Willinger's office. *Not too hot,* I remember, jerking clear. *Think yeast.*

I dry my hands on the stiff green washcloth. I stand in front of the toilet, feeling vaguely quarantined. It's not the ideal venue. It's not the place I would normally have chosen, but it's the only room in the apartment that feels private. I take a breath. I unbutton my shorts and lower myself onto the porcelain lifesaver. Even now, at the height of summer, the seat gives off a thrilling flutter of cold—the same flutter I get from hail stones, telephone solicitors. I lean back until my shoulder blades are resting against the tank and my buttocks are perched at the front rim of the seat and my spine makes a 45-degree angle with the toilet. I am comfortable. I am comfortable enough. I am arguably close to being comfortable.

My glass is on the floor, against the toilet base. My penis lies in my hand, looking as though it's just been discovered—tripped over, like a pine cone. How old it looks. So much older than the rest of me, so much more experienced. As I stare, a long, winding vermilion tributary marks itself across the parchment, flows upward into a tiny mountain of vein.

Through the door comes a lazy voice—a woman with half her face in a pillow, singing about a train that's coming in. It's Peggy, calling to me from her recording studio. But tonight I won't need her. Tonight, there will be none of the fumbling that took place in Dr. Willinger's office. I have plans—a special guest.

And yet, sitting on the toilet, I suddenly forget who my guest is. I forget everything except the bathroom I'm sitting in. I see the peeling brown wallpaper with its strange fox-hunting tableaux, the crooked steel stilts of the wash basin, the encrustations of mildew and mold where the bathtub caulking pulls away from the floor. With a start, I remember that this is my bathroom; this is where I live.

What a mistake! To think of conceiving a child here. In this apartment, in this repository of neglect. I feel it every time I come through the door; I feel everything. My job. My singleness. My childlessness. The gathered failures of Broomes and Reynoldses, bioaccumulating through the generations and converging in this bathroom, leaving this patina of mild, forgotten decay. Gravity, gravity everywhere.

So why should I be surprised? Why should I be in any way astonished to look down and see gravity doing its work, see the head of my penis wobbling, the body sagging into its bed of unkinked pubic hair? I pull; I yank; I whisper. But it has ceased to care for me. It would sooner twist off than respond. It is playing out on the movie screen of its own mind, undergoing a time-lapse shrink.

"OK in there?" Nattie calls.

"Fine!"

Do I sound desperate? I don't feel desperate. I feel myself cutting free of inadequacy, treating it like the spectacle it is. My dick is a bonsai dick. My dick is a shiitake mushroom, a dead frog. My dick is a blind worm. There's no end to the metaphor....

Through the door, Peggy's murmuring becomes more urgent. She's sitting up in bed now, stretching her arms. And something in her voice makes me sit up a little too. Once again I try to glimpse the man with her; I try to separate him from the swirl of microphone and flesh. Does he feel me staring at him? He must because he diverts his attention momentarily. He swings his head toward me, and I feel the shudder of expectation and surprise.

It's my guest for the evening. Nattie's brother.

He leaps to his feet with the clarity of a dancer. He sends a quick apologetic glance to Peggy, who lies there smiling and recumbent, waiting for him to come back. He takes a few gentle, appraising steps in my direction. He has wide drifts of strawberry-blond hair and big scoops of muscle—a catcher's build, powerful and heavy-legged. Still has his clothes on: a ribbed tank-top undershirt, one strap sliding down his shoulder; a pair of shambling dungarees, pulled down a few inches to give his penis breathing room. The penis is not a shiitake mushroom. It feints and darts, sniffs the air like a pet otter.

Nattie's brother says hello. His voice is husky, cracked, barely out of adolescence.

I say, *Nattie has told me so many things about you. I was so sorry to hear about your breakup. I know how hard it can be.*

He says, *I haven't been able to trust women since then. I can't bring myself to touch them.*

I understand, I tell him. *You need someone to restore your confidence. Make you believe in yourself as a man.*

I approach him very slowly, like a hostage negotiator. I speak very quietly, and as he watches me, the broad angles of his face open up, and something...curiosity, anxiety...stretches the corners of his mouth. He's waiting for me.

You need to be healed, I tell him.

He nods, once. His lips dampen in preparation. His eyelids fall to half mast.

I'm ready to do the work for both of us, but when I finally reach him, his hands move without prompting. They interlace around the small of my back and drag me closer. Our hips press together, and Peggy's watching us now from her floor bed, resting her head in her arms and moaning about biology, geology.

In my hand the map of my penis changes scale. The landscape acquires topography. The vermilion tributary coils, swells, overflows its banks. And suddenly my penis ceases to be a map; it becomes an organism. It raises its head. It learns to walk. It becomes wise. It delivers a valedictorian address.

And as I draw out its knowledge, Nattie's brother closes his eyes and yields. He flows into me and then flows out.

Ten minutes later, I'm standing just inside the living-room curtains. I've done something I almost never do in the summer: open the window. I'm waiting for the splash of hot chemical air on my face, but the rain has cooled things off, dampened the heat's vibrations, and a vagrant pity goes to those people sitting even now on the Mall, waving their limp toothpick flags, peering at firecrackers through the mist. How much quieter it is in this back-alley stretch of Capitol Hill. Even tonight, the only thing you hear is a dog's abbreviated bark, a bag of rubbish flung into a trash bin. Tinned laughter from the downstairs apartment, where a young, agreeably slouched man keeps his TV running morning to night.

At this very moment, Nattie is lying on my bed, inseminating herself. I handed her the glass as soon as I got out of the bathroom (a flush of shame in my face, as though my slingshot were being confiscated) and she seized it, hustled through the bedroom door, closed it behind her. Not a word, not an endearment. The business of baby making. I find myself wondering now how long it will take her, how the syringe will feel inside her. My ears strain unwillingly for her sound.

"Nick! Can you come in for a second?"

The door is opened maybe two inches. I wrench it open, and then I dance back out of the frame. I flatten myself against the living-room wall. "Oh, wow."

"Whoops," she says. "I should have...OK, I'm covered."

"No, it's not....I mean, you're standing on your head."

Where I had thought to find a face, I found feet. And in that half-second interval, the feet seemed to have appropriated the face's functions. The cork soles of her sandals had formed a swollen upper lip to the molars of her toes, and the lip bobbed and jutted with a drunken fluency. This, I think, is the part I will always remember: Nattie's feet speaking to me.

"Well, I told you about my mother and her tipped uterus," she says.

"I think...I think you were going to tell me."

"Oh, no, really? Are you sure? Well, my mother was trying to get pregnant. This was a long time ago. And her doctor told her every time she had sex, she should stand on her head to make sure everything flowed where it was supposed to. Incredibly goofy, but she did it, and lo and behold, Nick. Two kids! One right after the other."

"So you have a tipped uterus?"

"No, of course not, but this doesn't hurt, right? It worked for Mother, didn't it?"

I'm able to go back into the bedroom now. My eyes, still wobbling, lurch down the burled column of Nattie's body, settling finally on her face, which in its new inverted context has taken on a faintly obscene ventriloquial quality. Her hair spills across the floor, and her mouth moves in large robotic contortions as though the sound were being piped through the floor.

"Do you have to stay like that?" I ask her. "A long time?"

It's a token inquiry. I can't think who would discover her, even if she stayed until next July.

The muscles in Nattie's lower arms pulse; her fingers flex. She looks like she's getting ready to execute a full handstand. "Nick," she says. "I asked you in because I need you to talk to me."

"What about?"

"I don't know, talk about the kid. Tell me what the kid's going to be like."

But I can't tell her. I can't, because every time I try to envision our child, I end up combining the worst of both of us. My mind morphs our torsos, fuses our ankles and necks and chins, and the picture that emerges is never pretty. A girl, necessarily. Eight years old, oblong, misshapen, bunching out of her clothes. The kind of girl who breaks your heart just to look at her, the way Celia wounds me now when I see old pictures of her. And whenever I see this girl—our girl—my arms actually twitch at my sides as though they're getting ready to embrace her. I want to give her a lifetime's worth of immunity.

"I think it'll be a girl," I say.

"A girl. Uh-huh."

"Kind of a handful," I say. "One of those assertive kids. Not a bully, exactly, just very sure of herself, very territorial. I think, you know, I think she might push another kid out of the swing, but then later she'd go find him and offer the swing back."

"Ooh," says Nattie, "innate sense of justice, I like that."

"Very demanding. But kind of startlingly intelligent at times. Says things that kind of take your breath away, things about yourself."

"Wise," Nattie says.

"Very much wise. But not an observer because she's out there, right? No fear. She's mixing it up; she's loving the whole adventure."

She's everything I wasn't, is what I want to say.

"She's just like me," is what Nattie says. And the cork heels of her sandals rise toward the ceiling and shake, like a horse freeing itself of its bit.

Over the next week, I hear from Nattie precisely twice. Two E-mail messages with headings that read: "EXTRA URGENT! QUIT WHAT YOU'RE DOING!!" And when I open them, they turn out to be the usual innocuous fragments, the free-radical thoughts of Nattie Bryant. Monday morning it's:

I think I'm allergic to peanut butter.

A couple of hours later:

If it's a girl, we may not name it Courtney. I have met too many goddamn Courtneys. And they all curtsy.

And after that, nothing. I wait. I wait because waiting is all I can do. We still have two weeks, after all, two weeks before her body gives her the unequivocal sign—something more definitive than tacky mucus. And until then Nattie doesn't need anyone nagging her for temperature readings, wondering if maybe her breasts aren't getting a wee bit sensitive. But as the week slides by, I find myself hungering for news, for even the smallest, most ambiguous symptoms. I end up leaving a couple of short, nonchalant messages on her home voice mail. "No rush," I tell her. "Just wanted to see how you were doing." But she doesn't call back.

In a way, it doesn't matter, because everyone else in my life is rushing to plug the gaps. Shannon calls to tell me about the man she's been dating this week—a former Unitarian minister now shilling for the gun lobby. "You know, those people have some very interesting points to make," she says. My mother wants me to know that Hoy Phong left his job at the convenience store because they were personally demeaning to him. Celia calls to find out if her dentist is gay.

"Why do you want to know?" I ask.

It's true, I'm suspicious. I think maybe she's vetting another suitor for me, and as the memory of that last blind date sweeps over me, I want to say: *Don't. Please don't.*

"We have a bet going on at work," she says. "All these people have been going to this same dentist, and no one's quite sure about him, and I'm one of the people who's betting he's gay."

"All right, data. Give me data."

"OK, for starters, he's extremely, fastidiously neat."

"Well, sure," I say. "He's a dentist."

"But he told me when he goes camping, he packs everything in color-coded bags. You know, food in one color, toiletries in another. Underwear, overwear—everything's got its own color."

"OK, what else?" I ask.

"He used the word *ecru.*"

"What about the magazines in his office?"

"Um, *People.*"

"Yeah."

"And *Popular Mechanics.*"

"You're kidding."

"No."

"*Popular Mechanics.*" I let the title linger on my tongue. "Your dentist is an android."

"Yeah," says Celia, sounding oddly rueful. "That's what I figured."

One night, I even get a call from Greg. It's 8:30, and he's still at work, no surprise. But the call is a surprise. He asks how I'm doing and says I should really come over to dinner, and I'm startled enough to say sure without thinking about it. And even when I give it some thought, I can't be too scared, because I know Sally will be pleasant, and so will Greg, in his clumsy way. I could even make things interesting and bring Nattie. I could take her along on all the Broome family occasions—our next trip to Rehoboth even. She could be one of those pregnant bikinied women my mother stares at when they come walking down the beach. "No," my mother says. "I don't think I'd wear that in her condition."

Friday is one of those dawdling work days when congressmen have flown back to their districts, the staffers are dressed down, and the occasional constituent wanders in and flinches at all the blue-jeaned hilarity his tax dollars are supporting. Everyone in my office leaves at 5 and heads straight to the Hawk and Dove for pitchers of watery beer and free tacos. Everyone but me. I veer off at Second Street with a regretful wave. I explain that I have early dinner plans, but really I've decided that Nattie will call tonight, and I want to be there when she does.

It worries me a little that I'm doing this because I used to do the same thing with the Actor. If he were doing a show at, say, Woolly Mammoth or the Studio Theatre, I would sit in my apartment the entire evening, on the off chance he would call during intermission or during that long stretch in the second act when his character is sleeping offstage or certainly, certainly when the show was over, he was going to call and tell me who flubbed their lines, who messed up their blocking. And I would be clawing my eyes open, fighting off sleep, waiting for him to tell me where he wanted me to be. Nine times out of 10, he never called, and who would have suspected I could sustain hope for as long as I did, but I did. Maybe, just maybe, that was the source of my allure: that I had the courage to be so wholly pathetic.

Tonight, though, I do get a call. It comes shortly after 8:00, and the frequency of the phone—brittle, compressed, teetering into hysteria—tells me it's Nattie. It must be Nattie.

But it's a man. A youngish man with a light voice that hangs onto its vowels a little too long. He says, "Nick Broome, please."

"Speaking."

"Nick, this is Joe Bryant."

"Hi," I say, too quickly. I'm squinting, I'm staring at the ceiling. *Joe. Joe...*

"Nattie's brother?" he suggests. The way you point to something on a menu. As though there might be something else you'd prefer.

"Oh! Oh, hi! How are you?"

"I'm fine, thanks."

"I'm sorry, it took me a while to, to make the connection."

"I understand."

Nattie's brother. I'm talking to Nattie's brother. And he has a careful, nuanced voice—a voice nothing like Nattie's—with twanging syllables. And suddenly I remember: Texas. They're from Texas.

"She's told me a lot about you," I say.

I jerked off to you.

"Oh, right," he says. "Yeah, it's...hey, listen, I'm calling on kind of a request from Nattie."

"Uh-huh."

"She wants you to come see her."

I almost laugh then. It has such a peremptory sound: Queen Nattie bids you visit. "Well, where is she?" I ask. "Where is the queen?"

"She's checked herself into a hospital."

"Oh."

"A mental hospital."

"Oh."

I'm sitting on the couch—the place I'm always sitting when I call Nattie. And it's immediately obvious to me that she's on the other end of the line. She's lurking just out of sight, waiting to erupt into my ear, tell me it was all a joke and God, Nick is just about the biggest sucker in creation, isn't he?

"You mean she's *staying* there?"

"Yeah, and she's fine; she will be. The thing is we were just talking, and she said I should get in touch with you and let you know what's up."

Any second now. Any second she'll come bursting on the line. A squall of triumph.

"Are you OK?" asks Joe Bryant.

"No, it's, it's fine, I'm just...I was wondering, I guess. I was wondering if she's taking any kinds of medication. The only reason I mention it is there may be a slight chance she's pregnant."

And then quiet: gallons of air rushing through the phone line, crackling in my head. A wind of silence—I have to turn my hip into it, break a hole.

"I mean, she may be carrying our child," I say.

And then I hear Joe Bryant's caressing, chiming voice saying, "You know, you'd better come by the hospital. Why don't you come over tomorrow morning?"

Snookie Pie

nine

In the mental hospital that houses Nattie Bryant, the closets and drawers burrow into the wall, and the couches and beds buckle into art deco curves. There's not a corner in view. The only thing that holds its edges is the television set, which hangs from the ceiling of the common room, blasting an animatronic children's show. Nattie and I are sitting on the carpet so as not to block people's view, but no one is watching, not even the children.

"They won't let me shave my legs," Nattie says.

That's when I notice the purple crushed-velvet tights she's wearing. I've never seen her wear tights. I've never seen her wear purple.

"They took my bubble solution," she explains. "And the razor, of course."

I touch the thick cushiony pile just below her knee. "So this used to be panty hose."

It takes her a few seconds. She stares at her legs, then at me. Her eyes lighten with grace. "I'm touched," she says, "that you would think my hair is so soft."

My eyes wander to the surrounding walls, which are covered with pastel prints and framed passages from "If." I ask myself if Kipling would have approved of the people here. He would probably have admired the ones who, like Nattie, take pains with their appearance. Not the other ones though: the staggerers in their pajamas and bathrobes. One man carries his catheter bag with him, clutching it like a briefcase, and there's an old woman who wanders the hallway, muttering "Need to go. Need to go." And directly behind Nattie, a giantess in stirrup pants is playing table tennis with her young daughter. She lofts high-bounding balls to the girl, but the ball keeps getting away, and a harried-looking man keeps chasing it into the far corners of the room.

I ask Nattie how the food is.

"Summer camp," she says equably. "Mystery meat, mystery fish. I could take the food, but the sleep deprivation is killing me, Nick. Every 15 minutes they sweep a flashlight through your room, and every single time I wake up. I wish I could be like Martha."

"Martha?"

"My roommate. She just lies there snoring. All 300 pounds of her. Sounds like a jackhammer. Her doctors think she's lost the will to live, but they haven't heard her snore."

I'm waiting for Nattie's standard punctuation—the explosive barking "Ha!"—but she's on her best behavior today. It's as though someone has upbraided her for all her past excesses. She speaks with the caressing reserve of a garden club president, even when she's talking about the woman obsessed with Scott Bakula or the midget who makes obscene phone calls to high school basketball players.

"Thank God for the *Wheel*," she says. "*Wheel of Fortune.* Everybody gathers around the TV, and it's unbelievably quiet. Better than any pharmaceutical."

This much is the same. I'm still here, and Nattie is still talking (without her usual excitability, true, but still talking). The one thing, of course, she doesn't discuss, the one ambient topic, is our baby. *What's happened to our baby, Nattie?*

There's no way of knowing or even asking. Every few minutes, my eyes slide off Nattie's face and rappel down her body, down the dull brown smock in which she has draped herself, until finally, with an agonized sense of exposing myself, I stare at her belly, stare *hard*, as though I could bore through the skin and muscle tissue, through the dense fibers of the uterus, all the way to the embryo inside.

And I hear Nattie talking about pillow feathers—goose down and synthetic and the proper mixture of the two—and I'm wondering if I should respond, and then I hear her say: "I'm sorry, Nick."

And that's the last thing she says for a long while. Five minutes pass. We listen to ping-pong balls and tinny TV music and soft litanies. And then something changes in Nattie, sparks her back into consciousness. She is staring just over my left shoulder, and the beginnings of a wet smile pry her lips apart, and a voice behind me says: "Hey, where's my lanyard?"

"Ha!" she cries, rocking onto her back, covering her face.

A young man brushes past me, leaving a quiver of air behind. He is six-one or six-two, with blue eyes and small teeth, and he gives Nattie the full measure of his attention before he turns it on me.

"I told her when she came in here," he explains. "I said if you're gonna do those art classes, you gotta make me a lanyard."

"Oh!" Nattie pulls her hands off her face. "Nick, I didn't tell you about these classes. They herd you in there, right? They herd you everywhere. And they play, I don't know, John Tesh music, something terrible, which is supposed to make you scribble for 10 minutes, at which point you explain what the hell you just did."

"So what the hell was it?" the young man asks.

"What?"

"What did you draw?'

The question stops her for a couple of seconds. Stumps her. "I don't remember," she says, and a veil of abstraction sweeps across her face. "But what amazed me," she says, "what particularly amazed me was how specific people are. 'The *black*...'" She slips effortlessly into a Midwestern bray. "'The black represents my despair, which is what John Tesh always makes me feel. But the *green* shows the point in the music where I started to feel hope. And then the yellow's where the voices started coming back.'"

I sit on the pistachio carpet, almost laughing. A hand materializes in front of me. It belongs to Nattie's caller, and I assume it wants to shake my hand, but really it wants to draw me to my feet. And in its grip, I have the heft of pencil shavings.

"You must be Nick," he says. "I'm Nattie's brother."

Which, of course, I knew but didn't believe. The words are already crystallizing on my lips. "You're..." *Bald.* "Taller than I would have thought."

In fact, he is both balder and taller. In almost every way, he's different from the Joe Bryant I imagined: that compact fellow with the strawberry-blond hair and the washclothed face. That Joe Bryant was mourning his old girlfriend. He was screwing Peggy Lee. The real one is wearing cargo shorts and a ribbed short-sleeve shirt, very formfitting, and the form it fits is wide-shouldered, slim-hipped—the kind of body I have spent a lifetime aspiring to. You wouldn't even place him in Nattie's biological family except his face has the same dewy color, the compulsively straight nose and blue-green eyes. The more you look at them, in fact, the less distance you have to travel between them. All you need to do is stretch Nattie on a rack, shave her scalp, and seed her jaw with a day's worth of downy whiskers. Voila.

"Isn't he gorgeous?" Nattie asks me. She has hoisted herself into a standing position, clapped a proprietary hand on his shoulder. "Couldn't he be a model?"

"Yeah," says Joe. "Hair Club for Men."

And that's pretty much the last time the conversation includes me. The Bryants have checked into a suite of their own: exotic dog breeds, Slim Jims, a thrice-married cousin, a horrible Empire clock on *Antiques Roadshow.* They talk about anything that comes to mind, and something is always coming to mind, even here, especially here, and I suppose it should bother me, being planted in this teeming space with no one to talk to, but it makes it easier. I can begin the almost physical labor of detaching, and before I know it everything has detached: brain, heart, ears, legs. My eyes stretch across the space with an immoderate relief. I see an old man in a Diogenes nightshirt. And just off to the side, the see-through tank of the smoking booth, where patients sit exposed and soundproofed, like 1950s quiz-show contestants.

The problem, the *only* problem, with this state of mind is the effect it produces in other people. Every thirty seconds or so, Nattie and Joe steal looks at me that have no connection to what they're saying, and as the minutes pass, their sentences falter, and I realize that without doing anything I have become something they are helpless to do anything about.

"Hey, I should really get going," I say.

And neither of them makes a move to stop me. Nattie's face, in particular, is a study in resignation. Deep inside her, I suppose, some tiny gear is digesting me, getting ready to eliminate.

"I'll give you a call later this week," I say. "See how things are going."

And then I hear Joe say, "Let me walk you to your car." *Yer cawr*, that light San Antonio twang, a world away from Nattie's charging Eastern vowels.

"No, really," I tell him. "That's OK."

I'm even putting up my hand to stop him, but he says, "Trust me. It's hard to find your way out." He gives me a bouncer's tap on the shoulder and motions toward the door.

"Thank you for coming," says Nattie.

And before I can think of anything to say to her, we're walking—me and Nattie's brother—through the door and around the corner to the elevators. And as I round the corner, my eyes cut back and find Nattie again, frozen-faced and frozen-bodied, a monument to the war dead. Her jaw hangs open slightly, and her hands are folded across her solar plexus, and just as I pass from sight, one hand jars loose and offers me the smallest of farewells. And even this comes too late because I'm already passing from view, and here are the elevators, and here is Joe Bryant, and every pleasantry that rises in my brain perishes of its own absurdity.

Nice place. Nothing like that Olivia de Havilland movie.

The elevator arrives with a calm breathing out of doors. We step inside, and the womb closes around us. For five floors, nothing but the hum of the cables and generators and hoist ropes. Only when we reach bottom does the silence break, and it's Joe Bryant who breaks it. He says, "It was her idea to call you."

And as we walk down the matted linoleum hallway with its mustard walls, he says, "Apparently, she was on some antidepressants, and over the last few weeks, she stopped taking 'em, I don't know why."

Oh, yes. The tablets. The tiny tablets Nattie used to pop in her mouth at the Greek restaurant. She said they were vitamins.

"And the other night, I guess something bad happened 'cause she called her psychiatrist, and she said, 'You know, I'm really afraid I might do something. Please help.' So it really was Nattie's idea to come here."

"I'm sure she did the best thing," I tell him.

We push through the glass doors, into the bladelike glare of a July noon. The hospital has been designed and landscaped to look like an insurance office. It sits in a small parking lot in an upper-middle-class residential area in Falls Church, barricaded by lindens and oaks. Joe is walking toward a blue Chevy Venture vast enough to hold a baleen whale, but then he swerves left, past a Volkswagen Beetle, past a Volvo 850, stops finally in front of a gun-metal–gray Nissan Sentra with spots of bird shit scorched into the paint. He leans against the trunk, props a sandal on the bumper. Next to his left foot, a bumper sticker reads: HAVE YOU HUGGED YOUR ANGEL TODAY?

"Oh, I'm sorry," he says. "Is this your car?"

"Um, no. I thought it was yours."

"I don't have a car."

"Well, how did you get here?"

"A friend," he says.

Amazing how quickly I can summon her image. One of the regulars at his bar. Ash blond, dripping with divorce settlement.

"There's something you should probably know," Joe says.

"OK."

"I know you and Nattie were, you know, talking about babies and stuff."

"Well, that's true. Actually, we were...it was a little more than talking."

"Sure. Sure." His head bobs freely. "What you need to know is 'bout five years ago, Nattie had this *problem*. No, that's stupid. She had an *infection*, this bad cervical infection."

"Uh-huh."

"It was a big mess."

"I'm sorry to hear it."

"It's OK now. I mean, at the time it was scary, 'cause she spent a week in the hospital, but her life was never in danger apparently, and when it was over, she was *fine*. But just before they released her, the doctors said her uterus was damaged...you know, scarred." He sweeps a lazy hand across his scalp. "So Nattie says OK, what does that mean? And what they told her was she could not have babies."

"Oh." Standing in the parking lot, with my hands in my pockets, I am flooded with spurious authority. I could be one of those people who keep lines moving in public places. "So OK," I say. "So..."

"Well, that's what the medical establishment told her. 'Course Nattie never had much use for those guys. She's the kind, the weatherman tells her it's raining, she puts on her leather jacket, you know? So what I'm thinking happened is she realized after your...when you two tried the one time...she probably knew it wasn't taking, and that's what set everything off."

"Um." I tap my finger against my lips. "I don't know how she would know that."

"Sorry?"

"It's only been a week since we—"

"Right."

"—since we tried it, and normally it takes *two* weeks. To be sure. One way or the other."

"Well." Joe is looking at me now. "Maybe there's some other way of knowing?"

And that's when I remember: Just before she left my apartment, Nattie made a point of repacking her thermometer. Because she was planning to check her temperature at least twice a day. Because... "Because a woman's temperature rises after successful fertilization," I say. The words skein out of my mouth, like a Latin declension. "As much as eight tenths of a degree. Plus the...the breasts can become sensitive. But temperature is a more reliable indicator."

She probably checked it more than twice a day—on the hour, more likely. Every time her boss screamed at her, every time she got a hunger pang, she reached into that handbag, pulled the battery-powered thermometer from its tissue-paper wrapping, thrust it under her tongue. Oblivious, probably, to where she was or who was looking at her, waiting 30 seconds, a minute, squinting at the number, thinking there must be something wrong, it's supposed to be higher. Thinking maybe it's the batteries or the iced tea she had half an hour ago. Of course! Her mouth is still cold from the iced tea.

"You know, she's been to lots of doctors," Joe says. "She was always hoping they'd tell her it was a mistake, but they all said pretty much the same thing. So after a while, you have to assume they're right. But Nattie doesn't work that way. She always believed she could conceive if she found the right circumstances, you know, the right person."

Without any prompting, my eyes jump to the upper bank of windows, and I find myself waiting for her to loom, damsel-like, between the iron bars. "Poor Nattie," I say.

I only say it for something to say, but Joe gives me a frowning smile. "Thank you for taking this so well. You're bein' a real sport."

"Well...what?" I shrug listlessly. "What is there to say?"

"Oh, I don't know. Something like how dare she drag me into her crazy scheme when she knew she couldn't hold up her end. Something like that."

And it's taken me this long to recognize that he's the one who's pissed—pissed enough for both of us.

"Maybe you want to be alone now," Joe says, softly.

"No. That's OK."

And he takes me at my word. He plants his butt on the car trunk, as though he were easing himself onto a bar stool. And normally I would ask myself how someone could take possession of a stranger's car in this way, but all I'm noticing is the way his thighs flare across the metal, and

I'm recalling—as if I've ever forgotten!—that thighs were the thing I first loved in men.

"Why Nattie?" Joe asks suddenly.

"Why—"

"I mean, you probably got a bunch of people answering your ad. I was just wondering why you picked Nattie."

"I don't know," I say. "I liked her laugh. Um. I liked how she ate. Her name."

"What about her name?"

"I don't know," I say. "It sounds like Natasha."

"Who is?"

"Oh. She's this character in a book I'm reading."

"And the book is?"

"*War and Peace.*"

"Hoo!" Joe pulls his head back, gives his armpits a couple of yokel scratches. "Look at you. An in-te-llekchul."

"No, it's not..." I'm laughing in spite of myself. "I don't read it for that. It's escapism really. It's about getting married and having children. Dozens and dozens of children."

"Well, what'd they do with all those children?"

"Um, I don't know. Fed them blintzes? I'm not sure. I guess a lot of them died young, so the parents were probably hedging their bets a little."

"Huh," Joe says. "Kind of like Social Security. Makin' sure there's something around for later."

"Yeah, you could look at it that way."

For the next minute or so, we listen to the cicadas. They're loud this time of year. Sometimes they make a dry rattle, like a can full of coins, and sometimes it's just a waveless line of sound. Everything else is still, except for the fanning lines of a sprinkler in somebody's brown yard.

Joe slides off the trunk of the car, stretches his arms over his head. "Well," he says, "I've used up enough of your oxygen."

I stare at him.

"You've got places to be," he says.

Which, for most adults, would be true, but now that I've seen Nattie—now that I know there's no child—I have no place to be and nothing more pressing to do than vacuum under my bed, maybe purchase some frozen yogurt. Welcome to my freedom.

I stare at Joe Bryant, and in my head the usual klaxons break out: *He's straight, Nick. Woman-loving, touch-football–playing, Stooges-watching.*

So what is it that overrides all that and keeps me looking? Boundaries dissolve. The cicadas shake their tambourines. A mockingbird lets out a long, sustained cry, and a flatbed truck comes buzzing around the corner, disappears around the next corner.

And Joe Bryant cocks his head and smiles at me, and in my heart of hearts, I would call it an insinuating smile—I would swear to it in court. But it's not half as insinuating as what he says next: "Ye-e-esss?"

And the way he draws it out makes it feel like a question and a challenge and everything in between.

I don't know who moves first. It may be purely synchronous: two heads traveling the shortest distance between them. And it may be that my eyes are closed, but I see it all anyway: our heads drawing together, instinctively tilting in opposite directions; our jaws migrating toward each other. The first brush of lip, like the dab of a handkerchief. And then the second contact, deeper and fuller, with threads of moisture seeping through.

And me saying, "Do you need a ride?"

And him saying, "Thought you were never gonna ask."

ten

Three days later, we're driving into the passenger drop-off lane at Dulles Airport. Joe Bryant is flying back to San Antonio with the last of Nattie's things. Nattie is already gone—spirited away by her mother in a van. Gone without another word, leaving only Joe as collateral, and now the collateral is about to board a Southwest MD80, and won't be back for two weeks.

"Thanks for driving," Joe says.

The other departing passengers have followed orders—squeezed their clothes into small, hard stewardess bags on wheelies. Joe, by contrast, is hoisting an enormous backpack, like a Tyrolean exchange student.

"So I'll call when I get a chance," he says.

"OK."

"I don't know when that'll be exactly."

"Whenever is fine."

Behind us rise the white bones and parabolic roof of Saarinen's terminal. In a few seconds, Joe Bryant will disappear behind the smoked glass. He will testify that his luggage has never been out of his sight, that he packed it himself. He will sling a small carry-on sack over one shoulder, pass through the metal detectors, step past the woman with the metal wand. But for the next few seconds, he's here. Every part of him.

"It was very nice meeting you," he says.

An absurd diction; he can't sustain it. He giggles and then steals his arms around me, plants a covert kiss just under my left ear.

"Call me when you get there," I tell him.

"OK."

"And, you know, every-hour-on-the-hour kind of thing."

"Every half hour," he says.

"Fifteen minutes."

A dazed smile wells up on his face and slides off again. It's time for his signature line.

"OK," he says, "I've used up enough of your oxygen."

And since I don't have a signature line, all I say is, "OK, bye."

He gives me one last wink and makes a final turn. Within two seconds, he's inside the terminal. Through the glass I see his shadow darkening into a slate. I watch a few seconds longer, in case he rematerializes, and when I turn around, a woman in a rhinestone-studded blouse is embracing a man in a cowboy hat, and a hairy-armed Scoutmaster is shouting instructions to 10 boys in olive-drab uniforms, and a Washington Flyer taxi is honking at me to move my car. They're all completely surreal. I slip into the driver's seat, fumble for the keys, and then I remember they're still in the ignition. I press the clutch, feel the rev in the accelerator, and inch my way into the lane. A dog lick of air comes through the passenger window, and as I pull into the exit lane, an American flag ripples across my rearview mirror.

Joe Bryant's flight will not crash. Joe Bryant will not die violently. Joe Bryant will live long enough to require new teeth and hips.

For the next two hours, I dedicate myself to groceries, dry cleaning, washing my car, buying peaches at Eastern Market. I'm unbelievably strict about the peaches: I pinch them between my thumb and forefinger; I track the changes in hue. I force my thoughts in every conceivable direction, everywhere but *there*, so when I get home, finally, and find him on my voice mail, it feels like 10 years have passed.

"Hey, Nick! I'm using one of these damn airplane phones. The coolest thing, can you hear me? Oh, excuse me, ma'am, could you get your hand off my...hey, excuse me, that's for...hey, Nick, I gotta go, I'm gettin' a hand job like you wouldn't believe." A brief crackling and then Joe's voice comes back chastened. "Wait, I just remembered. These phones cost, like, 20 bucks a second, don't they? 'Kay, I'm getting off now. I mean I'm getting off the *phone*. I'll call you when I get to the airport. 'Kay, bye."

He couldn't sound much farther away. But then most everyone I know seems kind of remote these days. Shannon is in Lake Placid with her dad and his girlfriend. My friend George took the Metroliner to New York to catch the opening night of *Electra* at the Met. Greg and Sally had to fly to Albuquerque for the last-minute wedding of Sally's sister. The only people still around are my parents, who rarely leave anyway, and Celia, who is busy dating Nosferatu.

His assumed name is Larry. He is a never-married, 41-year-old dentist (aha!) with a Marine haircut and satellite-dish ears and the smile of the undead. I first meet him over light supper at my parents' house; I'm the one who opens the door when he arrives. I'm wearing my mother's apron and holding a hand beater because I've been ordered to whip the cream for dessert. Celia blanches a little to see me—she must not have known I was coming—but the hunch-shouldered man next to her already has his hand extended.

"You must be the dentist," I say, lamely.

"I'm one of many dentists," he says.

A rush of air warms my shoulder. My mother. She has dashed forward with a haste that she is already disguising with nonchalance. Her eyes, for want of clear instruction, end up locking on Larry's chin.

"Come, come," she tells the chin. "It's too hot to stand in the doorway."

We eat at the kitchen table. My parents' new ceiling fan, a little large for the space, whirls like a helicopter blade over our heads—if you lift your chin and speak, you can actually hear your voice warping. Everyone eats slowly, in deference to the heat. It's a sweet little meal: tomatoes and basil, grilled corn on the cob, potato salad, and some slices of Virginia ham, which my mother, true to her mother's legacy, has soaked in milk before cooking. My father has done Larry the honor of devising a theory on dentistry, which he imparts over a second glass of lemonade.

"Well, isn't it obvious?" he says. "Dentistry is about the fear of death. We keep our original choppers, and we never have to die. Be honest with me, Larry. Weren't people much wiser when they just let their teeth rot in their heads?"

"Um." Larry is quiet for a few seconds, searching for a patch of common ground. "You know, people probably didn't worry about their teeth in the old days because of the life expectancy. Because they died younger."

"Yes." The Rev. Broome nods. "They were wise."

"Dessert?" Mom says.

But dessert doesn't quite turn out as planned. The sponge cake was left in the oven too long and has hardened into a krugerrand. And in the excitement of Larry's arrival, I forgot to finish whipping the cream, which, in the heat of the kitchen, has collapsed into foam. The strawberries float in it like stranded atolls.

"Nobody has to eat it," says my mother piously.

It puts me in mind of the last dessert the Broomes ate together: the Entenmann's crumb cake, our birthday offering to Dad. I remember Mom trying to cut it with a plastic knife. I remember the cake fighting her every step of the way.

It's pretty clear: We suck at desserts.

But Larry takes two helpings and eats with a grandiose relish, and just when I'm starting to find his politeness excessive, I notice the deep trance he's in: bowed over his plate, chewing secretly, like someone who regularly has food snatched away. We sit around the kitchen table, watching him, and he doesn't even notice us until he finishes his second piece, and pushes his plate away.

"Once you're done with the cake," Dad says, "I've got some whitewall tires you might enjoy."

My mother is completely won over. She makes a great fuss of taking his plate away: "You're sure you're done? There's more, are you *sure*?" And later I hear her whisper to Celia about what a "cute little 'do" he has. (This from the woman who sends her eyes heavenward when I get my hair cut above the ears.) Back in the living room, my father has just shown Larry the block of wood he's been whittling for the last four months. It's now about one seventh its original size and no more recognizable than when it began.

"There's certainly some carving going on there," Larry allows.

A response I have to admire, but it doesn't lead anywhere. And so the conversation pretty much stops dead for the next two or three minutes, and just as I'm getting comfortable with that, Larry wheels on me and says, with a slight trembling of the skin under his eye: "Now it's *my* understanding that the whole Freudian explanation has been pretty much debunked."

It takes me a few seconds to grasp what he's saying. I've been staring too long at my parents' clock, which has a silhouetted man hanging off the bottom, pulling the outline out of whack. "Has been...?"

"It's all genetics now," Larry says. "They've debunked that whole domineering-mother–weak-father theory."

"Um." I'm staring at my father, waiting for him to dip his oar in. "You know, genetics is a lot of it. But of course, there are identical twins who don't...not that there isn't a strong correlation...."

"And the sex," Larry says. "My understanding is you guys are mostly oral these days."

"Um."

"I mean, more than anal."

"Well, that's—"

And because I am nothing if not obliging, I mount an unofficial tally, which begins with Joe Bryant and ends with Joe Bryant. And it occurs to me that I haven't had sex of any kind with him. Nothing oral, nothing anal. The barest hint of frottage. And yet the memory of being with him seems to demand a new class of license. If I close my eyes, I'm lying on an Arapaho rug on his apartment floor, my head butting an empty fish tank, my face maybe an inch from his, our fingers performing extended braille exercises on each other until the feel of denim and ribbed cotton grows indistinguishable from flesh. Who knows what kept us from going further? A certain delicacy, maybe; the knowledge that, a few miles away, Nattie was watching *Wheel of Fortune.* And yet nothing in those two hours seemed withheld. Clothing never felt so naked.

"Maybe 2–1, oral-to-anal," Larry is saying. "Or 3–1."

"Hard to say," blares my mother from the kitchen doorway. "You know, there's still quite a bit of anal." She comes toward us with a stately tread, a tray of coffee cups balanced against her chest. "Of course, barebacking carries a much higher risk of HIV transmission, but there are documented instances of..." She pivots, looking for a place to set the tray. "...of strictly oral transmission. Which makes me a little concerned about these bathhouses..." With her left knee, she shoves my father's foot off the table. "...where they have just the oral sex, over and over again. Now I know all about the sex-positive argument..." Carefully, she lowers the tray to the table, reaches behind her for the creamer and sugar bowl. "...but they can't honestly say it's safe. Not completely."

God knows where. *The Advocate? Out?* The PFLAG newsletter? I've lost track of all my mother's subscriptions.

She's smiling at Larry now. "Did Celia tell you she's never had a cavity?"

"Mom," Celia says.

"Not a single one. We're continually amazed."

"I complimented her," Larry says. "The first time she came to my office, I told her the dental profession has lost a lot of money on you. I said, 'I'll never get to know you because your teeth are too good.' "

"He also said I didn't floss properly." Celia reaches across the table, strokes the underside of his wrist with her fingers. "He said the gum over my left bicuspid was inflamed, and I wasn't—"

"That's true," Larry says. "But most people don't floss correctly."

"Is that so?" my mother asks.

"Oh, it's demonstrable. Of course, I'm very lucky because my teeth don't generate plaque the way most people's do. I'm part of a small class, about five percent of the population, and thus I really only floss to set an example."

He asks my mother if she's considered getting her teeth whitened. He tells her he can change her prevailing tint from beige to ivory within two weeks...another two weeks to chalk...and I realize then that this is a true-believing dentist, journeying into the world for converts, and that his sincerity imparts a kind of mystery. No wonder my sister didn't know what to make of him. *He used the word "ecru." He keeps things in compartments.*

"So Larry," my mother says. "You met Celia when she came to your office?"

"Well..." Larry starts to speak and then stammers into silence. Celia takes over but has to drop out after a sentence. They go on for about a minute like this. All I can make out, finally, is that Celia, during her lunch hour, accidentally dropped her purse off the M Street bridge, and that Larry happened to be standing below, pulled the purse out of the creek and ran it up to its owner, who was already halfway down the block. Beyond that, you're on your own. I have no idea, for instance, why Larry was frequenting Rock Creek during his lunch hour. I have no idea how Celia could have knocked her purse off a bridge.

Oh, no.

No, I take it back. I do have an idea.

The fortune-teller.

Mrs. Abbruzzi and the $93 that were supposed to buy Celia protection from evil spirits...if she took it to a bridge...took it and...*Christ, we discussed it*! How ridiculous it was to think supernatural beings had a use for U.S. currency. What a common scam it was, instructing someone to throw money off a bridge, not telling them, of course, that a confederate was waiting below to catch the bag.

She couldn't have.

"So then he gave me his card," Celia says, "and I said, 'How funny is that? I've been looking for a dentist.' Which, the interesting part is that was a lie, because I've been seeing Dr. Rosenzweig for about seven years, and it's probably the most stable relationship I've ever had with a man."

She leans into Larry and says in a stage whisper: "Until now."

"From the sky," Larry says. "A purse, falling from the sky. I don't know what that is if it isn't fate."

It wasn't fate, of course; it was Celia. That's what's obvious to me now. With no further instructions from Mrs. Abbruzzi, she went to the bridge nearest her office, waited until no one was looking, took her purse, and tossed it over the side.

"At first I couldn't believe it," Larry says. "I thought I imagined it."

And what a shock it must have been to find someone really *was* standing beneath the bridge. I wonder how long it took her to realize that Larry wasn't an accomplice of Mrs. Abbruzzi's, that an accomplice wouldn't be returning her money, that an accomplice wouldn't have this look of...what?...deeply qualified happiness. In those first few seconds, she couldn't have known anything for sure.

"Oh, Celia," my mother says, "your money must have been soaked."

"It wasn't much."

"Ninety-three dollars," I say, barely audible but audible enough, apparently, because Celia's face tightens into a mask, and the air in the room changes pressure, and Larry must feel it because his voice sounds smaller.

"It was only a little cash," he says. "No credit cards or anything. It wasn't even a real purse, was it?"

"Still," my mother says, "you should be more careful, honey."

"Money dries, Mom," Celia says. "It dries."

Emily Broome lets a few seconds pass. "But, no, I think it's absolutely fascinating. Oliver, can you...Oliver?"

The strange part isn't that my father has vanished—we're all kind of used to that by now. The strange part is he's actually wandering back into the room just as my mother says his name. He might have been standing in the foyer, waiting for his cue.

"Here," he says to Larry brusquely. "I want you to take a look at these."

In his fist is a sheaf of rubber-banded papers, and as they pass into Larry's half-willing hands, my eyes form a bridge with Celia's, and in that moment, we reconcile, and in that same moment, waves of weariness pass between us. My mother stares into her china cup.

"I don't know what you'd call these," Dad says. "Extortion letters is probably the best term. Their sole purpose is to scare me away from cigarettes."

"Well, that's interesting," Larry says, holding one of them to the light.

"You see?" says my father, pointing over Larry's shoulder. "There's a very childish ransom-note quality at work here. SMOKING KILLS. NICOTINE = DEATH. They come at least once a week—same subject, same Arlington postmark. Sometimes the sender throws in a picture of a black lung."

"Very interesting."

"Now I initially believed it was the secretary at my old church, because she was always nagging me about quitting. Then I decided it couldn't be anybody I knew because the messages contained small factual errors. *Now*, however..." The Rev. Broome straightens himself to his full six feet and two inches. His belly forms a spur of provocation. "I think those errors are a deliberate ruse to throw me off the track."

"Don't know why anyone bothers," says my mother. "I've been after him to quit for 30 years."

Dad's voice is heating up; he starts jabbing at the paper. "Don't you think there's a kind of veiled intimacy to these notes?"

"Well," Larry resettles himself in his chair. "They're very direct, aren't they? The skull and crossbones, for instance."

"Oh, very melodramatic. Quite a flair for it."

Larry does his best, poor guy: turns the letters upside down, looks at them from different vantage points, says some of the words out loud. (*Monoxide. Emphysema.*) "There's some strong feeling here," he says.

And that's about as far as he gets. After about five minutes, his face registers his failure, and before another minute passes, my father, with a choked expression, is restacking the letters in his palm, winding the rubber band around them.

"If only one of my children was a forensic scientist," he says, "we'd be in business then."

"Sorry, Dad," Celia mutters.

He presses his bundle against his heart, and just as he's disappearing into the foyer, we hear his gravely teasing voice: "I'd settle for a grandchild with a chemistry set."

One of Dad's macabre jokes. He means very little by it, possibly nothing. So why does it suck the air out of me? I'm sitting in the same room, and the seconds and minutes are suddenly dying before my eyes. Today, last week, the past six months: *dead*, because they have brought me no closer to conceiving a child, the thing I was put on Earth to accomplish. I have squandered my time on dentists, fortunetellers, ransom notes.

And so the rest of the evening passes like sentry duty. Dad putters through the basement, picking up and putting down tools whose proper function he knows only through rumor. My mother asks Larry if he has any openings in his office for an intelligent young Vietnamese man. I listen to the clangor of china and spoons, and it all becomes indissoluble from the ticking of my grandmother's clock, and it all says: *Dying. Dying.*

So as soon as 10:30 passes, I plead an early breakfast engagement, and I burst through the front door before my father can even make it back up from the basement. And driving home, I mourn, for the first time, I think, the child that Nattie and I never had. She rushes up through my gullet, this girl, lodges behind my eye, and I remember how, imagining her, I would become terrified for her. And I actually prefer that terror to what's left, which is Nattie gone, our baby gone with her, July halfway over, and me with less than six months to make a Broome.

At moments like these, my deadline has the ineluctability of creation. Every Newtonian and Einsteinian force seems to be converging on me at the same time, and I get flop sweat in the biggest way.

"What does it matter?" Shannon once asked. "It's your own deadline, it's completely artificial. Who cares if you don't get it done by the end of the year?"

No one, I suppose, but me. I feel as though I'm riding a wave, a little whitecap of daring calibrated to wash up on the shores of next year, and if there's no baby in my arms or on the way, the wave rolls back to sea without me. That's it. End of game.

Maybe that explains why children are triggering such a tender panic in me. Little Henry, for instance, the son of two high school friends of mine. I last saw him about a month ago, when he was barely 2 and obsessed with baseball—baseball bats, specifically. You'll be hanging up your raincoat, and from nowhere you'll hear his treble cry—"Bat!"—and you'll turn around just in time to see him cocking an umbrella or a plunger, shifting his weight onto his back foot, waiting for that inside-high fastball. "*Bat!*" And his mom will already be running toward him, running blind, really, because her arms are wrapped around her face. "No, honey, that's a lamp."

"*Bat!*"

The last time I was there, Henry got so exhausted from swinging that he ended up climbing into his dad's lap. By then the adults were yammering about, I don't know, buyer's brokers, Weber grills. Henry wasn't interested. He wanted to scale his father. Tom's a big guy too, so Henry hadn't even reached the shoulder before his legs gave out. He collapsed against his father's chest, and he decided then this was where he'd wanted to be all along, and so he stayed there, clamped in as tightly as a snowmobiler. Within two minutes he was asleep—just like that. His ear was tilted into his dad's chest, his breath rolled out in a quiet stream...my heart imploded. It's a daily event now. I don't even have to know the child. Just last week, the local news showed a 12-year-old Lanham, Maryland, girl who had just won the regional spelling bee—the winning word was *vinaigrette.* She stood there in her red jumper and oversize glasses, and she eviscerated me. I wanted to brush her hair; I wanted to squeeze the nerves out of her. I was crazy with longing.

What scares me is that this longing is sometimes indistinguishable from the feeling I have for Joe Bryant. That is, it is deeply physical and built on very little experience. Three days, in Joe's case, almost none of which I actually remember. We did talk a lot. I know his favorite dessert: orange sherbet with chocolate chunks. I know the last car he owned: a

1971 Pontiac Grand Safari, last driven in 1988. I know he hates turtlenecks and anything that even slightly constricts his trachea. I know the first man he slept with was his cousin and that he slept with this cousin two hours after he slept with the cousin's sister.

I know what it's like to have his arm wrapped around the lower part of my spine and how his breastbone feels, how his brown hand sits in mine.

Sometime Saturday afternoon, I grabbed him by the neckline of his undershirt. I said, "You're straight."

He lay there: sly, sleepy-eyed. "That so?"

"That's what Nattie said you were."

"You were too, probably," he said.

"Maybe when I was three." I gave it some thought. "And then again a few months in my 20s."

"Well, there you go," said Joe Bryant.

For 60 hours, we lay in his apartment. We kept the TV on but never watched. I wore his underwear, his bathrobe, his gym shorts. On Monday, we both called in sick to work. We ordered breakfast, lunch, and dinner from an Afghan restaurant around the corner. Other than the delivery boy, the only person who interrupted us was Joe's mother, who called on the hour to update him about Nattie's relocation plans. And faithfully, once a day, Joe visited Nattie—drove my car to Falls Church, came back two hours later.

"She's fine," he'd say. "Better all the time."

It was understood somehow that I would not join him for these visits. But the whole time he was away, I would revolve the two of them in my head, and when he got back I would peer into his mild eyes and wonder what it was about the Bryants. Why was it such a steep plunge each time?

"Hey, Nick! Come 'ere, that right ear needs some nibbling."

An hour after I get back from my parents, Joe calls. I don't understand at first what's happening because I've been asleep. I've just had a vision of Natasha, running down a brocaded hallway in a royal-blue down parka, unzipped, with the hood down. She must be running to answer the phone, the one ringing in my ear.

"Nick?"

"Unh." I press the phone against my face. I breathe the sound through my pores.

"This is your younger, prettier sister, Joe."

And as I come back to consciousness, the first thing I notice is his accent, more pronounced after a week in the motherland.

"What you been doin'?" he asks.

I tell him about my evening with the Broomes, about Celia and her wet money and her dentist.

He says, "Dentists kill themselves a lot, don't they?"

"Maybe."

"Hey, Nattie and me just got finished playing Scrabble, and you gotta tell me."

"What?"

"Is *maxi* a word?"

"Well, it's a, it's a prefix."

"Yeah, but a *word*? Nattie said it's a stand-alone word. This is the only way she can beat me, makin' up dumb, stupid words."

A child, I think. *This is how a child sounds. This is how my child could sound.*

"You tired?" he asks.

"Actually...you know, I'm an hour ahead and all."

"Oh, right, go back to sleep."

"Call me tomorrow?"

"'Course," he says.

"And say hi to Nattie if, you know, whatever..."

"I will. Good night, Snookie Pie."

I'm Getting My Tongue Pierced

eleven

"Hello, Daphne?"

"Yes?"

"Hi, this is Nick Broome. I don't know whether you..."

"Oh, Nick! Of course. How are you?"

"I'm fine, I'm fine. I know it's late to be calling."

"Never too late, Nick."

"The only reason I'm...OK, here's the deal. I've been thinking through our last conversation, which wasn't so long ago if you remember. And what I'm thinking is maybe we should revisit the subject. Only because it's been on my mind that we were possibly hasty in reaching our conclusion."

"Oh."

"Not that there was ever an obvious conclusion. I don't know. It's possible you've been reconsidering things yourself."

"Well..."

"It just struck me we had a certain rapport, and now that I've had more experience in this area, I'm beginning to think that's really the best you can ask for. With these kinds of arrangements."

"Yeah. You know, I've been meaning to call you myself.

"Really?"

"I was saying just the other day: 'I have to give Nick a call.' "

"Oh, well, there it is, really."

"I wanted you to truly be among the first to know."

"Know what?"

"Oh, it's too weird, Nick. I'm engaged."

"Oh. You're...OK."

"It's way beyond weird. Beyond anything, Nick."

"Well, wow. When did this happen?"

"A couple of nights ago."

"No, I mean, when did you meet the...the person you're...."

"My high school reunion! Is it not the corniest thing? My 25th reunion."

"Cincinnati."

"Oh, right, you remember! The funny thing, Nick, I was dreading this reunion. I *knew* it was going to be awful. I told myself, OK, you're going to leave after 10 minutes if you don't find someone to talk to, and *two* minutes later, I saw this very attractive man. But I couldn't remember him! I mean, I saw his name on the little My Name Is sticker, but he had to tell me which classes we had together, and even *so*, it was like we'd known each other all our lives."

"Huh."

"It was that instantaneous. It was melding."

"Wow."

"So that's...everything's changed, Nick. We're moving to Mendocino."

"Oh, congratulations."

"But not for two years. And we'd love it if you could make the wedding. It'll be very secular. Somewhere in the Caymans."

"OK."

"Sometime after hurricane season. Did I tell you he's a chiropractor?"

I can't say I'm disappointed. The more I think about it, the more I see this second attempt as my way of tying up the loose threads before proceeding to the next thing. And there *is* a next thing. Thank God, there always is.

I admit it takes me a little time to recognize it. It takes, oddly enough, going to Greg's house for that long-deferred dinner...and I might never have gone if I'd known what was waiting. A blind date! The last thing I would have expected from my brother. Celia, yes, but Greg? Did Greg really slap his head and say, "Hey, that anesthesiologist from Beltsville, the one with the spit curl and the wrists that make little snapping sounds. Perfect for Nick!" It's easier to see Sally having a hand in it, only because she doesn't know me as well and seems to take my singleness more personally.

Oh, the sleep doctor is nice enough, in a pink-elbowed sort of way. He keeps his hands folded in his lap; he compliments Sally on her tomato tofu pie. But what can I say? You can only discuss anesthesia for so long before a kind of hypnotic suggestion takes over. What keeps me awake, fittingly enough, is the image of Joe. Through the whole conversation, I keep thinking: *Wait until Joe hears about this. I can't wait to tell Joe.* And it's as though he's under the table, sniggering into the floorboards.

So the evening is not the disaster it might have been, which is not to say it is interesting. About the only thing remarkable is a tiff that breaks out mid-dessert between Sally and Greg—remarkable only because, to the best of my knowledge, they have never argued about anything. It begins when Sally puts her fork down and says, "Oh, Linda and Tom."

And Greg says, "What?"

"They're having another baby."

"Oh, that's nice."

"They're hoping for a girl."

"I bet."

And then Sally says, "Linda'll never lose the 10 pounds now."

And Greg asks, "What 10 pounds?"

"From the last baby. She made a vow she was going to lose it before she had the next one, but she'll never do it now."

"Is that a problem?"

And I can sense Sally pulling herself in a little, retracting the fibers around her nerves. "It's not a problem."

"I mean, you brought it up is all."

"Not because it's a problem, because it's...it's kind of funny."

"She's probably happy," Greg says. "She probably doesn't mind the 10 pounds because she figures it's worth it."

And then everyone is quiet, and it's as though we're all in the same bed, rolling away from each other.

"Forget I said anything," Sally says.

On the way home, I keep replaying the exchange in my head. And I keep juxtaposing it with the way Greg reacted last January, right after I told him I was going to conceive a child. I remember the way he started jamming his fingers into the tablecloth—right there in the Duchess of Windsor's restaurant—his face getting smaller and smaller over the floral centerpiece.

"Nick, what are you going to do with a child? Are you going to raise it yourself?"

"Maybe."

"You haven't thought this out."

"I've thought it out."

"No. If you'd thought this out...if you had thought this out, you would realize that being a single parent, whatever kind of parent you're planning on being, is very, extremely difficult, OK? Whether you're the mother or the father, if you're a single parent, kids have a harder time growing up, there's..."

"I know all this."

"...research, Nick! Kids from single-parent families are poorer than other kids. They're less likely to graduate. They commit crimes. They're unemployed. There's this whole body of research."

At the time it pissed me off. But now I almost have to smile when I think about Greg's faith in statistics. *There's research!* And in his defense, I have to say that having dealt with some extremely subjective people in the last few weeks, I'm beginning to see the value in hard facts. The world is awash with them; it just needs someone willing to sort them out. This is another way of saying I have gone back online—with a vengeance. I have spent hours calling up scientific texts and encyclopedia articles, ordering books (both medical and lay-oriented), visiting neonatal Web sites and gay and lesbian support networks, strolling through specially designated chat rooms, eavesdropping on parents from every trimester. It has been a pleasure, a *pleasure*, to learn in this way, and this is the result: I know now what I have to do.

"See, my mistake..." I'm explaining it to Shannon. We're sitting in the food court of the Longworth House office building, surrounded by low-rent lobbyists in funeral suits talking excitably to staffers half their age and by tourists in striped blouses and floppy T-shirts, slurping tubs of frozen yogurt. I'm eating a spinach salad with mounds of beets, and Shannon, because she is bored and cranky and waiting for a press conference that was supposed to start three hours ago, has treated herself to a Nathan's hot dog and Boardwalk fries.

"My mistake," I tell her, "was assuming the arrangement had to be a full partnership. But why does it have to be? How likely is it I'd find someone who wants to be a parent as much as I do? It's pretty *unlikely*, isn't it?"

"So fine," Shannon says, already impatient. "Where does that leave you?"

"I'm going to find a surrogate mother."

She sets down her glass of iced tea. She sinks back in her chair and applies her hands to her eyes like compresses. She says, "Nicky," and the hands slide down to form screens on both sides of her face. "Nicky, do you...I don't know where to begin."

"OK."

"I mean, do you even care what I think?"

"Sure."

And then her head moves from side to side like a blind musician's. "Do you know how fucked-up you are?"

"Why?"

"*Why?*" Her eyes bulge. "Nick, do you know how much something like this costs? Do you understand? You pay these chicks thousands of dollars."

"I know."

"On the order of $50,000-$75,000. Not to mention medical bills and living expenses."

"I know."

"So let's just start with the money. Where do you plan to get the money, Nick?"

"I have savings."

"Oh, where?" she asks, tossing her head. "In a little tin can by the stove?"

"Well, if you must know, I got a couple of thousand dollars from my grandmother when she died, and I figured this would be an appropriate way to, to honor her memory."

"Oh, now isn't *she* smiling up in heaven?"

To calm myself, I pull apart the paper straw cover on my tray. "Beyond that, I can work something out. I can go to a bank. Banks are always dying to loan you money."

"For this?" she asks. "You think the average home-equity application covers this?"

"Look, I'm not asking for your approval, OK? I just thought, you know, as a friend, you might be interested in hearing about my life, which is what friends do for one another—last I checked."

She leans toward me and spreads her hands in front of mine. "Nick," she says, "I *am* your friend. Which is what I'm trying to tell you: If you go this route, there's no guarantee she'll come through for you. She could easily skip town, you know. Hop a flight to, to Bora Bora and take the baby with her and then what do you do? No legal standing. No court in the world is going to lift a finger."

"I'm willing to take my chances."

She sits back, regards me with coin-slot eyes. She gives her forehead a couple scratches. "You're sure you don't just want to adopt? Find some nice private agency somewhere? A cute little Korean boy, Nick..."

"No." My hands curl into fists. "I *told* you. I want to father a child.

That's the whole point. I know it's not rational, it's just the way it is. That's all."

"So there it is," Shannon says.

"Yeah."

A sudden bustle around us: two Capitol policemen waddling by with empty trays; a receptionist from the office next to me, closing her Trollope novel; a knot of blue-blazered House pages, swinging ID chains around their necks with noisy importance.

And from Shannon a long, long river of air.

"All right," she says. "The *least* you can do is get a good lawyer to make it all neat. I want you to promise me."

"I promise."

"All right, here," she says. And with an irritated swipe, she grabs a Post-it pad from her bag, scribbles a name and phone number on it, tears off the top sheet, and slaps it in front of me. "This guy can be helpful."

I stare at the name for a few seconds, let the syllables dance through my memory. "Wait, didn't you used to date him?"

"Nick, I didn't say I was *speaking* to him. I just said he was a good lawyer."

Just then, three loud buzzers screech across the food court: The House has adjourned its business. One of the tourist children behind us lets out a small squeal, and drops a dollop of frozen yogurt onto her blouse.

"They're done," Shannon says, sucking her index finger.

"I guess so."

"Thank Christ," she says, rising abruptly in her chair. "Let's get this goddamn show on the road."

She bunches her wrappers, lobs them into the nearest receptacle, blows me a smooch, and strides away. The cell phone is already creeping from her bag, and as she passes through the glass door, threads of her conversation weave back through the granite columns: "Three *hours*...sent Cindy...fucking putzes..." And then she's gone.

Aunt Shannon, I think. That's what I'll have to call her. *Just because Aunt Shannon uses that language doesn't mean you should.*

Is it a promising sign, I wonder? That lately I've been viewing my friends and family through the prism of a child? I think Aunt Shannon, for instance, might be a little terrifying to a toddler—that wire hum of professional rage, that bellicose lip liner. My father, on the other hand, would have that baby cooing inside of a minute. He'd abandon all pretense of being an Episcopalian; something voluptuous and Catholic would creep into his demeanor; he would sweep the child into his arms, rub noses until his nostrils were chapped. We might not even recognize him by the time he was done.

And Joe Bryant? What would Joe Bryant do?

It's an abstract question, of course, and Joe himself is something of an abstract question these days. The night I place my ad, he calls to tell me a dear friend of his (she used to waitress at the Union Station bar) has a sloop she's sailing across the Caribbean and he thinks he might tag along for a week, see how he likes it, and there's a chance he'll go from there to New York to attend a three-day session of the Forum ("Used to be Est," he says. "Remember Est?") because a very good friend said it changed her life. Except he might be a little too sunburned to go—he'll have to see.

And the one question that should come out of my mouth—*Why aren't you coming home?*—never quite pops free. It's the ancillary mysteries that crowd to the front. Werner Erhard? Waitresses with sloops?

"What about your job?" I ask.

"Oh, I quit," he says.

Maybe it's the sound my breath makes when I suck it in. Maybe it's the quiet that follows. Something agitates his voice out of its normal rhythm.

"I know I told you," he says.

"No, you didn't."

"Oh, sure! You 'member when we called in sick that one day?"

"Yeah."

"Well, instead of calling in sick, I quit."

He's so breezy about it, he makes it sound like a self-evident choice. But how could it have happened without my knowing it? Was I even in the same room? (There's really only the one room in his apartment.) Was I asleep?

"It's no biggie," Joe says. "I told you I was gettin' sick of the place."

"Well, no, it's just...it's just you're unemployed."

"Oh, I can always bartend somewhere. It's very easy."

He tells me about all the contacts he has, all the phone numbers he can dial the minute he gets back. And knowing how easy it is, he says, makes it harder to come back, because he's not ready for work yet.

"I can always have a job," he says. "How many times do I get to go sailing?"

I don't know what to say, exactly. Except that, on Joe Bryant's list, I fall somewhere below the Caribbean and personal growth.

"Hey, Snookie," he says, sounding gravelly. "Tell me what you're doing."

And if this were a normal circumstance—if, say, he had just told me he was coming back, couldn't wait to see me, wanted to throw away two years' worth of appointment books—then I could take up his cue. I could say: Joe, I just left an ad on an electronic bulletin board, under the heading "Seeking Surrogate." Oh, and Joe, the text goes something like this (I've saved it in Word):

> *Hi: I am a single man living in the Washington, D.C., area seeking a woman to serve as surrogate mother. I am a responsible, hardworking employee of the U.S. House of Representatives. Applicants should ideally be 30+, already married, with children. Compensation and other contractual matters may be discussed in person. In vitro fertilization preferred. Serious candidates only, please. Refer all queries to my E-mail address. Thanks!*

I could tell him it took me roughly an hour to arrive at this, that it represents my 11th draft and still conveys less than a tenth of what I intended, that I spent half an hour alone agonizing over the "Thanks!" because I wasn't sure if it was appropriate to thank people for their uteruses.

What I say is, "Nothing. I'm not doing anything."

And then, because that feels inadequate, I lift my voice into a haughtier register; I strain, theatrically, for poetry. "I'm dreaming," I say, "of the moment when we're together again. When our...our cleft hearts may be one."

"Nick," he says, sounding very grave. "You mustn't ever lie about that shit."

twelve

I know, I know, the Internet is a global resource, but who believes it until you advertise for a mother? The first three responses I get aren't even from my own time zone. The fourth one is from Russia:

> *My name is Elena Treplaniov. I live in Yekaterinburg. I work in the town water service. At the moment I don't work. I live alone with my children at the present moment i'm divorced. We can't live as a kilo of butter costs more than 2 dollars. Now something about myself: no bad habits, I've 2 children: a son Ivan of 11 years (he is a pupil of the 6th form) and a daughter, who is 3 years. Being a healthy woman I can bear a child for the foreign parents. I would like to do it legally, out of Russia....*

I admit, there's a part of me that tingles at the mention of Tolstoy's land. In my mind, of course, it's always winter: troikas, samovars. There's a grown waif with wide, sumptuous cheekbones and seal-fur collars—Natalie Wood, maybe, in ice skates. And then I remember the last time I went for a woman named Natalie. And then I notice how generic the response is—the vague allusion to "foreign parents"—and the clumsy, third-party translation. And, maybe to protect myself from it, I cease to trust it. And that feeling extends to the next few pleas, which also come from foreign countries. Vietnam:

Very pretty. I give you baby, you see.

And the Philippines:

Hello, U.S. man. Filipino girls are best. I work in cigarette factory. Need strong Yankee take care of me. Filipino girls are most most best....

After that, there are three days when I don't get any responses at all. I don't sweat it, though, as much as I would with a newspaper ad, because the Internet is ephemeral, yes, but also forever. That's what I cling to. The bulletin board where I posted my ad has messages that date from four, five years ago: a Muncie couple trolling for agency recommendations; a Fort Lauderdale woman seeking advice on swollen feet. Crystallized moments of yearning that maybe even the yearners have forgotten by now. The point is I have time. Not much, but a little.

And a week later, my patience is vindicated. I get my first response from the Washington, D.C., area:

Mister, I am talking to you for my cousin Lupe, who is fine woman and mother. Lupe lives in Falls Church ,Virginia. She would be very good as mother to your baby. I am talking for her because the English not so good with her. My name is José. If you would like to meet Lupe, please E-mailing me....

Oh, a language barrier, sure, but all I see are the positives. They explode from my screen. Falls Church: a stone's throw from my parents' house. Hispanic: the chance to enliven a denatured gene pool, produce a child better equipped for the 21st century. And, come to think of it, there's something in the message itself, something in that twining of humility and pride. I get good feelings from José. He is honorable. He cherishes his family. Their cause is his cause.

So I send him a return message, asking for more details. The only thing he sends back is his phone number. Which is OK. It's OK because you have to figure his English may not be up to a more complex narrative and because one can only live off a computer screen for so long. Already I'm starting to hunger for a human's sound.

And José's sound turns out to be just what I expect: high and melodious and slightly childlike in its intonation, with an overhang of nasality where the English digs in. An affable six-string guitar voice.

"Hello, José," I say. "This is Nicholas."

No last names, I'm being very cagey—too cagey, maybe, because I end up having to prompt him.

"You E-mailed me," I say, "about an ad I put on the Web."

"The Web," he says.

"For a...for a surrogate mother."

"Lupe," he says, suddenly delighted.

"Right."

"So whadda ya think?" he asks.

"Well, you know, it's hard to say, José. I'd have to meet her first. Ask some questions, that kind of thing."

"You want to see her?"

"Yeah, that's...pretty much a standard thing to do."

For the next minute, a muffled thrum of voices: José's I can just make out, and one other, perhaps two. Gradually, a woman's voice threads through the tangle, and this is the thread I follow, because it seems to me Lupe must lie at the other end. *Lupe.*

"OK," José says, cutting back in.

"OK?"

"We meet, OK."

"OK. Where do you want to meet?"

"Where," he repeats, dazedly. Another consultation, shorter, less frantic, and José's back on the line.

"She would like to meet..."

"Yes?"

"...at the International..."

"Yes?"

One last whir of static. "House of Pancakes."

It's a game I play sometimes. Driving into a near-lying suburb, I will mentally peel off the accretions of the past few decades until the place stands in its original Eisenhower incarnation: America thrusting toward its future. So it is with Ballston. My mind pares away the black-windowed office buildings and the high-rise condos and the three-story town homes and the Hilton and the Tex-Mex joint. And what's left? A Chinese restaurant. A funeral home. A Methodist church with a white colonial steeple and a sign that reads FREE AFTERLIFE. INQUIRE WITHIN.

And more primordial than anything else, the IHOP, with its Dutch roof and little swath of plain, where sport-utility vehicles are already dueling for parking spaces. I arrive at 11:00 on Sunday morning, and it's fifteen minutes before I find a space of my own. I rush into the restaurant, flustered and already sweating, only to find that the air inside is 10 degrees hotter than what I just left. It feels even hotter because the place is so densely packed; in fact, the primary function of the patrons seems to be to give the heat texture. A row of fans beats ineffectually from the ceiling. Slicks of sweat gleam on people's wrists and foreheads, and two teenage white boys in wife-beater shirts calmly finger beads of moisture off the bridges of their noses.

But all I'm worried about is finding Lupe. And I'm kicking myself because I never asked for identifying features. I had counted, perhaps, on tracking her by ethnicity, never suspecting (stupid! stupid!) that Hispanics would make up 60% of the IHOP population and that, even after discounting the very young and the superannuated and the short-order cooks in their sporty berets, there would still be roughly three or four Hispanic women falling within the 25 to 35 age bracket. So I stand there, steamed and helpless, until a woman I haven't yet noticed begins waving. A woman seated against a rose banquette, her hand rotating in a calm, window-washing motion, the rest of her absolutely still, as though she's been pinned back by the table.

In the three seconds it takes me to get to her, I ask myself how I could have missed her. It's only when I'm actually standing in front of her that I realize she's about 15 years older than I expected.

"Lupe?"

She smiles. A fortunate thing, because her smile knocks a good six years off her face.

"Nick," I say, finally. "Nice to meet you."

She makes a demure motion with her head—a side-to-side motion that I can't quite place until I have a flashback to my high school junior prom.

She thinks we're on a date.

Which would explain the small amount of trouble she has taken with her appearance. She has tied her long, overtinted hair into a ponytail, draped two gold chains and a crucifix around her neck. She has donned a simple white blouse and khaki shorts and black boat shoes and paid some serious attention to her eyes, which look as though they've been pasted over with binocular eyepieces. The kind of raccoon rings a child might make with her mother's eyeliner.

"So here we are," I say, seating myself carefully in the chair opposite her. "Maybe we should order first?"

The waitress is already arriving as I speak. A big girl with a name tag that reads FLOR, looking unimaginably cross until she spots Lupe and breaks into a stream of volatile, happy Spanish. Lupe is known here, apparently, and not just by Flor. The busboy gives her a friendly salute, and she even gets a nod from the manager, a ruddy-faced, combed-over man in a lime dress shirt. They communicate like novitiates in a secret society, and it makes me wish my brother were here to translate. I remember visiting Greg once at Clinica Columbia and being charmed by the way the patients pronounced his last name: drawing out the single syllable, giving a faint roll to the *R* and then pulling away from the *M*, so you almost couldn't hear it.

Dr. Brroo, Dr. Brroo, it's my grandmother.

So I don't mind, really, that two women are talking over my head in a language I don't understand. It makes me feel the same way I felt in the hospital with Nattie and Joe: alone and incorporated. I wait until they're finished, and then I order the buttermilk pancake platter and a carafe of orange juice, and Lupe doesn't order anything even though I make encouraging gestures toward the menu and promise to pay. She keeps her arms folded on the table in front of her, and her eyes wander back and forth across my face.

From my pocket, I pull the reporter's notebook in which I have written the questions I am supposed to ask of a surrogate-mother candidate—the questions she is supposed to answer with a "yes." I have even drawn boxes next to each of the questions so I can write check marks or *X* marks.

"May I?" I ask, pointing to the pad.

She leans toward me, not welcoming or resisting, only, it seems, to get a better look at me.

"Do you...first thing is do you have children of your own?" I ask.

"Ch—" She squints her eyes.

"Children. Um..." I make a rocking motion with my arms.

"Ah!" The eyes light up now. "Yes, yes."

"You do have children?"

"Yes."

"Good. You know, you're probably wondering why I asked that. Supposedly, surrogates are less likely to keep the children they bear if...if they have kids of their own."

She waits a few seconds to make sure I've stopped talking, then nods solemnly.

"How many kids do you have?" I ask.

"How—"

"Um, do you have *uno? Dos?*"

"Ah, *two,*" she says, abruptly.

"Two kids. OK. And are you married? Currently?"

This produces the most complete blankness I have ever seen on a human face. My brain flinches and goes scrambling for a translation.

"*Es...esposa*?"

And just to make sure she gets it, I coil my right hand around my left ring finger and start rubbing, in a gesture that immediately registers as obscene.

"Ah!" She nods fiercely and giggles, and the laughter blows another 10 years off her face.

"So you are *esposa?*" I ask, nodding and smiling right along with her.

And just like that, the smile vanishes and the head jerks to a stop, begins a rueful side-to-side motion.

"No," I say. "No *esposa*. OK."

My pen makes its little *X* mark. Such a heartless motion.

"You know, it's not a big deal," I tell her. "It's just they like surrogates to already have their own family arrangements so...so not a big deal."

I stare at the sheet. My checklist expands before my eyes. It's beginning to look like a runic alphabet.

"OK," I say. "The next question has to do with financial security. Even though, of course, you'd be compensated and everything, there's the concern, I guess, that if you don't already have some financial arrangement, you might..." *Hop a flight to Bora Bora.* "...feel less secure about the surrogacy. So maybe you could tell me if...do you work? Job?"

The head nods.

"Where do you..."

She does something strange then: She rubs the table, moving her palm in small tight arcs across the painted-on burls of wood. Not quite able to follow, I mimic her, and as I do, I feel endless geological laminae of syrup adhering to my hand, binding it to the table.

"Here? You work here. Of course. That's why...that's why everyone knows you. You clean up and stuff."

And the head's really going now, grateful for the release.

"Nights," Lupe says, charmingly contorting her eyes.

"Right," I say, laughing. "You work nights. OK."

It's clicking in now, I can feel that. We needed a little time, but we're starting to connect. We're laying a foundation.

And just then I look at my list, and the words *College-educated?* fly up at me, and everything stops. I draw in a teaspoon of air and I close my eyes and ask myself if I know any Spanish word even remotely linked to education. I don't.

"So, so the next question has more to do with your state of mind. I'm curious to know, just how long have you wanted to be a surrogate?"

We stare at each other.

"For instance," I say, "Maybe this is something you've just recently given some thought to. Or maybe it's been a couple of years? Maybe you've been thinking about this for many *years*?"

Her face contracts—seizes up with panic. Her eyes plunge sideways, lodge somewhere to my left, and I wait for them to cut back to me, but they don't. So I turn to see what she's looking at, and I find a man looking back at me. A handsome, amused man with a ferocious mustache, sitting in the chair next to me, with his body angled halfway toward the window.

I say, "José?"

"Lupe didn't think you was gonna ask her stuff," he says.

His mustache wrenches toward his chin. Pashalike, he caresses the sloping mound of his belly.

"Well," I say, "that's part of the deal here. You know, we have to establish things like medical history and family history and...lots of things have to go into this process."

"She think you don't like her," José says.

"Well, that's silly." I half turn toward her. "That's silly, I don't even know her. It's, you know, it's a business transaction, and liking or not liking, that doesn't enter in."

Just then Lupe lets loose with a torrent of sound. Words, fragments go flying in every direction—up to the ceiling fans, back down to the checkered carpet, off the blinds and the hanging lights and the loudspeaker and the rose banquette. It goes on for a full minute, and even if I knew Spanish, I'm not sure I'd be able to follow it.

"Lupe say kids come, they pop out from her."

"Oh, well, good."

"She say last one come out on way to hospital. No doctor. Just come out."

Lupe's head is bowed now in an attitude of thought. I can just make out the graphite pencil she has inserted into the base of her ponytail.

"If it's any easier," I tell José, "I can ask you the questions. And you could translate."

He stares at his hands, which have woven together into a comb of wriggling digits. One hand suddenly breaks free and hovers over the table.

"Lupe got mother El Salvador," he says.

"Oh."

"Very old. We want her from *here*..." The hand describes a parabola between the Equal packets and the syrup canister. "...to *here*," he says.

"Oh, OK."

We ponder each other. José's eyes are fathom-deep with patience.

"So what does that have to do with being a surrogate?" I ask.

"You work for government," he says.

"Um. Oh."

My ad. My carefully crafted ad. *Responsible, hardworking employee of the U.S. House of Representatives.* I made a special point of putting that in so people would respect me more.

"You know," I say, "I work for the U.S. *Congress*, which is, which is strictly legislative in its...you know, there's an *executive* branch and then there's a *legislative* branch, and what you would probably need to do is contact someone on the executive side. That's probably your best bet."

José stares at his fingers again. He looks like he's on the verge of disciplining them.

"I can certainly find a name," I tell him, "and contact number, if that would be helpful. I could call you with that."

José's eyebrows arch upward. His mouth twitches and writhes.

"So..." I look at my pad. Pages and pages of questions stretch away from me. *Does anyone in your household smoke? During the surrogacy process, from whom can you expect to receive emotional support?*

"So why don't I give you a call?" I suggest. "You know, with the information we're looking for. And then the surrogacy issue we can defer until...until I've interviewed the other candidates."

Like who, Nick?

"And maybe further down the road we can talk again."

I'm looking at Lupe now, waiting for some reinforcement, but all she's doing is wiping away the rings of perspiration around our orange juice carafe. For all I know she's starting her next shift.

It's José who makes the next move. He places one of his hands on my knee and gives it a gentle squeeze. I'm embarrassed to say the tingle passes all the way up to my ears.

"Lupe got sister," he says. "Young. Very nice girl."

"No, that's—"

"More prettier than Lupe. The breasts."

The busboy saves me. He clears off one of his tables a little too efficiently, and the sound of exploding dishes collapses the space around us, whips José's head around and gives me an uninterrupted view of his left ear, or rather the three tiny buttons of flesh where his ear used to be. It's not the livid red spectacle I would have imagined. No evidence of violence, just a chain of tiny coral upswellings spaced so neatly across his head that they give the impression of language. The braille rendering of an ear.

And the strangest thought enters my head: *Did José's ear get chewed by a cowbird?*

Cowbirds have been on my mind lately. They are brown-headed creatures that decline the honor of building nests and instead lay eggs in the nests of other birds. Some birds pick up on the ruse, but most will happily incubate the new egg as one of their own. Cowbirds are usually termed *parasites,* which carries a certain peal of judgment, but nobody really knows how much care they invest in choosing the right nest. This may be where their love reaches its full fruition. Endless rounds of screening interviews, extensive aerial reconnaissance. Who knows what heights of diligence they are capable of? We might be surprised. We might conclude that being a cowbird is better than being an Atlantic herring.

"Lupe like the zoo," José is saying. "The panda."

And the sound of this suddenly familiar word changes Lupe utterly. She jerks upward in her seat, and her hands curl into what I take to be bear paws. Her top lip slides away to reveal a row of chattering, gnashing teeth.

"Chom chom," she says, and it's a good enough impression I can see the bamboo snaking through her mouth, and I don't have the heart to tell her Hsing Hsing is dead, and in my left ear I hear the low appreciative chuckle of her nephew.

"Kids love Lupe," he says.

thirteen

So what does a cowbird do if one of its eggs doesn't make it? How does it cope with such a public form of failure? I wish I knew. I'm estimating it will take me at least a week to get over Lupe. I'm already sealed in funk by the time I get home, and I don't say thank you when my landlord offers me a bong hit, I just keep walking up the stairs, sketching out my convalescence: low-fat mocha ice cream, clarinet concerto, Ronald Colman movie. And even as I map it out, I know it won't be enough.

But then I walk through the door, and the phone is ringing. And the sound produces a warming echo inside me. I don't have to convalesce. Someone has a plan for me.

The voice on the other end, though, is as far as an asteroid belt.

"Hey, Snookie!"

And it's not just the sound, it's the image behind it that's blurring out on me. It's as though someone were very slowly, painstakingly erasing him.

"I'm sick of sailing," he says. "I wanna come home."

"OK."

There's a crackle and a long pause.

"You can hear me, right?" he asks.

"Yeah, I'm...where are you?"

"I don't know," he says.

By which he means, perhaps, somewhere in the Caribbean. What else could be giving off that long, slow siphoning sound? It's the sea, washing Joe Bryant through my window.

"What about the Forum?" I ask.

"Can't hear you."

"What about the *Forum*?"

"Oh, I've decided I like being fucked up. I think it's part of my charm, what do you think?"

"I don't know," I say.

Joe says, "Snookie, I only got a few more days of this and then I'll be back. I promise."

"OK."

"Do you believe me?"

"Yeah."

He lets the question settle for a few seconds. And then he says, "You all right?"

I feel my eyes. They're damp and acrid, like grass clippings.

"Yeah."

"'Cause you sound kind of quiet."

"Everything's cool, Joe."

I skip the ice cream and the Mozart. I go straight for the prostration. And as I lie there on my ugly couch, I spend my time trying to reconstruct him. I start with all the things he cares for. Indian food, Cassandra Wilson, Tammy Wynette, Madeline Kahn. I try to remember the way his eyelids droop, the striations of his shoulder muscles.

A little after midnight, I fall asleep, quite abruptly, and I wake just as abruptly an hour and a half later. I stumble to my computer, blank-screened but still humming, and within a minute I'm back online, back on the surrogacy home page, clicking onto the bulletin board, scrolling down, down...

And then I see it.

> *Hello out there! My name is Claudia. I am completely into being a mom. I would love to chat at you, this is great. I live in Burke, I have serious feelings about children. I would so love to discuss this further. How would we do this? Enlighten.*

I'm not sure I trust myself to read it because, in some ways, it's better than I could have imagined. *Burke.* That's what really switches on the light in my head. Burke is just a couple of miles from where I grew up. (In those days, it was a post office and a lake.) And there's a good chance Claudia grew up there too. Knew the same people, ate pizza at the same greasy joint off Keene Mill Road, took fake ID's into the same Georgetown bar. So many possible convergences!

Later that morning I look at the message again, just to be sure, and it's the same message with the same promise. I barely trust myself to type the response.

> *Claudia, I was very excited to hear from you. I was wondering if you wouldn't mind giving me your phone number so I could call you at a convenient time.*

She responds:

> *The phone would not be the thing. Here's the deal. I have not yet told my family about my decision. I was hoping to discuss it with you first by way of making sure there was total compatibility before we proceed further.*

I don't want to go in blind this time—those panicky first moments at the IHOP still linger in my memory. So I type back:

> *Can you at least send me a picture?*

She gets back to me within five minutes.

Here it is. Let me know if you have trouble downloading.

And so the combined processes of modulation and demodulation drag Claudia, inch by inch, across my computer screen. She's as wholesome as a general store: mid 30s, strong jawline, hazy aquamarine eyes, and startled-looking eyelashes. A sensible, soccer-mom shag and a fair, robust complexion. Nothing of her below the neck, but her face gives off that hardiness you see in the women at Shopper's Food Warehouse, the ones who wear kids on their hips and waddle like farm girls carrying water from a well. Hard-flanked women; women you can depend on.

This is what I type back to her:

Let's meet!

We spend the next 10 or so exchanges trying to find the best venue. I'm thinking along the lines of Eastern Market, mostly because it's two blocks from my house, but Claudia expresses a preference for either the Springfield or Landmark Mall. *Of course,* I think. *She's a creature of the suburbs.* To avoid Shirley Highway, I suggest Georgetown Park, and she counters with Pentagon City, and that's where we ultimately settle.

We plan to meet Tuesday night, 8 P.M., in the food court, as close as possible to Au Bon Pain without actually being in it. I decide to get there early so I can watch her arrive. For reasons I can't articulate, it's important to me to see her walking across a large space. So at 7:45, I'm sitting on a hard green mesh chair, next to a composite palm tree that arches toward a compound-eyed glass ceiling. It's that dawdling time of mid-August when Washington silently empties out, so the only people left at the mall are Arab mothers in cloaks, teenage boys in long-billed ball caps, handsome, shaven-headed black men in relaxed-fit jeans, and a group of office workers screwing up their courage for a Macy's sale.

I sit there watching the last lines of blue ink drain from the sky, watching the glass elevator descend like a coal tram. I have the dim sense of being in a terrarium. On the table in front of me: a frozen Mocha Blast and a chicken Fo-ca-cha-cha wrap. I haven't touched either of them because I'm too busy looking for Claudia. I don't want to miss her when she comes. And since I don't know which direction she'll be coming from, I keep wheeling about, filtering and screening everyone who passes, searching for that auburn shag. Now and then I glimpse something and my heart pulls up a little, but always a cool analytic voice breaks in, says: *No. No, Claudia wouldn't wear leopardskin pants. No, her neck isn't crepey.*

And then, a few minutes before 8, I see someone who might qualify: off in the distance, a strapping, short-cropped woman ordering a volcano of rice from Panda Express. She stuffs her change, unfussily, into a large handbag and begins a slow arduous turn in my direction, and just as I crane my neck to get a better look, a girl steps across my viewfinder. A thin, pale teenager in a leather vest and fishnet stockings, with tiny, almost vestigial features and hair the color of corned beef and ears riddled with steel. She's about 20 feet away, and I'm waiting for her to veer off course, but she doesn't. She bears straight toward me, and I realize now that unless I stop her, she's going to set her tray on my table.

"I'm sorry," I call out. "I'm saving that seat for someone."

She says, "Are you Nicholas?"

I nod, dumbly.

"Claudia," she says.

And then she drops her tray onto the table with a percussive force and lowers herself irritably into the opposite chair. She pumps her elbows twice, as though she were priming an accordion.

Stupidly, I choose that moment to stand. I have some prearranged notion of shaking her hand, which even now I am having to suppress, and the result is that I simply stand there, my arms twitching, my brain sputtering.

"No," I say.

"What?"

"You're not."

She gives me a violent shrug. "Well, I'm Claudia. And you're Nicholas."

I see the smear of mascara under her bright vole eyes. I see the steel stud curled under her lip and the cuff link jammed into her nostril. I'm telling my mouth: *Close. Close.* But it's trying to say something.

"You're not the picture," is what it's trying to say.

And I must actually say it because she answers, "No, that's my mom."

And she says it so simply I wonder if I've missed something. I stand there trying to reconstruct our entire electronic history.

"OK," I say. "I'm very confused right now. Is your mother the one who contacted me?"

"No." Her face creases with puzzlement. "That was just her picture."

"Then...." My resistance vanishes; I drop into my chair. "Then that's really kind of misleading, isn't it?"

"Well, *yeah.* My mother, like, doesn't even look that way anymore."

Fearfully, wonderingly, I stare at her. She is almost mythologically pale—she could have wriggled up from an underwater cavern. Her lips are expertly daubed with a deep brackish purple. A row of pewter hoops forms an armored spine along each ear, and tiny silver globes pop out of her eyebrows. She's eating a cinnamon-coated pretzel dunked in something that looks suspiciously like chutney, and she's chewing with a birdlike nonchalance as though she's been eating with me all her life.

"OK," I say. "Just tell me something. Where's your mother?"

"I don't know."

"Is she here now?"

"Oh, right. Like I'd bring her *anywhere.*"

"So you drove yourself."

"Duh."

"And does your mom know where you are?"

"You know, why are you...like, you are so hung up on my mother. It's kinda weird."

Her nose and eyebrows converge, and her mouth folds into a sneer. A timeless, ageless expression. It has the curious effect of making me feel responsible for everything that happens to her.

"Would you like a soda or something?"

"Nooo!" The howl echoes halfway across the food court. If she were a 2-week-old crying for breast milk, I don't think I could feel any more helpless. But seconds later she's speaking in a completely different voice—the voice of a debate team captain. "So ask me something," she says, flexing her wrist. "Ask a question."

"This is ridiculous."

"Well," she says, "it sounds to me like someone needs to think outside his little box. I mean, how can you be sure it's ridiculous unless you, like, ask me something? Go ahead," she says. "I'm a totally open book."

My notepad is still in my pocket. I can feel the spiral binding rubbing under my belt.

"I don't know what I could possibly ask you."

But when I see her frail shoulders jerking all the way to her ears and back, I feel obligated somehow to give her something, repay her for her time.

"Where do you, um, go to school?"

"Lake Braddock."

"And do you...what's your favorite sport?"

"Sports are for dickheads," she says equably.

We go on for about 10 minutes like this: me sending up discrete inquiries, Claudia shooting them down like skeet. The experience seems to relax her. She leans back in her chair, crosses her legs, and from the corner of my eye, I see a black sneaker with three-inch soles bobbing like a toy sailboat.

And I think: *I'm old enough to remember Nixon's first inaugural, Janis Joplin, the* White Album. *I can remember when there were no malls. I'm old enough to be Claudia's father...*somebody's *father.*

"And what I think is really cool," she says, "is I am totally a *giver* by nature. That's, like, my nature. Which is what they look for in surrogate moms, right? 'Cause I mean, they like 'em to be social workers and stuff. And that's totally me."

"You do social work?"

"Well, I was a Keyette for a couple of years. And except for the clothes, I was way into it."

I know what I should be doing: crossing her off my list, forgetting it ever happened, grabbing my Fo-ca-cha-cha and running.

"Claudia," I say, "they also like surrogate mothers to be married. Already."

"Well, I have a boyfriend. Most of the time. But he is so totally inadequate, I don't think we should work through him."

"Why did you answer my ad?" I ask.

It surprises her a little. She curls her mouth into a moue of disapproval, mashes her pretzel with her finger. "Because you sent it," she mumbles.

"Well, yeah, but I didn't send it directly to *you*."

"Look," she says. "I could try to explain but it'd be, like, totally useless 'cause you're not going to get it so why?"

"Well, go ahead and try."

For a moment her bright dark eyes settle on mine, but it's too much. She whips her head away, stares across the half-empty tables. Ten feet away a tall breadstick of a man in a black T-shirt and camouflage pants is sitting down to fried chicken. She regards him with unfeigned interest—I half think she's getting ready to jump to his table.

"It has to do," she says, "with everyone I know bites, including me."

"So...?"

"So it'd be nice to do something that doesn't totally 100% bite."

I rub my hands together soothingly; I lower my voice into a school counselor's register. "Well, you know, that's very laudable. It's just...it's a matter of...how old are you, Claudia?"

"Old enough," she snaps. "I mean, I can fucking drive, all right?"

"So that means what? 16?"

"*Yeah.*" The contempt that only a teenage daughter could muster. It's a gift, I suppose: a preview of my future.

"Well," I say, "your being 16 raises a lot of very troubling questions. The whole question of legality, for instance."

And then her whole face gets working. The lips wince away from her teeth. The eyes squint shut. The forehead wrinkles into a music staff.

"Why is it a problem?" she asks. "I mean, you're *gay*, right?"

"Um."

"So it's not like there'd be sex," she says. "It all gets, like, mixed together and all. Like in a test tube."

"Well, yes, that's one way of doing it, but you're not...." I want to sound like an adult, but I sound like a child imitating an adult. "Sixteen is very young to have a baby," I say.

"See, now you're not even being historical. 'Cause, like, Marie Antoinette was 12 or something."

"Well, even if that were the case, that wouldn't...giving birth is a very traumatic experience. There's a lot of physical trauma involved."

"Oh, yeah, like you *know* this. Like you had a baby last summer."

"All I'm saying is it requires a certain degree of maturity. You know, to embark on something like this."

"All right. Fine. Fucking fine." She pushes her chair from the table, shoves her half-eaten pretzel into her handbag. "You know, you and my mom can go fuck yourselves." She grabs the bag off her chair and swings it onto her shoulder in a sharp, exaggerated arc, and I'm torn between wanting her to stay and wanting to watch her leave—the whole mannered display.

"Listen, Claudia. Please. I think you're very nice."

Almost certainly, I could not have chosen a worse word. Her face glows with white flame. Steam courses through her pores.

"Very *attractive* young lady," I say.

"Oh, fine. Thanks."

"I just don't think you're old enough for something like this."

"Of course I'm old enough!" She slams her purse twice on the edge of the table. "I'm getting my tongue pierced, like, next week."

fourteen

On her Web site, Debi lies prone on a polar-bear rug with her naked buttocks slammed against a computer terminal. Standing in my doorway, she looks quite different. Younger, for one thing—maybe 10 years out of high school. Her hair, which glowed like plutonium rods on my Compaq monitor, turns out to be your basic peroxide rinse with ostentatiously dark roots. More than anything, it's the clothes that surprise me: a single-breasted, seamed skirt suit in bayberry with matching earrings and strappy high heels. She even has a morocco briefcase with a gold monogram just beneath the handle. It depresses me a little to think this is what passes for seductiveness in Washington—as though we're all just waiting to screw a loan officer.

"Nicholas," she says.

A dainty, nail-polished hand clasps mine.

"Please come in," I say.

Still holding the briefcase, Debi moves across my floorboards with a deliberate, appraising stride—the same way Nattie moved when she came here on the Fourth of July. Of course, I had no idea then how erotic professionals really behaved. I didn't realize they would drift around your apartment, inspect your vase and your dog painting, and stop briefly before the potted ficus to finger the dead leaves at its base.

"Poor thing," she says to the ficus.

She smiles then, almost becomingly, and I notice the hard, crabbed, unvoluptuous set of her mouth, the absence of lip. I see the woman she will be 40 years from now.

"There was a guy," she says, "kind of slumped over in the courtyard."

"Right."

"Big guy with a mustache."

"Yeah, I know. My landlord."

She gives me a curt nod, sets the briefcase on the coffee table, and snaps it open.

"Would you care for a breath mint?" she asks.

It sounds vaguely like a come-on, and I'm trying to think of a suitable response, and then I see her drawing forth a tiny bag of peppermint-striped candy, silently proffering it to me.

"No, thanks," I say.

She pops one in her mouth, and takes two long draws.

"Love," she says. "Hard candy."

And again, from anyone else, it would be a double entendre, but there's something almost stupefyingly linear about her. With the tiniest of sighs, she lowers herself onto the raised-plaid couch, crosses her legs, and succinctly slides her skirt a few inches off her knees. Her thighs are almost too powerfully muscled for her profession—better equipped, maybe, for leading a step class—and her hands have the impersonal efficiency of a carousel operator.

"So," she says.

"Right."

"Don't you look nice tonight," she says.

"Well, so do you," I say, a little hurriedly. "That's a nice scent you have on."

"Thank you."

"Is it Polo? Maybe?"

"Black Diamonds," she says.

"And the shoes."

"The shoes?"

"Are nice too."

"Thank you," she says.

I'm sitting with studied ease in the armchair, thinking of all the things I should be doing: offering her a drink, putting on music—Johnny Mathis? *Peggy Lee?*—turning off one or all the lights. Everything I think of dries up and blows away.

"OK," I say, gathering myself in the chair. "Correct me if I'm wrong. It's my understanding that clients—they will occasionally just want to talk."

"Uh-huh."

"As opposed to the other thing."

"Oh, yes," she says, and then adds, "We call them talkers."

"Right."

"To distinguish them," she explains.

"Right."

"Would you like to talk?"

Her large brown eyes are resting on me with a surprising, discombobulating gentleness. *She's used to this,* I think. *This was standard fare in the days before Viagra.*

"Yeah," I say. "I think I would like to talk." My hands clap against each other. My feet beat out a tattoo on the carpet. "It's not really about *me* per se. I mean, in a *way* it's about me, but I'm more sort of curious to talk about you."

And whatever tenderness her face held vanishes, flushed out by a vein of suspicion. In the space of five seconds, I have become something she didn't bargain for: a cop, a missionary.

"I'm not interested in what you *do,*" I rush to explain. "It's more about your future plans."

"Uh-huh."

She takes a few more draws of candy; the chain of muscles ripples all the way down to her collarbone.

"Debi," I say. "May I call you Debi?"

She keeps sucking.

"What I was wondering, Debi, is...is this the kind of work you see yourself doing over the long term?"

Suck, suck. Suck, suck. "You mean like how long?" she asks.

"I don't know, maybe over the next year or two."

Her eyes go blank, and the rest of her face follows suit, except for the jaw, involuntarily rotating.

"Well," she says, "I suppose the health plan, you know, could be better."

"Oh, so you have a plan."

"It's really low option. There's no dental."

I lean forward until my elbows rest on my knees. I give her the full glare of my attention.

"So if someone were to offer you full health care for a job," I say, "a short-term job. Is that something you would consider?"

Her lips fold into an exaggerated kiss. "Well, it depends," she says. "You mean like for a month or something?"

"More like nine."

The lips fold back in. "Huh," she says. "I don't know." She strokes her nose. "It can't be heavy lifting because of my carpal tunnel."

"No, nothing manual."

"And it probably couldn't be anything, you know, illegal. Strictly speaking."

"It wouldn't be," I tell her. "It would be very much legal. It might...it might *preclude* your current job."

"Uh-huh."

I squint into her eyes. "Would that bother you?"

"I don't know. See, I don't know. I'm very much into people."

"You are. I could tell that. You probably like kids, for instance."

"They're OK," she says, sliding a finger into her mouth, wriggling something free. "As long as they're not crying," she says, "or eating."

"Eating."

"They can be very sloppy."

"True."

"And they don't wipe their mouth? If it was me, I would make sure they always wiped their mouth. Plus you're not supposed to smoke around them."

I lean back in my chair. My voice trembles. "You smoke?" I ask.

But I already know the answer. The breath mints! She needs the mints because she just stubbed out her menthol cigarette in the big fern pot in the front courtyard, right next to my landlord's head.

"I smoke more in the summertime," she says, "and holidays—because I work extra shifts."

"Have you tried giving it up?"

"Yeah, you know, a week, two weeks. But the weight always comes back. I think next time, if I have enough money, I'll just schedule lipo for right after I quit and that way, you know, it'll even itself out. Because you can understand, in my line, a pound here, a pound there. Not that you want to be a bag of bones, either. Nobody respects that."

"Uh huh. So gaining weight would..."

"Oh, God, who...I mean, why? I mean, this is what I figure: There's a whole lifetime to be fat. So if you're still young, you might as well be thin while you're able is how I think of it."

And the person who comes to mind is not Celia, the champion weight loser, but Sally. I remember the night she invited me and my parents over for dinner, and then, shortly after the decaf, excused herself, dropped onto the living-room hearth rug, and began working her external obliques. We watched her with an air of bafflement, like paying customers who wandered into the wrong movie theater. Greg explained this was Sally's routine, that it helped her sleep better. And my father, in a low voice, asked, "Does she realize?"

"Realize what?" Greg asked.

"You don't keep it forever."

"Keep what?"

"Your body."

And just then Sally grunted, and then once again, more loudly. She was starting to flag.

"Well, if anyone can, she can," Greg said.

He sounded dispirited, though, as he said it. And I can remember at that moment feeling a small flush of pride in Sally, in the way she confounded my family's expectations—confounded them, probably, without ever realizing it. And I remember also thinking that we ask a lot of bodies like Sally's. We want them to be many things.

And who, really, is asking more than I am? Unable to procreate in the usual fashion, unable to accept adoption or foster parenting or any of the alternatives once embraced by the reproductively disenfranchised, determined to lob some parcel of my genetic code into the embryo factory of the future, I am now trying to convince an employee of Gorgeous Girlz Limited to give up vanity, gainful employment, autonomy, bad habits. How exactly did I get to be this desperate?

Debi has moved now from sucking to crunching her candy. She grinds it down with cannibal zeal. And in the dark cavity of her mouth I catch powerful glimpses of white molar, I see a whole pitiless universe.

"Hey," she says, "you're zoning out on me."

She tugs the hem of her skirt back to her knees. Her thighs merge and disappear under their bayberry wrap. It's like the retraction of a birth.

"So," she says. "Tell me about this job."

My head drops back against the cushions. The ceiling pulls away.

"Never mind."

She says, "Excuse?"

"Never mind. I'll pay the full hour."

Debi's employer accepts three major credit cards, but I decide to make it easier by writing a personal check. Of course, I'm assuming that handing over the check will end the transaction, but something—some latent chivalry, maybe—makes me insist on walking her out. As we step through the lobby door, the landlord is nowhere to be seen, but even without him there's a pharmaceutical smell to the air: fumes of rain. A woman down the street is watering her hosta, sending showers of insects into the path of a streetlight.

Debi holds her briefcase from the bottom, like an artist's portfolio. She applies a damp finger to the hair just above each ear.

"Good night," she says.

Her voice is ready to leave, but she's not. She's actively hesitating, and I wonder what could possibly be keeping her, and the only thing that comes to mind is her work ethic. She wants to earn the money.

"Well, good night," she says again.

She hoists herself up on her toes—it reminds me how big I am—and before I can demur, she leaves a little impress of moisture on my lips. My eyes, instinctively, have closed to her touch, and when they open again, they're peering over Debi's shoulder—at a man who has positioned himself next to the apartment directory and is staring back at me with flickers of irony and contentment.

The Caribbean has done something remarkable with Joe Bryant's skin, stained it a deep tawny brown upon which his postcard-blue eyes float like agates. He is almost entirely liquid. He is the ocean he just left.

"Snookie," he says.

And all the rituals of transition abandon me. I don't say good-bye to Debi. I don't introduce anyone to anyone. I don't explain a damn thing. I walk over to Joe Bryant and wrap my arms around his neck and sink in. It turns out he's not liquid at all.

The Broker

fifteen

These are the things I know now about Joe Bryant: He has a 32-inch waist—I checked the back of his jeans. He plays volleyball on the Mall, serves as a ringer for congressional softball teams. He is frightened by lady-vampire movies.

He reads poems to me. He'll call at one in the morning to tell me what Auden wrote after the moon landing. He wants to perform "Howl" in Union Station. He wants to celebrate Keats's birthday by running up the Spanish Steps.

He teaches me things too. One day he yanks the stamen out of a honeysuckle flower and shows me the perfect little liquid pearl dangling off its end. Another day he says, "Nick, your first hit of cocaine is always your best. Don't let anyone tell you otherwise."

An afternoon in September: We're helping one of Joe's friends move into the Cairo Apartments, and Joe is leaning against the trunk of someone's Subaru Outback (not *his* car; never *his* car). His pelvis is thrust forward just a little, he has a bottle of Poland Spring water in his right hand, and his left hand is pulling up the fabric of his shirt, peeling the drenched cotton from his skin, rubbing the end of it across his face...and there it is, the line of brown hair, the love trail running down his belly.

And for a moment all I want to do is press my face in that exact spot. And I think about how it must have looked the winter Joe got back from Costa Rica: welts running from his chest to his navel. As though someone had been dripping hot wax on him. His health plan sent him to an old Jamaican doctor lady who took one look and said, "Ah tink it's cheeguhs. You got to pull dem out, cut dey heads off." Joe wasn't buying that, so he found a nice Malawian doctor in Silver Spring who told him he'd been stung by a small jellyfish indigenous to a narrow band of the Pacific Ocean.

"You don't feel these babies when they sting," Joe says. "They just kinda work through your system. Which when you think about it, isn't that kinda like being gay?"

So we spend two hours trying to isolate our "stings"—those moments in our childhood when, retrospectively, we can see our sexual destinies coalescing. For me it was watching Robert Conrad in *The Wild Wild West*. For Joe it was seeing Arlene Francis on *What's My Line?*, tugging her false eyelashes back to their proper length after the Mystery Guest eyeshades came off.

"Oh, and she was always gloating," Joe says. "She always knew who it was."

One Saturday afternoon we drive out to the Eastern Shore and rent a Skipjack, and Joe sails it down the Wye River toward the bay. In the dusk, the river water is soft and brown. We don't see any Atlantic herring, it's true. No ridley turtles or cowbirds. But we watch ripples turning into blue crabs and fish snapping insects out of the air. We see snowy egrets, a couple of vacant osprey nests, and far away, a bald eagle, motionless in a tree. On the southern bank, a herd of sheep, conspicuously bored; and farther down the river, a porticoed Georgian farmhouse with terraced fields and a manicured lawn running all the way to the water.

Everything is warm and still, and the silence has something to do with Joe's silence, and I keep thinking something is going to emerge from it. Something does. Driving home that night, Joe takes one arm from the wheel and drapes it around my shoulder. He says, "I think we should move in together."

Such odd symptoms: an explosion of air behind my breastbone, a surge of blood in my throat. Elation, I guess, although the more I think about it, the clearer it becomes that we've already moved in together. Most of the time, Joe sleeps at my place—the bed's bigger, and the space seems to fold around us more completely; and my mind, instead of floating to the far corners of the room, stays put. I lie there with Joe Bryant's head on my chest, or I roll on top and stare down into his half-shut eyes, and I wonder: *How? How do people end up with each other?* There I am, pressed against a man with a smooth golden dome and a heavy rib cage and a 32-inch waist, and his blue eyes are shining back at me, and I have no idea how it happened. Or when it stops happening.

"All right, he's a bartender," Shannon says. "But what is he really?"

"He's a bartender."

"No, I mean, there's a career path. It's been interrupted, but there's a path. An *idea* is going on."

"That's the only idea."

She gives me a taut, forbearing smile. "See, Nick, bartending is not an idea. Bartending's what you do until an idea comes along."

And yet when she meets him, she doesn't think to ask about his ideas. She doesn't have time, really, because Joe grabs her around her waist and lofts her in the air like a bed sheet. "Nick *said* you was pretty!" She never quite comes back to earth, because she has found in Joe a miracle of empathy. He strokes the sleeve of her pinstriped jacket. He feels every single one of her pains: childhood, high-protein diets, men's betrayals. He throws himself on them like a bomb-sniffing dog.

"Of course, I was constantly made fun of," Shannon says, "because I had big eyes and skinny legs."

"Which are *assets* now," says Joe.

Truthfully, I couldn't have coached him any better. After lunch

Shannon grabs me around the neck and pulls my ear to her mouth. "This is a significant improvement for you, Nick."

I would have preferred putting off the meeting with the Broomes, but one night over the phone my mother makes her bimonthly inquiry—"Anyone we should know about?"—and I take too long to say no, and in that half-second of hesitation my mother gleans everything.

"What's his name?" she asks.

"Well, it's Joe."

"Joe," she says. "Joe."

She likes the straightforwardness of it. She asks if he's big. I say tall but not as broad as me. She asks if he's an actor. I say, "No, bartender." She asks when we can all meet. And there! It's on the books.

The one saving grace is no one will be cooking this time. My mother has decided that people can't get acquainted that way. So, through some combination of torpor and fate, we end up at a Red Lobster in Falls Church, squeezed into a horseshoe-shaped booth. Dad and Joe sit facing each other, and I'm pressing shoulders with my mother, and just before the lobster arrives, my car alarm misfires—I can hear it through the restaurant wall. By the time I get back, cherry-faced and perspiring, the lobster has been sitting for 10 minutes, and conversation has lapsed into a grave decorum. My gambits exhaust themselves within seconds. I mention a razor I bought at Costco, and my mother says, "Oh, well, there you are. I don't belong to Costco." I tell them about a senile senator who wanders into traffic, and my father says, "They should probably shoot people like that."

Midway through the meal, I see the light of inspiration flare up in Joe's eyes. It gives me the queasiest feeling.

"OK," he says, clapping his hands together. "Everyone's gotta answer the same question."

A pall of confusion settles over my parents' faces. Their eyes quiver like shaken raisins.

"We're not sure what the question is," my father admits.

"Oh!" Joe raps himself on the temple. "The question is: Who was the first person you ever had sex with? No cheating!"

Some atavistic survival instinct pulls down the shades of my eyes. When they scroll up again, I am astonished to see my mother, with a deeply apologetic smile, hitching her thumb in my father's direction.

"Aw," says Joe. His face screws into an expression of genuine compassion. "Well, that's OK," he says. "Who was your *second*?"

And then something even more astonishing: the sound of my father's laughter, cannoning off the walls. I'm not the only one who's startled. From one end of the Red Lobster to the other, skeins of white bibs ripple toward us.

Driving home that night, Joe says: "Your dad has a good sense of humor."

"Well, it's a little dark is all," I say. "A little buried."

"The best kind," Joe says.

The following Saturday, Greg and Sally join us for a barbecue in my courtyard. The day after that, Celia and Larry meet us at the National Zoo. Whatever anxiety I bring into these meetings dissolves within minutes—to be replaced by an entirely new anxiety. It has to do with how well Joe performs under pressure and also how curious he is about the Broomes. I can't help thinking he's auditioning us. He gathers more about my brother's clinic in 10 minutes than I have in 10 years. He quizzes Celia about cash-balance plans and expresses such a profound interest in teeth that Larry spontaneously launches a tutorial just outside the reptile house.

"So what do you think is in plaque?" Larry asks him.

"Um, there's...bacteria...."

"Right." A stern nod. "What else?"

"Germs?" Joe guesses.

"No, that's the same as bacteria."

"Oh, I give up, I give up."

"*Food* particles..." Larry peers into Joe's eyes, as though he's trying to prod a dormant memory. "And?" He waits a few seconds longer. "And *saliva*," he says triumphantly.

"Saliva," says Joe.

And by this point, I expect some lilt of mockery in Joe's voice, a conspirational wink, but he never cracks, not once. He's too interested. He wants to meet everything on its own level, which may be why nothing ever seems to surprise him. There's a moment when we're standing outside the panda house (a sweet memory of Lupe wafts through my head) and behind me I hear Celia asking: "So, how did you guys meet?"

Not a tough question, not by any stretch. But I can't begin to answer it without incriminating myself. And that's when Joe actually steps forward, jutting out his chest.

"My sister introduced us," he says.

Which is true enough,when I think about it. And I like too, the element of intentionality it suggests in Nattie's behavior. I can't help thinking that even if she did nothing explicit, she still *meant* for this to happen, and everything else was just a way of getting us here, and it gives me a pang now and then to think she's not around to enjoy it.

I did receive a postcard from her: a more sequential effort than I'm used to.

> *Hi, Nick. Mom and I just went to a church in San Antonio to get her springer spaniel blessed. Lama made his own little baptismal font in the back pew. Mother says we should have taken him to a Buddhist temple, except she's not sure how Buddhists feel about dogs. This is my life for now—only for now.*
>
> *I miss you. I miss our Greek place.*

No mention of Joe—not enough space probably—but then Joe and I rarely mention her either. If her name ever leaks into our conversation, it calls down a shroud of silence, and I have to forcibly remind myself that Nattie is alive and chafing...and for all I know plotting her next raid on parenthood. I don't for a minute think she's given up. They haven't *dreamed* of the pharmaceutical that could do that.

But it's not a subject Joe and I ever linger on. Frankly, I think he's embarrassed by how we met—and maybe by me too. Sometimes I can see my aberrations stamped, one after the other, on the ticker tape of his mind: *Tried to knock up my sister. Reads Tolstoy for escapism. Cries when he sees children in denim overalls.*

Joe, by contrast, spends large stretches of time in kid-free environments. One night a week, I visit him in the downtown hotel bar where he works. An elegant, wood-lined space with beveled mirrors, tawny light refracting through upside-down wine glasses, nonprofit employees with glasses of scotch planted under their chins. And presiding over it all Joe Bryant, in his hieratic white shirt and black pants: the high priest of Stolichnaya. Entering his temple, I feel a strange dreamlike humility, as though I have been sent on an errand I only dimly understand. I swing my legs onto the stool, I bow my head, I close my eyes. I hear Joe Bryant say: "Snookie want a Snook Shake?"

That always breaks it, of course: entering the closed universe of our creatures. They multiply at a fantastic rate. We invent three in the course of a single dessert. I'm not sure I could even list them all, but there is a core to which we keep returning. Snookie Pie, that's me; and Skunkie, that's him; and then there are variations on the theme: Snookie Bird, Skunkie Bear, Fishy Fish, Billy Bison. Each character has his own vocal register and a single individuating quirk: Barfly, for instance, longs for Beer Nuts, and Mr. Tomato is pining for his long-lost boyfriend Oregano. Oondra does nothing except say "Oondra" over and over again, in slightly different intonations. Same with Palpope and Zimpool.

Sometimes I wonder if this is the same thing autistic twins do: build parallel worlds with carefully constructed syntaxes. If you attached a radio transmitter to either of us and followed us to a grocery store or a movie theater or somebody's house, you'd wait maybe 10 minutes at most, and then you'd hear Joe make a sound like "Mrrk, mrrk."

And then you'd hear me: "Hello, Fishy Fish. How are you?"

"Mrrk, mrrk."

"That's nice. Have you had a nice swim today?"

"Mrrk, mrrk."

"Oh, the Tidal Basin. That's a little cold, isn't it?"

We need very little prompting. All it takes is browsing through the vocals section at Tower Records on a warm, soupy September afternoon, and before I know it, I'm leaning into Joe's ear and lifting my voice into a high, strangled cheep: "Snookie no like Harry Connick."

"No?" asks Joe, unfazed.

"Snookie sing better than Harry Connick."

And so Snookie starts singing "It Had to Be You," landing especially hard on the "you" and, with each succeeding word, wandering further from the original key, ascending finally to a ham-radio frequency that should be making Joe wince but instead draws a dreamy smile across his face, and I'm halfway through the song when suddenly Snookie Pie vanishes. I stop singing, I set down the Harry Connick CD, I walk to the other side of the store. Joe joins me there a few seconds later.

"What?" he's saying. "What's the problem?"

"I was getting on my own nerves."

I tell him that because I can't tell him what's pressing on the inside of my mouth: *You're not my kid.*

How could I? When he doesn't even know I'm still trying to be a father? How can I say that the energy I devote to acting like a child—treating *him* like a child—could be better spent making one?

You're not my child, Joe. You're not running down a muddy field in a blue parka.

And yet there are moments—I have to acknowledge it—when I do feel an almost biological connection to him. It's there the afternoon I pick him up at Union Station. He's coming back from a wedding in Boston, and I'm standing at track 8, feeling much the way my own parents must have felt waiting for me to come home from college. And that memory swallows the present, and I half-expect Joe to stagger out in a misbuttoned, untucked flannel shirt and parachute pants, with a big canvas bag of dirty laundry slung over one shoulder and a complex, multichambered backpack slung over the other.

And it hardly matters that when he finally does arrive—two minutes early—he's wearing a herringbone jacket over a crew-neck shirt, and his head is freshly shaven, and the only thing that evokes college is his tiredness. He's traveled straight through from Boston, and he has the ashen expression of someone who's been three times to the club car, and he must realize how he looks because when he sees me, he balls up his hands and makes tiny rubbing motions in front of his eyes, like a baby just before nap time.

I laugh, and the laugh jams in my throat and becomes a sorrowful burble, and for a second, I could swear he's mine.

And something about that paralyzes me. I can't make a move in his direction. All I can do is echo him: Make the little fists and rub them in front of my eyes.

He's moving slowly. The overnight bag thumps against his leg. His head falls to one side, and he smiles—the barest etching of a smile—and he says, "I missed my baby."

And that's the shocking part, the really unsuspected part. That it could work in both directions. At the same time.

It's almost too much to bear. Something in me wants to fight it with all I've got. One night my friend George comes over to play Monopoly, and Joe insists on being the dog. *Being* the dog. Picking up his little dog marker and hopping it from square to square and yipping like a Scottish terrier: "Arf! Arf arf arf!" When he's sent to jail, he makes piteous whines until he's released. And each time he passes the little car marker (George's) he lifts the dog's leg and makes a loud, extended pissing sound.

George handles Jacobean manuscripts for the Library of Congress, and so I'm not sure he's seen anything like this. I have, of course. And my response is much the same as it was in Tower Records: joy and then a sudden bottoming out, as though somewhere inside me a drain has unstopped itself.

When the game is over, Joe celebrates his victory by flipping over the playing board and flinging the paper money into the air. Blue, yellow, orange, pink: The play dollars shower down on him like dead leaves, and I'm already on my feet heading for the bedroom.

Joe finds me there a few minutes later, the pillow pressed against the top half of my face. I'm breathing very deliberately: in, out, in, out.

"Snookie sad?" he asks. His voice is so soft it feels like mist.

"Shut up."

"Skunkie get sad when Snookie sad."

"Go away, Skunkie."

"Skunkie smell bad when he sad." He buries his snout in my neck. Great hoggy snorts issue from his throat. I can feel his nostrils dilating against my skin, his tongue slurping the space just below my ear. "Skunkie smell so bad," he growls, running his nose up and down my neck.

All right, all right. I'm laughing. He doesn't give me a choice. But I really wish laughter had more nuance, because I would like it to say: *This is pleasant but it is not acceptable. As substitutes go, this is not acceptable. You have parents. I have parents. Whatever we are to each other, it's not that. Someday my Internet ad is going to elicit interest from a naturalized U.S. citizen of voting age, and what then? What happens to Skunkie Pie then?*

Joe stops and pulls away—not far, a few inches. His eyes have an unusually quiet gleam, and his mouth has fallen open in a gesture of unconscious amusement—I once saw an orange tabby with the same expression. I touch his chin, which is damp from rubbing against his own spittle.

"Look at you," I say. "You're all saliva."

"I know," he says. "An important ingredient in plaque." He's back in his grown-up voice. "Skunkie very bad," he says.

"Skunkie very bad. He needs to let Snookie make some coffee for our guest."

But I can't get off the bed yet because Joe won't budge. He's looking at me head-on. All the role-play has burned away. Nothing left but raw tenderness, and it's almost disabling to watch. I think maybe it's better that laughter doesn't have a nuance.

I reach out and stroke the stubble on his head. And I say, "I'm OK."

He says, "OK?"

"OK, baby, yeah."

sixteen

Nicholas!

Tuesday morning, early October. My daily check of the surrogacy message board—a comforting, fruitless ritual—but today, out of nowhere, these words come climbing off the screen.

Call me as soon as possible. I think I can be of real service to you. Please call on my cell phone, and let's discuss further.

The exchange is local. The message is signed: *Lyle Kibbee.*

Lyle Kibbee. The name gathers on my lips. My hands rehearse the business of calling, I'm actually reaching for the phone until I remember that Joe is here. He dragged in a little after 3, swept into bed like a blast of Freon. Even now, his wrists are curled under his chin for warmth. I want to wake him just to tell him he isn't cold anymore.

But now I don't dare. I scribble the phone number on the back of a bank deposit slip and I stuff it into my pocket, kiss Joe on the cheek, and walk to work. And I let another hour pass before I call and leave a message for Lyle Kibbee.

He calls me back 20 minutes later.

"At your service," he says.

"I think you possibly answered my ad?"

"Yes, I did. Now tell me why."

"Why...?"

"That's really the important question, isn't it, Nicholas? Why did I get such a good vibe from your ad? Why did I say, 'I need to talk to this guy'?"

"You'd probably have to tell me."

"I can't. All I can say is I read it, and I thought: *This is a person I want to work with.*"

"See, the thing is I'm not sure what you do."

"Fair question, Nicholas. What I am is a dream implementer. Now if you want to be *technical*, if you want the *technical* term for what I do, I'm a surrogacy broker."

"Oh. I didn't know there were such things."

"Now why would you, Nicholas? We're a rare breed, we're almost *sui generis.* Our job is simply to link up aspiring parents with surrogate candidates."

"OK."

"You can read all about it on my Web site. Now I would guess...I don't know you, I've never met you...I would guess so far you've been going the traditional route."

"I...you know, I don't know if I'd call it traditional."

"What I mean is you probably haven't considered the gestational surrogacy option."

"Oh, right."

"That's where you fertilize an egg from one woman, which is then implanted—"

"—in another woman's womb. Yeah, you know, Mr. Kibbee, that sounds kind of complicated."

"Oh, well, I'll tell you what that extra dose of complication does for you, my young friend. It weakens the maternal bond."

"Uh-huh."

"Which makes it less likely...God forbid, but we know how people are...less likely for the surrogate to withhold custody from the IP."

"IP?"

"Intended parent. We're in Washington, yes? We must use acronyms."

"Right."

"Listen, Nicholas, I hate talking on the phone. I mean, I can't tell anything about you, you can't tell anything about me. So when?"

"When?"

"I don't want to rush you, it's not about rushing. What I'm envisioning is strictly a fact-finding exercise, a getting-acquainted, see-how-we-work-together kind of thing. The only problem, Nicholas—"

"Nick's fine."

"Time is a little bit of the essence here. Because I'm only in D.C. for the next couple of weeks. D.C. is just one of the regions in which I operate, so time is a little bit of the essence, and I would love to see if there's some way I can help you. I guess that's what I'm trying to say, Nick. I want to help you."

We should live so long to hear these words. The only trouble is I've gotten used to doing without help. It's become a small point of pride with me that Shannon is the only person I ever confide in—and usually several weeks after events have transpired—and even Joe hears nothing of my progress, doesn't even know enough to know there is progress. I'm an independent contractor. Proud of it.

But time, but time. Last March I had the luxury to be austere; autumn is different. Some evenings I walk out the front of the Longworth House office building, and to my left, a red, molten, soft-boiled egg of a sun is bleeding across the horizon, lighting up the Washington Monument like a cigarette. A pocket of cold air inflames the lining of my nose, and all the things I usually love about this time of year—the leaves on the Bradford pear trees, geese honking across a parking lot—tickle me with dread because I'm running out of time.

It's true, there are hours, even days, when my deadline loses some of its power. I'm hanging with my officemates at the Hawk and Dove or spending an afternoon with Joe in St. Michael's, shopping for coffee tables, and I'll feel my resolve springing a leak. I'll think: *Well, maybe, if it happens by February, that'll be OK. March could work....*

And there are days, too, when I think maybe my family might charge into the breach. I look at Celia and Larry, for instance, and I ask myself if two people could be more suited for marriage, for baby in the baby carriage. They never appear to argue. They never let more than a foot of space separate them. They are like those people you see smiling in the checkout line, forgetting to cross at street corners, staring benevolently into rearview mirrors. People with deep private joys.

But it turns out Celia and Larry aren't like that. And it's Celia who breaks it to me. She calls me at work one morning and asks what I'm doing for Thanksgiving. I tell her I'm doing the usual: eating with Oliver and Celia.

She says, "I'll probably be joining you."

"I thought you were going to be at Larry's parents."

"No," she says. "I don't think so."

"Change of plans?"

"Kind of," she says. "We kind of broke up."

She's genuinely surprised when I probe for an explanation. "Oh, well, it's just...that's what people do...." So I keep pressing, as gently as I can, and I'm about to give up when she snaps: "He doesn't want kids. OK?"

I stare at the receiver.

"What do you mean he doesn't want kids?" I ask.

"He told me. He said, 'They don't cook. They don't clean. They eat your food. Why bother?'"

"Oh. That's...yeah—"

"So nip it now, that's the best approach. It's not...you know, I'm still young. I'm more young than old. There are lots of men in the world."

"Sure there are."

"Lots of dentists even."

So I arrange to meet Lyle Kibbee—that night. And because my mind goes blank when he asks me to pick a restaurant, I end up suggesting the Greek restaurant on Pennsylvania Avenue. I'm frankly stunned by my betrayal—letting a stranger onto Nattie ground—but when I get there, I realize it's not the same place at all. It seems to have sprouted grime, the way a face sprouts freckles, and the man who shows me to my table isn't the rubber-faced grandfather I remember but a large, flushed, panting man who speaks in abrupt Eastern European cadence. I ask him if someone's waiting for me, and he says there's nobody. But as soon as he seats me at one of the upstairs tables, I see there is somebody: a smallish, oblong, bearded man, positioned by the window at the very table where Nattie and I used to sit.

"Lyle?"

He doesn't answer at first, just squares his shoulders, slowly refolds the napkin on his lap and sets it on the edge of the table. "At your service," he says.

But he doesn't move in my direction. Ten seconds pass, and I realize we're at an impasse. We're both, for reasons I can't possibly divine, trying to save face. I'm the one who breaks first. I back my chair out, gather my place setting, and carry it over to his table.

"Oh, if that's OK," Lyle says. "The view's nicer here, don't you think?"

And then he turns on me the full efflorescence of his smile, and for a moment that's the only part of his face I can see, that zipper of tannin-stained teeth. The rest is just beard—black, lycanthropic beard—smothering his lips, rambling up his face like a colonizing mold. It takes some doing to parse out the other features: a thin, brackish wash of hair; a wedge of nose; lunettes of gray skin dragging down the eyes; and finally the eyes themselves, small and droopy with infinitely dense black irises, like collapsed stars.

"You'll have to tell me what to order," he says.

"Oh, well, chicken souvlaki is usually what I get."

"Does it drip?"

"Does it—"

"Drip." He's pointing to his peach oxford shirt, unbuttoned at the top, fastened tight around the chest. "I just got it dry-cleaned," he says, smiling bashfully.

"I've never had much drippage."

The man who showed me to the table is the same man who takes our order. I'm beginning to think he's the only one working here. He gives off an air of agitated martyrdom. Creeks of sweat bleed through his shirt. He doesn't want to stay long—he's already striding away when Lyle asks for a glass of merlot.

"He forgot to take our menus," Lyle murmurs.

"Yeah." I'm wiping the edge of the table. "It's usually a little better here."

"Not a problem," he says. "And Nick? May I just say? It's a nice town you've got here."

He's not joking apparently. Something about his tone makes me think it really *is* my town.

"I've never met a surrogacy broker before," I tell him.

He shrugs—a large, stylized, comic gesture directed to the heavens. "What can I tell you, Nick? There aren't many like me. Maybe there's no one like me."

He tells me he used to work for a surrogacy agency in Westchester County. Loved the work, loved the clients. Began to chafe, though, at all the bureaucracy: too much paperwork, not enough people work. ("Everything takes too long. The screening periods *alone* go on for months.") One of his clients convinced him to go out on his own, even put him in touch with a couple in California. They were so pleased with his work, they mentioned him to two other couples. Before he knew it, he was freelancing on both coasts. That was five years ago, and today, he says, he has more work than he can handle.

"People are hungry, Nick." He's refilling my water glass for me, very carefully, as though it were a graduated cylinder. "They *want* their own child. Adoption's always there, adoption's great, but there's nothing—am I right?—nothing like having a little *piece* of yourself in the world." He peers up at me. "You know what I'm talking about."

"Yeah, I do."

"I don't have to tell *you*."

The waiter brings us salads we didn't order. "Oh, and a glass of mer—" Lyle starts to say, but the waiter is striding back down the stairs.

Lyle folds his hands primly in front of him. "You must have questions," he says. "Please, fire away."

"We can wait for dinner."

"I think we will be waiting for dinner."

"Oh. Yeah. There was one thing I noticed. On your Web site? You don't have a mailing address."

"No, why? It would be pointless—why? I'm a virtual operation, Nick." With his left hand he sweeps invisible clutter off the table. "I tell you what, I could bring you over, show you my shiny downtown office, dazzle you with, with green-leather ottomans, and you know what? You'd be the one paying for it. Because all that stuff gets passed onto the client—every chair, every paper clip. I travel light, Nick."

"Uh-huh."

"And I work nonstop. I've got eyes and ears everywhere. I can find surrogates at a cocktail party, a newspaper kiosk. I have that instinct, Nick. This is something you're born with. You see a woman—across a crowded room, as they say—and right away, there's an emanation. I'm being spiritual here, but you understand me. A certain emanation, a light. And that's when you know." His whole body becomes possessed with the telling. The mounds of his shoulders twitch; the fingers fling little buckets of air my way. "Now that doesn't mean they're always *willing*," he cautions. "But I've found when you explain the benefits, when you catch them in the appropriate circumstances, it's amazing how quickly they come around. Oh, and here's our souvlaki! Splendid! And if I could...glass of—"

Having a meal to eat doesn't slow him down at all—it just shunts him onto a second track. And after a while I'm hard-pressed to distinguish his speaking from his eating because they seem to spring from the same communicative impulse.

"I will tell you this, Nick. (The souvlaki is very fine.) I've never had a surrogate turn on me."

"No?"

"None of that Baby M business here. You work with me, you won't be spending the next 10 years of your life in the courtroom, paying for some lawyer's third Miata. I'm careful with my contracts, Nick. Not one of them has ever been challenged."

He tells me about some of the surrogates he's worked with. Fascinating women, he says. Some of them very maternal, some not at all. Some in it for the extra cash, some just wanting to pass the time a little faster. High school geography teachers, French-horn players, traffic cops, cruller makers, pool cleaners...the whole socioeconomic spectrum.

"Oh, and army wives. Army wives make fabulous surrogates, but you have to catch them at a certain window of boredom. And the thing is you can never tell anything from a woman's build, because Lizzie, for instance, was a doll. A china figurine, Nick. Picked up dog doody in the park, sang with an Irish hip-hop band in Venice, California. So delicate, you thought you'd break her just breathing, and this girl popped out babies like Pop-Tarts. Oopsy, up comes another!"

We're alone—not another diner in sight—and Lyle is talking, and a glass of merlot has mysteriously appeared at his elbow, and everything we say from now on feels permanent, as though we're carving it into the space around us.

"Do you have children, Lyle?"

I can't tell if the question surprises him. He pauses for the barest second.

"I have not had that privilege," he says. "It's been suggested that what I do is a form of compensation. For that deficit. And I won't say it's wrong. I won't say it's right; I won't say it's wrong."

He rubs the stem of the wine glass between his palms.

"Let me tell you what I believe in, Nick. *I* believe—if you'll allow me to be corny—I believe it's important to live an exemplary life. By which I mean the life you're *meant* to live, the being-all-you-can-be kind of life. And clearly, in your case—I don't know you, I'm going out on a bit of a limb—in *your* case I think that means children. Having a child is what allows you, Nicholas Broome, to reach your highest potential. Now I know I'm talking big talk, *but...*" He leans into me now. All his energy gathers in his eyes. "...you feel perhaps something along those lines, Nick. Am I so far off?

"I won't say it's wrong," I answer. "I won't say it's right."

He smiles, less abundantly than before.

"Dare to be great, Nick. That's all I have to say. The rest is up to you."

Around us all I can see are empty tables, chairs waiting for occupants. And I'm thinking if I worked hard enough, I could put people into these chairs. I could fill them with people who don't even exist yet, and we could all throw ourselves a party, and this party would be talked about for many years to come. Even our waiter, unhappy as he is, would smile a little telling people about the night the Broomes came by.

"You're right," I tell Lyle. "It is up to me."

seventeen

Lyle insists on paying for dinner, but I won't hear of it. I tell him to think of it as a down payment. He's a little affronted by that.

"Oh, Nick! Don't worry about the money. I know, I know, it's always the first thing people think about, and really? It's the last thing. Because the money always works itself out. I've got sliding scales, I've got loan officers I can put you in touch with. The money always works out. Now, that said, there *is* an up-front $50 fee for processing your application. *But* I don't want you to pay me a dime until you've called my references."

He sends me home with a curriculum vitae, articles of incorporation, and a portfolio of testimonials—faint, third-generation texts that date back only a few years but exhale an elderly methanol perfume. They come, as advertised, from every region of the country but merge into a single dominant chord: people crediting Lyle with saving their dreams, their marriages, giving them the family they never thought they would have. I keep checking the prose for signs of dictation, for urtexts, but the idioms range all over the place, and here and there my eye snags on a convincingly eccentric detail.

Lyle called us at 2 A.M. from a pool hall in Sheboygan just to make sure we'd made our appointment....

He told our surrogate she should stop eating so many bananas because it was too much potassium for a baby....

I end up calling the author of the most recent testimonial: a woman in Northampton, Massachusetts, who picks up the phone with such an expectant breath it kills me to have to tell her who I am. She rebounds quickly enough, and her voice relaxes into a singsongy rhythm, which can't be for me, and sure enough, she begins cooing the other man's name.

"Benjamin," she says. "Mommy's on the phone. She's on the *phone*, isn't she?"

A quick plunge into the adult register.

"What Lyle did was he just kind of kept everything on track. Which was important because—that's a big toy truck—because our surrogate got a little wacky on us toward the end. She wanted us to pay for—beep, beep—all this stuff. Like flying her mother out, calling this psychic hotline...taking Swedish lessons, stuff like that. And Lyle really kept her on track, you know. Not in a bad way—no, that's Mommy's foot, that's not—he just kept reminding her of her obligations, and God bless him, he got her to come around. Without him, I can't imagine how it would have turned out."

"He's an interesting person."

"Yeah, I would say he's very intense is what he is. But he gets the job done, and as far as I'm concerned—whose Jeep is that?—that's exactly what I want. Someone dotting every *T*..."

"Yeah."

"*I* is what I mean."

"Yeah."

"How *is* Lyle? I haven't talked to him in, God, months."

"He's good. We had dinner the other night."

"Oh, dinner," she says. "Good."

And in this way our conversation winds quickly to its close. There's nothing left for me to say except: "Good luck with your kid."

And she says: "Good luck with yours."

And just by saying that, she casts a prickly brightness into my mind's compartment. All the old pictures come back: The boy in the parka, the girl with my father's eyes, these children I have created out of the axons and dendrites of my brain, just waiting to be realized. And all it takes, apparently, is filling out my application, making out a check for $50, and setting my bloodhound loose.

The first part, at least, is surprisingly pleasurable. Unlike the testimonials, the application is professionally produced: an 8 1/2-by-11 brochure with the company name stamped up top in cobalt blue: SURROGACY SERVICES OF AMERICA. The questions unspool for eight pages— but without the inquisitorial drive I recall from the sperm-bank applications.

What do you think compels you to be a parent?

If you could dream your child to be anything, what would it be?

A pleasing, impressionistic rhythm, and as I linger over my responses, I get a small jolt from realizing that I am no longer a suitor. I have no viability assessments to pass, no motility thresholds to cross. It's enough just to want. I want.

How important is it to have an egg donor of similar:

...race?

Not important.

...religion?

Not important.

Lyle calls me at work a couple days later to see how I'm getting along.

"Almost finished."

"Precipitous," he says. "Why don't you drop it off at the Capitol Suites on your way home from work?"

"Oh. That's only a couple blocks."

"Mmm-hmm."

"I didn't realize you were staying so close."

"Well, I figured for the next week or so, why not? There's another couple I'm talking to over by Lincoln Park."

This throws me off a little. Lincoln Park is a 10-minute walk from my apartment. It's almost inconceivably near. If Lyle has clients there, why not Stanton Park? Why not the waterfront or Logan Circle or Happy Valley? And suddenly it's almost too overwhelming to contemplate, this chain of underground parents circling and cinching the District, one link invisible to the next. We pass each other, probably, in the Safeway aisles. We stand in line at the Department of Motor Vehicles, never guessing the fraternity in which we're enrolled.

So it's a surprise to walk into the lobby of Capitol Suites, with its cantilevered green overhang, to find Lyle alone, sitting on a red-and-gold sofa with his feet on a stars-and-stripes ottoman. In his patched Harris tweed jacket and his open-collared peach oxford, he reminds me of those retired bureaucrats who sit in cafés every morning at 10 reading three newspapers. Except what Lyle has in his lap isn't a paper; it's a miniature photo album bound in purple cellophane. He proffers it to me like a box of cashews.

"My wombs," he says.

"I'm sorry?"

"Gestational surrogates. Here, sit."

I check first to make sure no one is watching—I feel exactly like someone about to be fellated—and then I fold myself into the sofa, lowering my head to its horizon. Lyle leans toward me with the insinuation of a hypnotist; his stubby thumb worms through the laminated sheets.

"I've worked with all these girls at one point or another," he says.

At first I watch from a clinical distance, but before I know it, I'm bending forward, and my brain, my eyes, all my senses are feasting on Lyle's surrogates. Beguiling women: fully clothed and half-smiling. For a professional photographer, perhaps, they would have composed themselves, but in the presence of Lyle's Polaroid Instamatic, they sprawl like 19th-century courtesans. And the names scribbled under their pictures sound like nothing more than confections. Do you want me to be Tami? I'll be Tami.

"You'll note the wide variety of body types," Lyle is saying. "People always talk about the so-called breeding hips, but I've always felt it's the size of the cervix that really matters. Often you will find rather large girls who end up needing C-sections, and conversely, these...these *birds* with cervices the size of manholes, no pun intended. You never can tell. Take Janie..."

His index finger comes to rest on a dark, erect, reedy woman with harsh protruding cheekbones and a mouth set puckishly to one side. Her hands are latticed protectively in front of her pelvis.

"This is the womb I have in mind for you," Lyle says.

And just then, Janie starts changing scale on me. I could swear she's actually shrinking on the page—I have to squint to get her back in sight.

"She's from Woodbridge, works in security at JCPenney. Very hardy. Runs half-marathons when she's not gestating."

"Uh-huh."

"A real workhorse. Drops the baby, calls a month later to ask when the next one's coming."

"Wow. She seems kind of young, Lyle."

"Well, yes, she would. I never work with girls over 30. In fact, I find that college girls are usually the ones best suited to the work. For a variety of reasons."

The photo album is sagging open like a broken jaw, and Lyle is watching me, and so are all the members of Congress whose faces line the walls of the lobby.

"Well, anyway, this is just for giggles," Lyle says and slams the album shut. A small protest of dust flies to the ceiling. "Where we *really* want to spend our time is finding your egg donor. Because the GS—you know this already—the GS is just the vessel, but the *donor*. I mean, that lucky gal is going to be contributing half of your child's genetic material. So you really can't be too choosy."

He presses his hands prayerfully against his mouth.

"Now what I'm going to do is review your materials, get a better sense of who Nick Broome is. And then I will start putting out feelers for a donor. What I do is I make some preliminary calls, and once I get a good vibe from someone—and I may even have two or three candidates by then—what I do is I get back in touch with you, and we review the qualifications. Does that sound like a plan?"

It does sound like a plan; what kind of a plan I can't be sure. But the onlooking members of Congress seem to approve, and Lyle approves, so what can I say? I say sure. Sure, Lyle.

He shakes my hand, pats me on the shoulder. "There's a good fella," he says.

And that very night, he calls me at home. "Nick, I was just going over your application, and I wanted to make sure I got one part right. You mentioned tennis as a hobby."

"I play sometimes."

"Very well, you *play*. Do you also watch?"

"Um, sometimes."

"So would it be important, the athleticism? Is that something you'd like to see in a donor?"

"I guess. Only because it would mean they're healthy."

"Very good," he says. "Thanks very much."

The next day he calls me at work a little after 2, just as my boss is heading down to the floor to defend grain subsidies.

"Nick, I was noticing that your father is a man of the cloth."

"Yes."

"So, religious affiliation: Is that an issue for you?"

"No, I think I put that down. It doesn't—"

"Oh, you put it *down*. But I find it's helpful...only because there's a gap sometimes between what people *think* they should say and what they...and since it's not my business to pass judgment—"

"No, I really don't care about that stuff."

"Very good," he says. "Very good."

He calls me twice more over the next two days, and always there's that quick brightening of the voice just as the conversation is coming to an end. "Very good. Excellent." A reflexive retail inflection, and the more I think about it, the more I realize he *is* in retail. And so it all begins to make sense, or a close approximation of sense, and I find myself gradually welcoming the calls, the way perhaps a bride looks forward to hearing from her wedding planner. And after a week I begin initiating the calls—trying him the first few times on his cell phone and then just ringing him directly at his Capitol Suites room. Almost always he picks up on the first ring. He's the 24-hour matchmaker, and his voice gives off a thrum of industrial energy, and I marvel that all this horsepower is being expended on my behalf. I'm not sure I can contain it all. There are moments when even his voice is too much for me—the dark, grainy timbre, the rinsed vowels—I have to pull the receiver away just to give myself space.

And there are moments too, when the voice cools and compresses into my brain, and I could be talking to myself. It doesn't matter where I am—alone at home, sitting in my dingy work cubicle, surrounded by colleagues who are more or less doing the business of the American people—when I'm talking to Lyle, every trace of self-consciousness slips away, and I can talk about anything.

"Lyle, what if the first embryo doesn't take?"

"Oh, you see, you and your egg donor would fertilize several embryos at the same time. And the ones that aren't transferred to your GS are simply frozen and then, if necessary, we transfer them at a later time. Very simple."

"And would the egg donor in any way be connected to the GS?"

"No, once the eggs are fertilized, you generally don't see the donor again. Which I have to tell you is better that way—for everyone, trust me."

Hearing Lyle's voice in these contexts is almost the same as seeing him: We could be back in that tassel-curtained lobby, leafing through wombs. And when the weather's fine, we really do see each other—we meet for lunch on the southwest side of the Capitol. We lay our sandwiches on the same stone bench where I used to read Tolstoy, and as I watch Lyle rip apart his scallion-scented chicken-salad sandwich, it occurs to me he might fit very well into Natasha's world. With the slightest reconfiguration, he could be falling out long-distance with Napoleon, hanging with serfs, bearing children even. Plump, prosperous children like the ones passing us now, bused and airlifted from every state and every land for three days of mandatory history, their hands shoved in their pockets, their heads encased in quilted hoods. Lyle and I make no more imprint on them than a pair of Corinthian capitals. A tray of clouds has appeared from nowhere, and the air has turned cold and damp, and the leaves on the Capitol lawn are the color of scabs.

Lyle says, "You're a homosexual is my guess."

The thing is I've been waiting for this, and even so, it catches me off-guard. I give him the quickest of glances, just to make sure his face is in line with his voice.

"Would it make a difference?" I ask.

"No, I think it's delightful." He arches his back luxuriantly. "It gives you leverage, Nick. Listen to me, any heterosexual can be a dad...squirt squirt, done...but *you*, you have to come to people like me, which is to say you exercise choice, which is the same as power. Once we take sexual attraction out of the equation, we become *powerful.* Women know this. They're the gatekeepers, they know."

He's so convinced, I hate to contradict him. But increasingly, it strikes me that this power he is referring to is just a bewildering array of options: an entire universe of women subject to no classifying principle but Lyle Kibbee's black-eyed squint. Whereas sex is the ultimate in gatekeepers. I mean, sex enters the picture, and for those few minutes (months, years) no one else need apply. So that if Joe Bryant, for instance, could have children, Joe Bryant would be the person I had children with. And wouldn't we all be better off in the end—or at least less tired? Just Joe and me and our bundle of DNA—our very own nativity scene.

But, of course, even if Joe could have kids, would he? Honestly, would he? The signs aren't good. He's 30, his primary mode of transportation is a Schwinn, he hasn't balanced his checkbook in two years, and his main career objective is to quit whatever job he's in. All of which makes him, in Washington, a nice change of pace, but dad material? Is he dad material?

So here I am again, vetting a boyfriend for parental potential and flunking him and wondering if maybe I'm setting the bar too high. Would I even pass my own test? I'm still a renter. My car is 12 years old. I have no grand career plan. My salary has been stuck in the middle 30s for as long as I can remember. I have next to no disposable income. What could I possibly offer you, my child?

Only the certainty that you are wanted. I want you more each day. I want you like oxygen. And the wanting only gets worse the less I speak of you; it wrenches everything else out of alignment. I find myself doing strange things, like going to the movies with Joe and then deciding I can't afford to go to the movies. We're standing there right on the theater's threshold, and I'm shying like a colt.

"Maybe we can come back for the cheap show," I say.

And Joe, who has less money than I do, says: "Honey, you knew how much movies cost before we left the house."

"Oh, well, it's..." I fling my hands in the air. "Christmas is coming...."

And maybe that's not very convincing, but it's got to sound better than saying I owe thousands and thousands of dollars to two women I haven't met yet. And even leaving that aside, even leaving aside Lyle's finder fees, what about the expenses to come? Rattle toys and teething rings and spill cups and those troikas people use to ferry their children around Capitol Hill. I could hawk everything I own and still not have enough for the high chair.

My thrift unfortunately expresses itself not in budgets but in spasms. I'm the type who blows 50 bucks on dinner and then balks at dessert. I spend 80 bucks to see a touring musical at the Kennedy Center, but I won't give a dime to their parking overlords, so Joe and I end up hustling 10 blocks and sprinting across a highway just to make the opening curtain, and as I listen to him puffing along beside me, I want so much to explain.

For God's sake, there's a reason! There's a reason I'm such a mess!

But I can't. Or at any rate I don't.

And what makes it worse, really, is the nagging suspicion that he's got something under wraps too. He's coming very slowly to a decision that I won't know about until long after it's been carried out. I can feel that restlessness working through his system, the itch to be gone. He says he wants to volunteer for a gubernatorial campaign in New Hampshire. He wants to spend the winter in Lisbon, ride bikes in the Canadian Rockies, pick apples in Oregon, fly beef from Argentina. Fantasies, sure, I could blow holes through most of them, but there's no getting around the pronoun, the *I* that gets attached to them.

When I was a kid, I used to hew very closely to my parents whenever we were in public places. I was convinced they were just waiting for a large enough crowd to make their break. And when I wasn't tracking them, I was making contingency plans for the moment when they did finally shake us. I figured Greg would have to get a job, and I would do the cooking, and Celia would keep the house clean, and in retrospect the setup has a romantic quality, but I remember feeling very hard and pragmatic at the time. I was going to be a survivor.

And it's that same feeling I get some nights with Joe, lying in bed with him, monitoring his breathing. *When is he going to bolt?* I'm steeling myself in advance; I'm already reassigning his functions. Because I could get George to rub my feet, if I begged, and when I need colorful language, I can always call Shannon, and Celia's good for dumb jokes—she E-mails three every day—and my parents enjoy the occasional movie. And the sex...the sex is easy to get, isn't it? If you're very determined?

Oh, I could get by. I just don't want to. And I could keep closer tabs on him, but he's much more elusive than my parents ever were. He has his job, his friends—all these crowded places I can't follow him into. And even when he reemerges, he's often slightly, momentarily altered. It's most noticeable, I suppose, after one of his monthly cocaine salons. I don't usually see him until the next morning, and still I can't get over the change. It's not the hangover symptoms; it's him. He explained it once. "When you're doing coke," he told me, "you feel like a rock star. The next morning you're a rock star who hasn't cut an album in six years."

I'm never judgmental about this stuff—minister's sons tend to bend over backward that way—but I still feel a little seed of resentment sprouting inside me. Who asked him to be a rock star anyway? Who *needs* rock stars?

It all comes to a head when I least expect it: on a Saturday morning in November, two weeks before Thanksgiving. A strange Scottish sort of morning, with lowering clouds and strands of rain, and shining through it all, the yellow leaves of a birch tree on the northern side of my courtyard. Joe has just staggered back from Xando with a wet latte grande, and he has the usual symptoms: He's rubbing his face, wiping his nose, complaining about his allergies. He's shuffling across the living-room floor in topsiders that are two sizes too big—they're mine. He's tugging at an oatmeal-green V-neck sweater—mine. It's a safe bet he's wearing my underwear and my socks too. It's the way he is, that's all, so why am I pissed off? I wait for it to pass, but it won't, and then I watch Joe pulling down the neck of his sweater—*my* sweater—and a good six inches of skin peeps out, and normally his skin is a good thing to look at, but this morning it's not.

"You went out like that?"

Joe drags his eyes open. "Like what?"

"You just, you threw that sweater on. That *wool* sweater."

"Yeah."

"With nothing underneath."

"Uh. Yeah."

I'm sitting on the arm of the sofa to calm myself. "See, the thing with wool sweaters is you're supposed to wear something *under* them. You know that scratchy feeling you get? That's your sweater talking to you. It's saying 'Joe, please wear something. Under me.' "

"Wow," he says. "I had not fully appreciated the, the capacity for speech in a sweater."

I press my palms to my forehead. "No, what it is, it's this cavalier thing you have with my things. You wear my sweater, and wearing my sweater comes with certain rules."

"Rules."

"It's the same when you use my tennis balls; it means you give them back to me when you're done. You don't take them back to your place and throw them out. For example."

Joe sets his coffee on the kitchen counter. "Gee, I'm glad you haven't filed charges on me, Nick. 'Cause, you know, a lesser man probably woulda."

"Yeah, OK, this is what happens. I ask you to behave like a grown-up and you, you *run* in the opposite direction."

And then he does something. He flares his shoulders back as though he's shrugging off a coat. And I think: *That's not his. He stole it from the Actor. The Actor used to do the very same thing when we were fighting.* I'd always assumed he picked it up in a high school production of *Grease*, and now it turns out to be more universal than *Grease.*

"Anything else?" Joe asks.

"I'm...give me time."

"'Cause I was just gonna suggest maybe check with your buddy, see if he's got some other issues we should discuss."

"My buddy?"

Joe jabs his chin at me. "Yeah, I don't know his name? 'Cause every time he calls? You keep saying, 'Call you back, call you back.' You know, you might think about—"

"Joe."

"—bein' more *discreet*, you know, the next time."

"Joe, it's not that. Christ."

"Not what?"

"It's not bad. It's not a bad thing."

He's frozen on the living-room rug, with those extravagantly cocked shoulders, and I'm sitting on the arm of the couch wondering how I let the high ground get away.

"This is a guy," I say. "He's helping me find a surrogate mother, he's just...a *broker*, and he finds these mothers for you, and it's his job, and his name is Lyle."

I know it should be a relief, opening the window like this. But all it does is make me suddenly, preternaturally conscious of everything: an old *Smithsonian* magazine on the coffee table, the birch tree in the courtyard outside, the stubble on Joe's jaw as he sits next to me.

"So there's some reason you couldn't tell me this?" he asks.

"I don't know. It's not that easy. You know, it's...this is my *thing*, it's my *project*. I didn't think you'd approve."

"Well..." He lets out a small cloud of air. "How could you know unless you told me?" Then he pauses, and even without looking at him, I feel the barometric pressure dropping. "Unless maybe," he says.

"Maybe what?"

"Maybe I'm just not part of the calculations here."

"OK, now? I have no idea what you're talking about."

I start walking for the kitchen, but Joe calls after me. "Oh, see, to me it kinda makes sense. You don't tell me about the kid 'cause I don't fit into that. I'm just, I'm the trailer, right? You're waitin' for the main feature."

"God, this is—"

"Well, OK."

"*This* is—"

"Tell me I'm wrong, Nick. Tell me. You see *me* in your life, you see a *kid* in your life. The both of us, that's how you see it."

I wouldn't have believed he could become so lucid this quickly.

"All right, Joe, what do *you* see? Do you see yourself, do you honestly *see* yourself as a dad? You think you're ready for that?"

"I might be."

"So...so that means what? You stop bringing home nickel bags? You get a job that lasts more than six months? Hey, while you're at it, buy your own car!"

His mouth screws upward.

"You know," he says, "I don't think I need you lecturing me on what it means to be an adult. I got a mama does that for me, so I don't need you."

"Fine. Then go be *her* child. 'Cause I can't afford two."

Amazing how quickly it happens—like a wind shear. We're actually rocking on our feet. Joe's face goes hard. Slowly, very slowly, he peels my sweater off his back. He yanks the door open, stands on the threshold, tawny and bare-chested, like a jeans model. Then he kicks my shoes off his feet. They bounce off the couch onto the floor.

"Let me know if I forgot anything else," he says.

He's gone before I can move.

Ten minutes later I find his coffee sitting on the counter. It takes me another hour to pour it down the sink. It takes much longer to shake the vision from my head. The vision of Joe Bryant—topless, shoeless—navigating our city, hopping into taxis and Metro cars, leaping over grates. Doesn't he want to put something on? Doesn't he know winter's coming?

eighteen

He doesn't disappear—not at first. Habit drags him back a few more evenings but only after I've gone to sleep and only a certain distance into the apartment. Most mornings I find him sleeping on the living-room sofa. Unlike me, he never wakes up with its plaid pattern stamped onto his face, but then there's nothing else on his face either. I peer into his hard proletarian mask, and I realize I have become somebody's job—which is not so bad until I remember how Joe feels about jobs.

We exchange maybe 10 words a day, and even that is a form of labor. We leave the stereo and TV off. We sit on opposite ends of the couch, and when one of us leaves the apartment the other says, "Bye," without raising his head. It's all very deeply ritualized; we might have been carrying on like this for years.

And then one night he doesn't even make it through the front door. The couch is empty the next morning, and when I come back from work the following evening, virtually every trace of him has vanished: the address book, the colander, the extra pairs of underwear on the hall table, the bong named Heathcliff. The only thing he's left behind is a robustly pink ceramic piggy bank purchased by his mother at an estate sale 20 years ago. Just above the pipe-cleaner tail is the dedication he scrawled on the occasion of our two-month anniversary: *To Snookie Pie, For Rainy Days. Love, Stinky.*

The bank was empty when I got it, and I'd be surprised if it's accumulated more than two dollars since. A little coffee change from Joe, extra pennies from me: enough, apparently, to give Joe the sense of having a joint IRA. He would shake the thing sometimes when he was restless. "Where's it gonna take us, Snooks? New Zealand? Where's the pig going to take us?"

In his mind he was always on the move, and so as soon as I see the piggy bank resting on the kitchen counter, I figure he's made good on his promises. And when I call his bar, I'm not at all surprised to learn he's given his notice.

"Quebec," says the guy who's taken his shift. "Some seasonal gig at the Chateau de Frontenac."

Which sounds about as plausible as New Zealand, but I don't doubt that he's gone somewhere on the way to somewhere else—even if it's just around the corner.

Over the next few days, I must touch that piggy bank about 10 times a day—a quick referential tap the first few times and then a longer planing motion and then a simple landing and resting. I leave my hand there for so long, sometimes I expect to pull off great swatches of pink.

"Ceels."

"Nicky! How are you?"

"I'm...why do you ask?"

"Oh, no...I was..."

"I just wanted you to know, there's this trial separation thing going on. Between Joe and me."

"Oh, Nicky."

"Everything's fine, I just wanted you to know. I mean, it's *fine*."

"Oh, I'm sorry."

"No, Ceels. I was thinking it works out well because over the holidays we could be like the Misery Twins. Making, you know, bitter remarks every five minutes or so and wearing everyone down until they're just, they're staring into the cranberry sauce because we're *siphoning* the oxygen from the room. It could be fun...."

"Oh."

"What?"

"No, the thing is we've gotten back together. Me and Larry."

"Oh."

"A couple of days ago."

"Wow."

"I know, Nicky, it's...the timing is..."

"No, congratulations. I mean, how did it..."

"Well, it turns out he was joking. When he talked about not wanting kids? No, he wasn't joking. What it was: He thought *I* didn't want kids. Because we never discussed them, and I would always get very, very *quiet* whenever I was around them. So he thought I didn't want them, and so his saying what he said was his way of saying that was OK, he was OK with that."

"Even though..."

"Even though he's perfectly *OK* with kids. Someday. If that's what we decide we want to do. You know, it's an option, whenever we're ready."

"Well, good. That's good."

"I know."

"No, Ceels, it's *good*."

"I know, I know. I just...I would have loved to be your Misery Twin. I would have been honored."

I tell the rest of the family that Joe has gone home for Thanksgiving. Celia doesn't openly contradict me, but a giveaway gloom infects her at the dining-room table whenever she looks at me for too long. At one point Dad is sounding off about his most recent stop-smoking letter—"The energy is definitely tapering off, Nick. I'll show it to you, there's a very clear muting effect"—and he casually suggests showing the collected correspondence to Joe. "Joe hasn't seen them yet, has he?" And at that moment, Celia's pity actually congests in my head, trickles down to my bronchial tubes.

She's upset, I know: She thinks I'm alone in the world. She doesn't know I have Lyle—in multiple media. As soon as he found out government employees can receive E-mail from civilians, he began firing off three, four messages a day, and not only are they getting longer, they're beginning to acquire a perverse gravitas.

Nick, until just a few centuries ago, did you know, it was commonly believed that men alone were responsible for procreation? The assumption being that the woman was simply a receptacle for the man's seed.

Now the discovery that women in fact contributed to this process...and no one has seen fit to comment on this...coincided almost exactly with the onset of the Industrial Revolution. And so their effects have been conflated. When in fact what broke down the male animal was not the machine, it was realizing he had to share responsibility for life. By which discovery we became the equivalent of half-men, a condition that persists to this day, God help us all. :)

He CC's everything to himself. Ten, 20 hours may pass between messages, but they each pick up where the last one left off, and when I reassemble them in my head, they form a continuous harangue.

And once they were onto chromosomes, forget it. It's so clear. XX, that's women; XY, that's us. The letters refer directly to the chromosomal structure, do you see where this is going? The Y is A MUTILATED X. Missing a crossbar. How do we get back our crossbar? By reclaiming control of the reproductive process. We buy the eggs FROM the woman. We control the destiny of those eggs. We reclaim our authority. Whole men! :)

It has sequence, it has surface coherence, it has emoticons, and so I can't directly compare it to Nattie's messages, but there's enough resemblance to give me pause. It seems every time I usher away one eccentric, another comes hammering on the back door, and so I'm forced to ask: Is it traveling down an alternative road that leads you to these people, or am I just a lint brush, snarling off the loose fibers of the world?

I make a mental note to ask Shannon what she thinks, but when I next see her, she's too full of epiphany. She has just returned from visiting her father in New York ("He used to make me shave the back of his neck, did I tell you that?") and on the Metroliner home, she sat next to a woman who had, like Shannon, missed her weekly Al-Anon meeting.

"So we had our own meeting, Nick. Just the two of us, on the train. Best one I've ever been to. In fact, honestly, it kind of invalidated the whole notion of regular meetings. Oh, wait, I have to tell you."

"Yes?"

"You're *not* still thinking about surrogacy, are you?"

We're patrolling the aisles of Blockbuster, the one that squats with an indecent brightness next to the fire station on 8th Street, and we're staring at the new-release titles that were new two years ago, and until this moment, I was feeling very cocooned. I was assuming it would take her the rest of the evening to get to my business.

"It's possible," I say.

"Well, all I can tell you is do *not* do that egg-donor thing."

"I'm curious. I'm curious why you say that."

"Oh, please." She jabs me with her elbow. "It's completely barbaric— no, not that movie, I hate Gwyneth—did you read the article?"

"What article?"

"The article I was reading on the train, next to the Al-Anon woman, which tells all about what happens. With these 19, 20-year-old girls who can't afford college. They sign themselves up." Her eyes widen like a campfire raconteur. "The doctors induce premature menopause— 20-year-old girls, Nick, having hot flashes—no, I hate Julia too—and then the doctors inject them with *more* stuff, swing them the other way so their ovaries are, like, the size of basketballs.

And then comes the little suction tube up the wazoo, *sucks* the eggs right out."

I can't prove it, but I do believe everyone in the store is edging away from us. I believe fathers are shaking their heads, mothers are clapping their hands over their daughters' ears, and the cumulative body of judgment is too much for me. I duck into the horror section and stare at a row of Roger Corman movies.

"Well, it's not like they could *lay* the eggs," I say finally. "Like in a twig nest."

"Nick, this is institutionalized, medicalized rape."

"They're adults, Shannon. They volunteer. No one ties them to the bed, no one, no one *yanks* out their ovaries...."

"Oh, well, let's not even get into the volition thing. I mean, we can't even go there."

Against her better judgment we take home a Vincent Price movie, but we never get around to watching it. We just slip into a long, indeterminate stretch of VH1, something about dead teen idols. An hour into it, Shannon asks how Joe is doing, and I'm distracted enough not to bother with a plausible lie.

"He's doing a job up in Quebec," I say.

And even as the words come out, I'm aware that this is how one speaks of contract killers. Does Lyle speak this way? Does he talk about "doing a job down in DC"? Is he chomping on a Havana cigar as he says it? I end up having to call him just to dispel the picture. As usual I find him in his Capitol Suites room, sounding almost giddily lucid, as though he's been swigging mouthwash from a paper bag.

"Nicholas! To what do I owe this very distinct pleasure?"

"Lyle, I've been...I've been thinking stuff through, and I really need to talk to you about this egg-donor business. Because I'm just a little concerned...."

"I can't believe this."

"What?"

"The psychic connection is extraordinary. I was just about to call you."

"Oh, you were?"

"Nick, listen to me. I've found a donor!"

"You've..."

"Now don't go nutsy on me. We've had some preliminary discussions, and from all I can tell, from my considered professional judgment, it looks like a fit. But we won't know until we schedule a meeting. Because the two of you must talk, yes? Now, it's my experience that the first meetings are usually quite brief—a minute tops—because we know immediately, don't we? It's like love, Nick. Are you ready to be in love?"

Her name is Bathsheba.

Twenty-eight. Five feet six, 135 pounds. Healthy, active nonsmoker. Hails from Baptist stock in Detroit. No siblings. Mother: homemaker. Father: auto worker, union organizer. Came to D.C. ten years ago, got her JD from Georgetown Law. Recruited by prestigious K Street firm, partner track, left shortly after having her son, citing firm's failure to accommodate reduced schedule. (Currently in litigation with firm over back pay.) Working now in day care but eager to reenter the legal community, perhaps in nonprofit advocacy sector. Interests: opera, cooking, social justice.

"Very devoted to her son," Lyle tells me. "Recently divorced the father, so she is single, but that's less of a concern with a donor. It's the single *wombs* you have to worry about."

"Uh-huh."

"Now she's older than I usually go for, but she's still within bounds. And having met her, Nick—we had coffee last night, delightful time—she definitely possesses what I call the fertility aura. Which I know sounds mystical, but I'm rarely wrong about these things. Now I asked her when we could meet, and she said the best time would be weekdays, around lunchtime. So how does tomorrow look for you?"

"Tomorrow."

"You could always call in sick or, I don't know, doctor's appointment? How do the feds do it? You should probably allow for two hours max, but most of that's travel time. She wants to meet in Malcolm X Park."

"Oh, right."

"The upper tier. Now I have an appointment just prior, so maybe you could meet me there? Around 1:00?"

"One. OK."

"I don't want to make any promises, Nick, but I will say I have a good feeling, and I'll leave it at that. Oh, by the way. You've probably guessed already...."

"What?"

"The Biblical name."

"She's religious?"

"African-American, Nick, to use current parlance, which I felt sure would not be—"

"No."

"—a *problem*, judging from—"

"Not a problem at all."

And so the next day, a little after 12:30, my car begins the long crawl up the 15th Street hill, and for once I'm not thinking about Joe. Or Lyle, for that matter, or even Bathsheba. All I'm thinking about is climbing, which, in my mind, is just a compromise between forward and back. And when I park my car on the west side of the street and cross to the other side, part of me wishes I could just keep climbing. Then I see the stairs: a set of stone steps emerging miraculously halfway down the block. I take them at a sprint, two steps in a single leap. And luck is with me because it's a long staircase; it winds through an underpass and it takes its time, and I jump over heaps of green bottle glass, my nostrils pick out the clear, sharp tang of urine. I'm climbing, and the steps are coming to an end, the sky is broadening its shoulders, and the ground is clearing on every side.

And suddenly I'm standing at the western entrance of a park. The very place I'm supposed to be.

And stretching away on either side is a great lawn, as long as a landing strip, lined with pines and magnolias and ringed by benches. For a moment I think I've been transported back to the University of Virginia, back to Jefferson's neoclassical green, but this one is different, it's *moving*...running south and hurling itself toward a stone balustrade. And beyond the balustrade the rest of Washington falls away in a swoon.

Meridian Hill.

I remember now. Before anyone called it Malcolm X, they called it Meridian Hill. They still do. And that was Jefferson's doing too, wasn't it? Jefferson decided that the Earth's prime meridian passed through this point, and who were we to say differently?

And what better place? What better place to meet the mother of your child? You stand here on a warmish day in autumn. Unemployed men, cut free of time, loll in baggy T-shirts. A 30-something office worker strolls through the grass with her eyes shut. An old janitor slumps under an oak tree, and a green-shorted albino jogger bounds down the concrete walkways.

And children. Pods and pods of children, whirling and ungoverned, bouncing rubber balls, hopscotching, running away from harassed-looking adults in jumpers: a great chain reaction of children.

And seeing them moves something in me, shakes me out of my reverie, and I walk again, tracing a slow line around the park's northern perimeter. I don't feel hurried at all. There's time. There's time for the kids from the multicultural middle school, taking angry drags from cigarettes. Time for the finches and the grass and the bare saplings in their mulched pedestals, noisy with crows. I move through it all at my leisure, knowing, of course, at some point I'll have to stop moving. But what surprises me is how soon it happens. Halfway through my loop, my eyes swerve east and lock onto Lyle Kibbee.

"Thought you were going to walk right by us," he says.

He's sitting on a bench, his fingers curled like spiders on his knees. My face must be an utter blank, because he gestures with melodramatic furtiveness toward the woman on his left. It's such a harsh jabbing motion I half-expect the woman to pull away—I'm pulling away myself—but she doesn't appear to notice. She sits erect as an equestrian, staring across the common. A handsome, short-cropped woman in a great woolen shawl, with a dyed straw bag resting against her ankle.

"Have a seat, Nick." Lyle pats the area of bench to his right. But as soon as I sit, I realize he's blocking me, and the only thing that gives me a shot at Bathsheba is my height, which allows me to peer *over* Lyle's head and absorb her in installments. First the shawl, with its browns and yellows and deep reds. Then an ear, small, vestigial, sketched in almost as an afterthought. And then the head itself, a naked prow.

"Nicholas Broome, this is Bathsheba Williams."

"How do you do?" she says. She doesn't turn, not an inch. Just vibrates a little, a low vibration that swells up from her rib cage, spills through her throat and mouth. Thrilling.

"I'm fine, thank you," I say.

And Lyle says, "I'm so glad we were able to do this."

Nobody answers, so he releases a long sigh of contentment, as though words weren't necessary. He lays a soft hand on Bathsheba's shoulder. "You know, Nicholas actually grew up in this area."

"Oh, yes?" she says.

"Which I think is so interesting. Only because the population here, being so transient..."

"Mmm-hmm," she says.

Her gaze is locked straight ahead, and I have to wonder if there's something out there on the grass transfixing her, but all I see are a mother and three kids, tossing a tennis ball, and a shaven-headed black man with his head in his hands talking to himself. And right now I'm wishing I were back with the Actor because *he* could do this; he could impersonate someone who could talk to a woman on a bench in a park.

"My brother," I say, "works not far from here."

"Oh?" says Bathsheba.

"He works for a clinic. Clinica Columbia—maybe three blocks from here."

"He's a doctor?"

"Very dedicated, very long hours. Always stays at least an hour longer than everybody else."

Who would have thought I'd be using my brother to score points with a woman? My brother, least of all. Of course, Greg would be the first to question this whole business. He would ask why I needed to score points in the first place. He would wonder why Lyle wasn't asserting my authority or *his*, or something. Something should be changing.

My eyes strain once again to find Bathsheba. "You work in day care, I understand."

And now, for the first time she turns to me, in a glacial, stylized sequence, her head wheeling by degrees, rising and falling in what I take to be a confirmation.

"There's this center," she says, "where I used to leave my son. Rainbow Room Day Care. They had a position open."

"Oh!" Lyle cries. "Is that them over there?"

At the southern end of the common, a taut, pigtailed woman is bellowing through a megaphone at a ring of pasty children. "If you love Jesus and you know it," she sings, "clap your hands."

"No," says Bathsheba. "That's someplace else."

And already she is turning away from us, wheeling her face back toward the green in that same oiled motion. And as I watch, her lips slowly pry themselves apart. A sliver of gum emerges and then three large upper teeth.

Behind us a car engine strains up the hill. A park ranger roars down the sidewalk in a Ford van, and a young boy with a basketball runs in the opposite direction, screaming, "Ah, ah, ah."

"Nick works in Congress," Lyle says.

"You mentioned that," Bathsheba says.

"Correct me, Nick, if I'm, if I'm putting words in your…but it occurred to me you might be of use in Bathsheba's job search."

"Um."

"People you know, perhaps. Well-placed individuals who could really use someone with Bathsheba's skill set."

Once again it steals over me, that feeling I had with Lupe and José, that sense of being almost criminally overrated.

"I could do some checking on that, sure."

Lyle looks at me for a moment, then shrugs. Either he's disappointed with my response, or he's already forgotten what we were talking about. He laces his arms behind his head and lets his legs slide out on the pavement. Through his feet, I see a splash of Aramaic symbols.

"Lovely day," he drawls. "Wouldn't...winter..."

"And dear Lord," croons the voice on the megaphone. "Thank you for the punch and the cookies...."

A minute. That's what Lyle said. It would take no more than a minute, and I'd know, and it would all be clear.

So maybe this is one of those decisions that becomes clear only in retrospect. Maybe the thing to do is to store every impression as it comes, on the expectation that I will have to recall it later. Thirty or 40 years from now, they will quiz me, and I will have to remember the man in the grass and the sun squirreling itself behind a cloud and the scraping of wooden slats against my back.

And I'm working so hard to commit it all to memory, I almost don't hear the high, labored sound just to my left. It's Lyle, clearing his throat.

"Now, Miss Bathsheba, I think what Nick would like to hear...and Nick, correct me if I'm...specifically, what is it that *appeals* to you about being an egg donor?"

Her head doesn't move. Just a tiny flurry around her jaw, and even this is enough to make me notice, for the first time, the white whorl of a scar floating across her cheek.

"And how much," Lyle continues, "how *much* you would enjoy providing eggs to somebody as suitable and deserving as Nicholas here."

She studies her hands. Her jaw makes another tiny revolution.

"Well, you see, what I've been doing is examining certain options. And in terms of options, this has a certain...it leaves me free to pursue other options."

Lyle rears back. He cups a hand mockingly to his ear.

"Hoo! That's not very ringing, is it? Nick, would you call that a ringing endorsement?" His voice ratchets upward into a frequency I've never heard before. "As my late mother used to say, 'You're gonna have to do better than that, missy!'"

A ripple passes through the wide column of Bathsheba's neck. She compresses her lips.

"I want very much to help people realize their dreams," she says.

And at this point I'm not thinking how unnatural Lyle's words sound on somebody else's lips, or how unnatural they would sound even on *his* lips. All I'm seeing are Lyle's references, the book of testimonials he sent me home with after our first meeting. Affidavit upon affidavit...and not one from a surrogate. And if there was one thing Lyle's references kept bringing up, it was how firm he was with his surrogates.

Our GS started giving us trouble, but Lyle brought her in line...

Lyle impressed on her...didn't stand for nonsense...

Took her into the other room, we have no idea what he told her, but she never said boo again....

Amazing, really, to think of Lyle having that kind of sway over anyone. But then you have to do something, don't you? You have to do something, or something has to happen to you before Lyle can enter your world.

"And Nick, maybe there's something you'd like to say to Bathsheba?"

But when I look up, Bathsheba isn't looking at me, and neither is Lyle, and no one seems to be expecting much of anything from me. And so we sit there: me and the mother of my child and our black-bearded chaperone. Sharing a single bench, a single purpose...a family in the making.

Are you ready to be in love, Nick?

I turn once more to Bathsheba, and I find her bent almost double. From the chamber of her chest this *sound* is emerging. Laughter. Big, scratchy, raucous laughter, so different from her speaking voice, so large and vulgar I expect all the pedestrians in Meridian Hill Park to stop what they're doing and pay attention. But this is the city, after all, and so the only one paying attention is Lyle, who is on his feet, dancing around Bathsheba like a beagle.

"Oh, she's not well!" he's crying.

"Lyle," I say.

"Is it the heat, Miss Bathsheba?" He's calling to her as though from a great distance, and the sound of his voice only adds to her hysteria. Before long, hiccups wrench her frame, and the hiccups are only another source of comedy, until finally she is nothing but laughter, a gale of laughter, washing in waves down the green, over the balustrade, all the way to the Potomac River.

And the woman on the megaphone is at last concluding her prayer—"In Jesus' name, amen"—and Lyle is still dancing, a mad, fluttering dance, and I could almost believe it's Bathsheba's laughter jerking his arms, sparking his feet into jigs. And he's speaking the whole time rather calmly, saying things like: "Oh, it's very warm for this time of year. All these *vapors* are coming up from the earth. Is it vapors, Miss Bathsheba?"

I don't go home right away. I wander out of the park and down an adjoining block, and before I know it, I'm standing in front of my brother's clinic. It certainly wasn't my intention, but there's the stained brass nameplate—CLINÍCA COLUMBIA—and there's the buzzer just beneath it. The brown brick facade, with the NO LOITERING sign and the fans in the windows. Large baroque weeds poking through the sidewalk and the foundation. Potato chip bags, slashes of graffiti. And somewhere on the third floor, my brother, in the high-ceilinged room he shares with two other doctors.

I push through the oaken door. I walk the three flights of concave stone steps, and shove open another oaken door. A wave of fan-driven heat greets me. Cast-off family-room chairs and an unvarnished metal desk, and a few feet behind it, two women: one of them a plump, smooth-skinned Hispanic woman with two children in her arms balanced like grocery sacks.

"I think she need to come see you anyway," she's saying, "'cause lately she all confused? She think my granfather still livin'. He is dead six month ago, but she don't remember."

"OK," says the other woman, the slightest edge in her voice. "Bring her in tomorrow, we'll take a look."

"I don't know, tomorrow my oldest boy got tournament to go."

"As soon as you can, then."

"OK, 'cause she real confused. I mean, this person is 90 years old, so I don't know...." The rest of her thought dies away the moment she sees me hanging by the door. Her two kids swing toward me to get a better look, and the other woman whips her head around.

"Can I help you?" she asks.

My face pulses with heat.

"I'm sorry," I say. "Do you have a phone I could use?"

"Pay phone," she snaps. "Back down the stairs, turn left, and it's down the street."

But that particular phone is dead, and I have to walk another three blocks to find one that works. I dial Lyle's Capitol Suites number from memory, and the whole thing comes out in what feels like a single breath.

"Lyle, it's Nick. It's not very long after I saw you. It's maybe 15 minutes. I'm standing in a phone booth on 15th Street, and what I wanted to tell you was I don't want Bathsheba's eggs. I don't want anyone's eggs. No surrogates, no eggs. And it's not...it's not like I have other ideas, Lyle, I'm fresh out, but it's *this* idea, Lyle. That's what I can't do. Which I know won't make sense to you, and I know you've done a lot of work, so come up with what you think is an acceptable figure, and send it along, and I'll be happy to pay, OK? And thanks very much for all your time and effort. I can certainly see why you're...and if I ever run into someone with that, that *need*, you can be sure I will *happily*...so thanks. And I'm sorry, Lyle. I'm sorry it didn't work out."

When I get home, there's a message from him on my voice mail. I think it's the shortest message he's ever left me. He says, "Nobody fires Lyle Kibbee."

nineteen

That's not his last word on the subject. He E-mails me the very next day, and it's not so much an afterthought as a complete swerving of tone:

Now that I think about it, Bathsheba was not emotionally prepared to be an egg donor. I should have seen this. There is a certain emotional maturity which is called for, which of course has nothing or very little to do with age; for instance, a donor I knew in Laredo, was barely 18 and alarmingly self-possessed, the way you expect saints to be.

This seems to spark him toward a more elegiac mode, because the next few E-mails teem with memories. A surrogate mother in Wilmette who snipped her child's umbilical cord and kept it in a jar by the TV. An intended mother in Eugene, Oregon, who got spooked after dreaming she had adopted a horse.

It took all of my persuasion, Nick, to keep her from canceling the contract. But of course it wasn't persuasion; it was reminding her what was at stake, daring her to be who she was—which you can be too, Nick. All the things you are.

It's not just E-mail. He calls me at home too, when I'm least likely to be there. I come back from work and find batches of two, three, even four messages.

Nick, I was at a party last night in Glover Park. Met an acupuncturist. More later...

Heard about a Foreign Service gal just back from Colombia. Irish-Scottish, extremely intelligent...

Never mind about the Foreign Service gal—she's had her tubes tied. I'm on the case though, Nick. I'm working for you.

So it's true: You don't fire Lyle Kibbee. You can't.

It amazes me now to think that when he first blew into town, he couldn't stay more than a couple of weeks. And here it is five weeks, and the possibility presents itself that he doesn't have anywhere else to be, and in a certain sense, that's not surprising: Every freelancer has boom-and-bust cycles. What's surprising is the guilt that comes sweeping over me. I feel legally responsible for Lyle, and I keep revisiting our conversations to see if there was some covert message I should have taken away, and I wonder if maybe I should have ended things more gently or at least given it another minute's thought.

And so as the days pass I become convinced that I owe Lyle one more minute. But when I call his room at the Capitol Hill Suites, a stranger answers, and when I try the front desk, they tell me he's checked out. And so all I can conclude is that Lyle doesn't want my minute, he doesn't want me to know where he is, and this is why he has so carefully avoided direct conversation. Who knows? Right now he could be patrolling a hair salon in Richmond, an FBI training seminar in

Quantico, working his black eyes like compass needles, sniffing out that effluvium of fertility.

So Lyle is, by my count, the second person I have sent wandering into the desert. Who would have guessed I had such power? And if I do, why can't I apply it to a more practical end? Why can't I make a baby?

I have three weeks left. *Three weeks.* And I am no closer than when I started and maybe a small distance back. And here we are, entering the season of miracles, which should give me hope—life wants to happen, doesn't it? Life will do anything to make itself happen—but I think of miracles roughly the way I think of lotteries. They bless other people. They thrust their enlarged personal checks into the faces of Iowans.

So I go through the holiday motions, because what else is there? Work motions and shopping motions, card-writing and wassail-sipping motions. I take a quick lunch with Shannon, an early-music concert with George. I turn on PBS and watch English boys sing "Once in Royal David's City." I listen to my landlord explain why the holidays turn him into an anarchist when what he really means is Antichrist.

One night, my mother calls to ask if I want to join her for the annual chopping-down of the Christmas tree. And this should qualify as one more motion, but I can't quite follow through this time because I remember how last year my mother vowed never again to have a big tree. And I had assumed this meant running off to Hecht's at the last minute to get a two-footer for the coffee table, and I'm just about to suggest it when she cuts me off.

"Oh, come on," she says. "Christmas."

One thing at least will be different about this year's trip. Hoy Phong will be joining us.

"Honey, he's been dying to see a tree farm, and I want him to have this because it's incredible the progress he's made the past couple of months. The English is so much better, the interview skills. Oh, I don't think I told you."

"What?"

"Larry. Celia's Larry."

"Right."

"Is talking about hiring Hoy. As a part-time receptionist."

"Really?"

"Which couldn't come at a better time because Hoy has just met the nicest girl, very sweet, Austrian. Muesl or...*Liesl.* So it's all starting to come together for him. I can honestly say I've never seen him with this much self-esteem. He's glowing, Nick."

And maybe it's because my mother has primed me, but Hoy does have a matador's sheen as he coasts his Ford Taurus into my parents' driveway Saturday morning. He executes a grand jeté on his way out of the car, then pauses to tweeze a pair of errant leaves from under his windshield wiper. His hair has been professionally moussed into thousands of quills, and his body is laved in a rich fennel scent.

"Hoy," says my mother, "I don't know if you've met my son."

Something else is different this year: the weather. A renegade heat front has settled over the D.C. metropolitan area. It's 75 degrees when we leave the house and nearly 80 by the time we reach the tree farm in Loudoun County. The air is sappingly warm; no one has quite dressed for it. Plucky, scrubbed, Yule-dependent women bustle past in red leggings and ivy-green sweatshirts, smeared with felt and beads. They're hell-bent on celebrating Christmas, and I wonder what energy source could be powering them, and then I remember the vapors—the vapors Lyle said were rising from the earth—and suddenly it all makes sense. They've been inhaling vapors. You could scream "Give up!" until you had no voice left, and they'd still be reaching for that next Dixie cup of hot cider.

"Who's got the saw?" my mother asks.

Hoy reaches under the driver's seat and hoists a red-handled saw to the sky, like Excalibur.

"All right," Mom says. "Let's try the Scotch pines first."

But she doesn't like the look of the pines, so we make for the Douglas firs. We walk through fields of straw-grass; we step across the tiny yellow brains of sage oranges, smashed by the wheelbarrows people use to ferry back their trophies.

My mother stops in front of a strapping, conical 10-footer. "This could work," she says, and that's the only cue Hoy needs. He pulls out the saw, throws himself to the ground, and starts edging through the trunk—a clean, sweet, musical motion. In less than a minute, the fir lies docile at my mother's feet.

"I think that's the fastest one that's ever come down!" she says.

Hoy lofts the tree onto the barrow, stares at it respectfully, then makes a courtly gesture in my direction: *After you.* I pick up the barrow by its handles and drag it toward the baling machine. Within a minute rivulets of sweat are streaming down my jaw. Just ahead of us, husbands and wives—their faces damp, their mittens hanging unused from their pockets—watch trees disappear into an enormous diaphragm and reemerge in long, hairnetted bundles.

My mother has walked ahead to pay. Hoy treads serenely by my side.

"Nice of you to drive," I tell him.

"I drive all time for Emily."

Emily. For Emily.

"Well, it's nice of you to do that," I say. I'm feeling very charitable right now. Hoy is the kindest person in the world; so is everyone else.

"Oh, not me," Hoy says. "Emily afraid to drive."

"Well...no, I mean, she drives to see *you*, doesn't she? She goes once, twice a week."

"No, she walk Metro station. She take Metro. I pick her up."

If I squint, I can just make out my mother's trim, square-shouldered figure at the tail end of the cashier line. Her wallet is already out of her bag, unclasped. Her head is still and obedient. I haven't seen her drive a car in three years.

"She think she gonna die," Hoy explains. "Like when engine start. You know: Vroom, vroom, die."

It's hard to tell whether he's getting any pleasure out of this. His eyes never once cut my way.

"She send notes to your dad," Hoy says.

"Notes?"

"Smoking kill. Cigarette kill."

Just then, one of the tree's branches lodges under a wheel, and the barrow shudders to a halt, and as I lurch against it, I catch the passing incredulity in Hoy's eyes: *Emily son can't push cart.*

"My mother sends those notes?"

"*USA Today*," he says, brightly. "My neighbor got big bunch *USA Today*. That's what she use for letter. She cut up *USA Today*, plus magazine. She glue together. I mail for her."

Fifty yards ahead, my mother chooses this moment to turn. Her eyes dance through the crowd, searching for the two men who brought her here, and when she finally spots us laboring down the hill toward her, she can't restrain herself. Her hand launches toward us; the fingers waggle like a rooster comb.

I'm silent most of the way home. And not from sulking. I'm just busy overturning some assumptions, and that takes time. There's the assumption, for instance, that the family you start out with is the one you end your days with, when, in fact, families grow old and fail, just like the people in them. And if you're, say, a woman at a certain time of life, and the sons you started with are a little too distracted, too compromised, to assist you in letter-writing campaigns, why not go out and get yourself a new one?

But the thing is, Mom, I've spent the better part of a year trying to extend the Broome family, and I'm not sure I would have gone to the trouble if I'd known you were doing it on your own: acquiring Vietnamese immigrants and dentists and who knows what else? I mean, what's left for me to do?

"You know, Hoy," my mother says. "I think this is the fastest we've ever made it back from the tree farm."

It's a little after 2 when I leave my parents' house. Hoy is already wrapping strands of white light around the tree, and I think under normal circumstances I would stay to prove my worth, but I have an unscheduled stop to make. From my parents' street, I make the usual left, but instead of accelerating toward the highway, I slow down and pull onto the narrow southern shoulder and flick on my hazards. Across the road sits the "electrified house"—the sore of my father's eyes—with its rivers of Christmas light. The sun is high and bright now, so the electricity hasn't been switched on, but you can still make out some of the features the owners have added to this year's display: a gigantic pinwheel on the side of the house; overhead, a suspension bridge; in back, an electronic waterfall. In the midst of all these public works, the crèche is easy to miss—crammed between the nutcrackers and the reindeer and a little off kilter so that Mary staggers north and baby Jesus threatens to tip out of his cradle. In the naked light of day, the Holy Family looks glumly skeptical: They're wondering, maybe, if this is really the best the inn could do, and I suppose I'm wondering the same thing. Sitting in my car, I feel very tenderly toward them. I feel the same way about the people who own the house. I want to knock on their door; I want to fling myself in their arms.

See, I'm trying to make this baby....

But it doesn't look like anyone's home. The place has the grim, over-adorned emptiness peculiar to this time of year. I give them another few minutes to appear, and then I drive home.

My landlord is there to greet me. He's sitting in a beach chair in the middle of the courtyard, wearing flip-flops and a Polynesian shirt that hangs so low it's hard to be sure there's anything underneath. He's drinking what looks to be a violet mai tai.

"My special brew," he says, squinting into the sun. "I could *not* begin to tell you what's in this shit."

"That's OK. You rest."

It's when I'm reaching for the knob on the entry door that I notice the rash on my forearm: a serried formation of pink. When I touch it, I can practically feel the hive of toxins buzzing beneath the surface. Poison ivy maybe. Or just something from my mother's tree that rubbed against me when I lifted it from the cart. Who would have thought Douglas firs could be this dangerous? Only Hoy, probably. Hoy wore long sleeves and gloves.

My apartment is chokingly warm. I walk straight to the nearest window, muscle it open, and stand for a few seconds, inhaling the earth's vapors. When I turn around the first thing I see is Joe's piggy bank sitting on the end of the kitchen counter, more garishly pink than ever in the amber light. My good-luck charm. I give it a quick, dry scrub with my hands, and then I set it down again.

I lie on my couch, waiting for an idea, but the only thing that comes is sleep. It comes quickly too, and it would probably stay, but sometime before 4 P.M., the phone rings. Such a powerful sound! It slashes through the tissue of my brain and somehow *becomes* my brain so that I answer quickly and softly, the way you answer in a dream. "Hello..."

But there's just a click and a dial tone. And the anticlimax of it is too deep to ponder. I lie there for a minute with the phone resting on my collarbone, and then, more from reflex than anything else, I press the reset button...and I hear the telltale thrumming.

A message.

All this time I've been lying here, and there was a message waiting to be heard! And as I enter the coordinates, I feel that surge of hope that unheard messages always inspire in me. For the next few seconds, anything is possible. There's a sperm bank that *will* take my sperm. There's a woman who *will* bear my child.

So it's the usual surprise to hear a voice I already know.

"Hey," says Joe Bryant.

I haul myself up on the couch.

"Snookie, it's me. I'm back in town...I didn't go for long. I saw Nattie though; she says hi. Um, this is hard. I'm thinking I was a little quick on the draw, Snookie, I was...well, the way I see it is people need to have at least 10 or 20 bad fights before they seriously consider not having anymore. 'Cause that's what *adults* do, right, Snooks? So what I figure is we got *easily* 19 to go, and maybe even a couple more, so...shit...listen, I was thinking maybe I'd stop by in a few, and you know, if you want to see me, it's cool. Whatever, it's cool. So I'll see you in a bit, maybe."

I look at my watch: a quarter to 4. And he left the message...when? He didn't say. He never says. It might have been an hour ago, five hours ago. It might have been him just now calling to see if I was home.

So something should be happening. I have the groggy sense that something should be happening. The apartment should be cleaned. The toilet should be scrubbed.

But no, I cleaned, didn't I? I cleaned very recently.

And as I whirl about the apartment bustling—uselessly bustling—I hear a sound. Familiar, of course, but in the context, strange. It's the sound of someone at the door, buzzing to be let in.

And I'm so flustered I don't bother using the intercom. I already know who it is—because he's been down there for hours, probably, waiting for me.

I lean into the buzzer. I hold it down because he'll need time, he hasn't been here in a while, and that front knob can be a little tricky if you don't...push it *in* a little bit and then turn it counterclockwise and even then it sticks sometimes....

My ears strain for the sound of his footsteps on the stairs, but I don't hear anything, or I don't hear anything I can separate from the rest. But what did he do with his key? He never gave it back, and if he still has it, he could be using it now, but isn't the likeliest explanation that he lost it somewhere? Somewhere in Quebec or...or Texas....

And now I *do* hear something. Not a tread at all, but a high, steady tone—a vibratoless keening. Hypnotic, the more you listen to it, and so when the knock finally comes, it comes as an undertone to this main theme. And it's only then I realize I'm still pressing the buzzer. It's been buzzing for a full minute, and for all I know, the entire population of southeast Washington has entered the building. But I'm only interested in one of them. I have no idea what I'll say. I'm not prepared for anything, and maybe that's the best way to face him, free of plan, and so I fling the door open, and I'm glad I don't have a plan because it's not Joe at all. It's no one who even resembles Joe.

It's Lyle.

He stands on my threshold, with a manila folder pressed against his narrow chest and a smile trembling through his beard. He's wearing scuffed Timberlands and an oxford shirt—peach, of course—which he's half-tucked into a pair of rumpled khaki trousers. His voice, when it comes out, is deep and comical: the voice of a horse puppet.

"Hulloooo," he says.

I take three steps back, and Lyle takes one step in, stands just inside the door.

"I don't want to keep you, Nick. I felt sure you'd want to hear about this very promising candidate I came across yesterday, and being in the area, I thought I'd just bring over some of her materials. So please, be my guest, look these over—"

"Lyle."

"—at your convenience and let me know what you think. I should tell you I've temporarily discontinued my cell phone service, so maybe the best thing is for me to call you. Tomorrow, maybe..."

"Lyle."

"Or maybe dinner. That Greek place was very nice. Some Greek places, I find—maybe it's a function of the feta—the food tends to talk back to me...."

And he's off. There's no stopping him. All the cuisines he's sampled over the past year...Wichita Falls...Fort Wayne...startling gastrointestinal effects...the medicinal qualities of curry, unless it's the wrong kind of curry, which means you have to look for a very specific region in India, you have to ask the owners where they...

And in the face of all this language, all I can do is put out my hand, like a traffic cop.

"Lyle," I say. "I don't think...I must not have made it clear. We can't have dinner. We can't have *anything*, because I don't want a surrogate. I'm just...I'm not in the market anymore."

Smiling foggily, he crosses and recrosses his hands across his chest. "Well, Nick, if you have some concerns about the process, I'm happy to address them. Or if you'd like to talk to people who've gone through this, I'd be happy—"

"No, Lyle, I've talked to people, I've...it's me, it's *me* deciding this is not what I want."

One hand drops toward the floor, still clutching the manila folder. The other dances lightly on his chest. "Well, gosh." He clears his throat. "I'm trying to restrain, I'm trying to *curb*—"

"I'm sorry."

"—my feelings of disappointment."

"I'm sorry you feel that way."

He starts to speak, then claps his hands over his mouth. His eyebrows constrict, and for a moment I think he's getting ready to cry, but in fact, he's gathering steam.

"There's so much selfishness in this world, Nick. And I had assumed, I had *hoped* you were an exception to that, but I'm beginning to think I was mistaken." A quick pair of thumps on his chest. "I'm beginning to think that maybe you're like all the others, and the larger issues of life, by which I mean people's *sacrifices...*" Another thump. "...the *sacrifices* people make on your behalf, these have no meaning."

And now he's moving: backing away, and then circling, and gradually the circle he's making becomes an ellipse, and the ellipse flattens into a straight line, a groove in the front-room carpet.

"This isn't a consumer choice, all right? This isn't a matter of 'Oh, never mind, I don't want that mission table after all.' This is about *life*, Nick, and there are people, flesh-and-blood people out there on the front lines of reproduction, busting their, excuse me, *balls* for you so that life can happen. Life *wants* to happen."

Can it be coincidence? Can anything else explain it, the same thought striking both of us within the space of 24 hours? Not even a thought, really, an intuition. Life wants to happen. Inorganic matter, exposed to ultraviolet light, becomes organic. Primal soups of methane and ammonia burst forth with amino acids, proteins and enzymatic reactions and nucleic acids and cells. Life. *Life* wanting to happen. And this is what binds Lyle and me in our masonry, and I could almost embrace him—*brother*!—if I weren't afraid of springing the coil in him, if he weren't standing in the middle of my carpet, gazing through the walls. I'm afraid even to blow on him.

"Lyle," I say, "I think you need to go."

It's not my voice, I don't think, but something does call him back. His head jerks up. A few yellow teeth peep through the carpet of his beard; his fingers paw each other back to life.

"You know, Nick, I'm just a little short on cash today."

The room goes quiet.

"Not having had time," he says, "to get to an ATM, owing to the fact that I was rushing over here..."

A shiver runs through his throat, and he falls still—maybe the only moment of true stillness I've ever witnessed in him. It doesn't last long. From some invisible engine deep inside him, a spark flies up, and the gears start humming again.

"Maybe you could tell me," he says. "Is there an ATM nearby?"

The thing is I'm all prepared to give him directions. I'm very good at directions. It's just that for a few seconds he stops being Lyle. My eyes wander across his untucked shirt, his unlaundered trousers, his beard. *When was the last time he trimmed his beard?* And I ask myself what would I do if I saw this man walking up to me on a street. Would I just keep walking?

And just the act of asking the question alters the nature of our relationship. I can't look at him anymore.

"I'll loan you something, Lyle. If you're short."

"That's very kind of you, Nick." His mouth is shuddering. His whole body is shuddering. "If it's not a problem, I could use, say, five dollars? For the cab?"

I'm so relieved I spin around, I scan the room for my wallet, and it takes me half a minute to find it, and why should it take so long when it's sitting there right there at the end of the coffee table? I yank it open, I fumble through the bill compartment, and the whole time Lyle's voice circles me, ventilating the room.

"Maybe six would be best," he's saying. "With the zone system. You know, I can never figure out that system; it keeps changing on me. I have yet to meet anyone who can explain it...."

Three 20s and two singles: my entire cash supply. And how much of it goes to Lyle? I gently tug on one of the twenties, draw it out of its chamber, and then I tug the second one into alignment. And then my finger reaches for the third 20, but it hesitates, draws back. And a voice inside me snarls: *Go on, Nick. Give it up.*

And when it comes, it comes as pure sound. A splintering, heaving, dying crash. Such an imposing sound that I'm still listening to it a minute later—still listening and only dimly aware that the light has gone out—and I'm pitched face forward on the floor of my apartment, and my head is disintegrating, melting onto the floorboards around me. And now the light is starting to come back on—it's never been off—and my head is firing off explosions, one after the other. They're radiating from the back of my neck through my eye sockets; they're laying a trail of fire across my temples. My eyes snap shut, and even so, the light gets through, and each particle of light calls out a new pain.

Slowly my eyes open again, and the world comes back in increments. I see a large rose shard, shaped like a teepee, with black markings on it, and next to it there's another shard, slightly larger, attached to a pink squiggle of pipe cleaner. Behind it and surrounding it, more shards, a plain of pink rubble. I'm trying to reassemble the shards in my mind, and suddenly they form a picture, and a great bubble of laughter bursts from my stomach. It shakes me so hard I'm moaning.

Joe! Your piggy bank hurts like a motherfucker.

I've made it onto my knees now, but standing is a whole new adventure—it's a mountain climb. My lungs aren't used to the altitude, and neither is my head. I thrust out an arm, and by some miracle, it finds a segment of wall. And from the wall, it's only a few yards to the door. And getting to the door is like learning to walk again. Big tottering steps, like a baby raptor, and it seems to me I'm actually *un*learning how to walk, even though my brain is at last swimming into focus. I can make out the sectors of my terrain. I can separate the floor from the door and the lamp from...from my wallet, spread-eagled a few feet from the couch. I can fix the wallet in my viewfinder, I can pick out the empty tiers where my credit cards used to be, peer into the gaping billfold.

I can look down and find, pinioned in the fingers of my right hand, three $20 bills.

I suppose it's a measure of my lucidity that as I inch through my front door and down the darkened stairwell, I'm calculating Lyle's take. If he'd done it my way, he'd have $60. His way, he gets two dollars and access to a couple of maxed-out credit cards, no longer operational once

I get to a phone...I do have to get to a phone...I need to call the credit card people and the driver's license people and probably...probably the library card people too; he may have taken my library card.

Inside my head tiny cannons go off in close sequence, and from the distance of the first-floor landing, the front door looks impossibly heavy. But I find that when I abandon the comfort of the stair rail, my body charges ahead of its own accord, and the momentum is enough to force the door open, and what do you know? I'm standing outside my building, in the blinking daylight. The sun is blazing in my hair. Every pore and nerve is blazing, and I'm suddenly aware of my *surface*, the warm air on my face, the prickling mound on the top of my head swelling upward like a condominium.

I dab at the condo, gently, I brush it with my fingers. Its only response is a slow caress, warm and viscous, and when I pull my hand away, it comes back a new color: a thin wash of red. And gradually the sensation of red duplicates itself everywhere—across the back of my head, down my ears and neck. I pass a hand across my face, and that comes back red too, and it's hard to avoid the conclusion that I've been split open. And it should be shocking, seeing how much of me is being lost, but I'm quite clinical about it. *Of course*, I'm thinking. *Head wounds bleed freely. I fell off my bike once, and I thought I'd never stop bleeding.*

I'm very proud of my clarity. I would like the world to see just how clearheaded I am. Here I go: one step, two steps. I know exactly where I'm going—down the steps, into the front courtyard. Nice day...hard to believe it's December...just got back from a tree farm in Loudoun County, sweating like you wouldn't believe….

And then things get a little less clear because the sky drops a large white moon in front of me, and the moon turns out to be a face: a face with a walrus mustache and two small pink eyes. It looks, for all the world, like Joe's piggy bank, healed, restored, and I reach for it, but it sprouts a mouth.

"Oh, fuck," says my landlord. "Oh, Christ."

Now this is something I hadn't considered: the effect of my appearance on others. It was thoughtless of me. An apology forms on my lips, but the face isn't there anymore. I spin around to find it, but I spin too quickly, and the courtyard spins faster. For a few seconds I'm caught in the whirl, and I fully expect it to take me somewhere, but all it does is drop me onto all fours like a golden retriever. I can't tell you how much better this is. I take a couple of practice crawls, and before you know it I'm crawling like a pro. Not in a circle either, a genuine straight line, and at the end of this line is a new apparition: tall, saucer-eyed. It has Joe Bryant's head and Joe Bryant's neck, and it is in general more solid than you expect apparitions to be. I crawl toward it, and pretty soon the apparition starts moving to me, cutting the distance. Very kind. It even lowers itself to my level so that when my body finally gives out, there's a lap waiting for me.

"Sir!"

It doesn't particularly sound like Joe, but it's hard to hear because there's so much movement going on. There's a light cotton sweater, for instance, which is being whipped off and bundled and placed under my head. And there's this voice, which could be Joe's, and it's asking something, which I'm about to answer until I realize I'm not the one being asked.

"Excuse me! Sir? Do you have any hydrogen peroxide or anything?"

And then, from far off, like a cowbell, comes the voice of my landlord. "Neosporin."

So he's lucid too! A happy day.

"OK, good," says the voice over my head. "That's good. And maybe a towel would be nice. And some warm water."

It has to be Joe Bryant's voice. Something's just twisting it out of its natural register.

"And sir?" he yells. "If you could maybe call an ambulance too."

I'm already laughing: I know what's coming next. I'm almost mouthing the words as they come out.

"Remind me," says my landlord. "The number."

"First digit is 9," Joe says.

"9..."

"And then the rest is easy. It's 1-1."

"1-1. 9-1-1."

And he must actually be gone because I don't hear him anymore. There's nothing to listen to except my heartbeat, which sounds sluggish and peeved, as though it's being poked out of sleep. But I don't have to listen; I can do other things. I can smell Joe Bryant, for instance. He smells like grass and loam and peaches. Clementines.

He leans his head over mine, squinting back juice. I hear myself say, "Sorry."

"Sorry—why?"

"I'm getting your sweater dirty."

"Bloody" is what I meant to say. *Bloody.*

"It's yours anyway," Joe says.

"Oh." I press one of my hands to my forehead. "I thought when you..."

"I thought so too," he says. "But I found this last week, propping up my TV stand."

"The TV stand."

"And you know, it always fit me better."

"Probably."

My legs have stretched themselves to their full length. My arms are floating on the courtyard bricks. I'm sailing across this courtyard; I'm sailing onto the shores of Joe Bryant. What a long trip it's been!

And the sun is caking the blood on my hands and on my face, and my mouth is beginning to find new language. There's something I want to tell Joe.

"Maybe you should rest, Snookie."

"No, I am. Could you talk? Could you do that?"

"What about?"

"I don't know."

When he starts speaking, there's a little tremor he has to get rid of. It's gone very quickly.

"OK, once there was a little boy named Snookie. Snookie *Pie* was the full name."

I close my eyes, but Joe tugs them open again.

"And one day he was walking through a forest, and he met a boy named Skunkie. And he said, 'Skunkie, you sure do stink.' And Skunkie said, 'Yes, but I got redeemin' points.' And before you know it, they were living together in Snookie's tree."

"It's a tree?"

"Shut up. Big ol' cottonwood tree. And whenever it was kind of blowy, gusty, Snookie and Skunkie would hop on one of those, one of those cotton puffs that comes off the tree, and they'd go sailin'—for miles they'd go. And they were havin' such a good time with their cool little cotton thingies, they figured, what else do we need? Carpe, you know, diem, caveat emptor."

He's speaking Latin. It's so touching.

"Qué sera sera," I say.

"Those were the very words that Snookie and Skunkie uttered. Did I tell you this story?"

"No."

"Now don't get me wrong. Snookie and Skunkie got plans, all right. *Big* plans. They just don't know what they are yet."

"Yeah, can I go to sleep?"

"Not yet, Snooks." He sweeps a hand across my brow. "Not your bedtime."

"OK."

From somewhere behind us a siren starts doing scales. Maybe it's my ambulance—it's always hard to be sure in the city. And you can't know how close it is because the Doppler effect comes into play, doesn't it? The closer the sound, the higher the pitch. And when it's right on top of you, that's when it sounds highest of all. But the pitch has never really changed, not in an absolute sense; it's just a trick of perspective.

I lie in Joe Bryant's lap, perfectly happy, watching the sun go away. About two minutes before the ambulance comes, I remember what it was I wanted to tell him. I grab him by the collar of his T-shirt, haul myself up until my face is level with his. I speak very slowly and distinctly because I don't trust myself to get it right.

"We need a new piggy bank."

The Holy Peach Tree of Texas

twenty

In the triage room of George Washington University Medical Center, my mother, Hoy Phong and Joe stand just inside the plastic curtain, watching a doctor stitch up my head. Mom is taking extraordinary pains to control herself, but something has to give, and it gives just as the doctor is pulling through the last length of suture.

"Do you see what happens?" she cries.

The doctor glances up; 20 feet away, a man in a wrist cast jerks his head around.

"Do you see what happens when you insist on living in the city?"

Even now, with my scalp anesthetized, I can see that having stitches frees me from the need to explain. And so as they stack the bandages onto the shaved section of my head, I close my eyes and tune into the sounds around me: a man in the next stall, retching; a young woman whispering into her grandmother's ear; the treble voice of a child. I find myself oddly luxuriating in our fellowship. I think we must have veered off course so we could intersect here.

"Do you think Hoy would live in the city?" my mother asks. "He knows better."

Joe is supposed to wake me up every two hours to make sure I'm OK. Each time he does it, I have the sensation of falling out of a dream into a deeper dream. I can barely make out his face, and I have to take it for granted that it's really him. Ten o'clock, midnight, 2:00: he's very punctual, and by the time 4:00 comes around, I have come to expect it; I'm drifting back to sleep almost from the moment he wakes me. And then I feel his hand: sliding down my chest, pausing briefly at the nipple, tugging at the waistband of my briefs.

I protest, feebly. "I can't move...."

"Don't worry," he whispers. "You won't have to do a thing."

The shiners stay on my face for a couple of weeks, and they are something to behold: large inky pools spilling out from each eye. My officemates come up with the usual nicknames—Raccoon Boy, Panda Man—but to my mind, I most closely resemble an allegorical figure. I'm pretty sure Hogarth could have used me. Poverty. Licentiousness. Hunger. Any of those would work.

At Joe's urging I file a report with the local police. The woman I talk to has a glossy face, and she's chewing on a large wad of gum, which means I have to ask her to repeat herself. She responds by slowing her speech to a crawl.

"Did. You. Get. A. Clear. Look."

"No, I heard that part."

"At. The. Perpetrator."

"No," I say. "The room was too dark."

Sometimes, at night, I get a twinge thinking about Lyle. It's always the same scenario: He's trying to use one of my credit cards—at an airport or a menswear store. Alarms shatter the air; iron bars crash down. Lyle whirls and claws the air as armor-plated police squads bear down on him. It's already too late to warn him. I hope they'll be gentle.

Natasha never does makes it to the Broomes for Christmas dinner, but it's a fuller house than usual. All the siblings are here, of course, and

Sally. Plus Larry and Joe and Hoy and Hoy's new girlfriend, Liesl, a grinning, beet-haired girl who holds down a half-time job at the Hair Cuttery. She has wrapped a rather small sweater around quite remarkably large breasts, and now and then Hoy forgets what he's doing and stares into her cleavage. At these moments his face takes on a look of rapturous shock, which endears him to me a little.

It's good. It's good having new people for Christmas. If nothing else, they alert you to your family's essential and undying strangeness. When Joe, for instance, starts cutting up tomatoes for the salad, I watch my mother skid to a halt on the kitchen tile, I hear the little pocket of air escaping from her throat, and it's like watching it for the first time.

"Joe," says my mother, "I'm sorry, I didn't tell you. That's not the tomato knife."

"Oh, it's OK, Mrs. B. This one's working fine."

"No." Very quiet, very firm. "That's the onion knife. And the cutting board you're using is the poultry board. It's my fault, I didn't tell you."

Something similar happens when Liesl volunteers to help my father with the dishes. He tolerates the company at first, but before long, the threat of new ideas becomes too much for him.

"You know, Liesl, the Dobie cloth is really better for that. Oh, there's a spot there, see? Dishwasher doesn't get that. Let me take just one more pass at that spoon."

My father believes in cleaning every dish and piece of cutlery before it ever reaches the dishwasher. Usually, the only way to expedite the process is to wait until he goes out for a smoke and then shove as many dishes into the machine as you can. But this year we're stymied because my father, without any fanfare, has decided to stop smoking. He is making do with nicotine patches and with straws, which he chews whenever he gets cravings and then absent-mindedly spits out. You find his droppings scattered all around the house in places you least expect to find them—medicine cabinets, the undersides of rugs. They have the persistence of a religion.

That evening as I'm getting ready to leave, my father pulls me aside. He takes a small, gift-wrapped package from his pants pocket and silently hands it to me. The wrapping comes off very quickly in my hands—I get the feeling it wasn't even taped—and inside is a tiny wooden figurine: a single, pea-sized knob resting on top of a large, rounded snowman torso. It takes me a few seconds of staring before I recognize it as the piece of wood my father was whittling last spring at Rehoboth, the same one he was showing to Larry a couple of months ago. By now it's probably a sixth of its original size.

"I figured if I didn't stop, there wouldn't be anything left," he says.

"Oh, thanks, Dad. It's nice."

And then he says, "If anyone can make sense of it, it's you."

He's silent for a few seconds, and suddenly he's very loud—he's laughing hard enough to rattle china. "I'm a terrible artist!" he cries.

The figurine ends up on the mantel over my gas fireplace. I make a point of looking at it every day, sometimes first thing in the morning. I'm not sure I'll ever make sense of it, no matter what Dad says, but I *am* able to project things onto it: children, of course; cartoon animals. I get my best results, though, when I treat it abstractly, and then it looks either lost or, depending on the light, found.

Next to it sits the new piggy bank Joe got me for Christmas. This is a wooden model, with no tail to speak of and strange swaths of purple mascara under its eyes. More than once Joe has offered to bolt it down—just in case.

Two days after Christmas I get a postcard from Nattie.

> *Nick. Happy holidays, and don't let my brother pull any shit with you. Tell him I remember what he did in the Piggly Wiggly, and I will tell unless he shapes up. I am now dating, believe it, and am exploring the old-fashioned form of conception—luck! Ha! Nattie.*

The night after I get her card, I dream that Joe Bryant has converted to Islam. He walks around the apartment with a small smile and a blond cowled robe and a paperback copy of the Koran. He won't pick up after himself, he won't answer when I call him, and after a while, I get so frustrated I grab him by the shoulders and give him a shake. "What's *wrong* with you?"

"I'm getting ready to leave," he says, "this very minute."

His lips don't move; he must be speaking directly from his larynx. I ask him why he wants to leave, and he pauses as though he's not sure I have security clearance.

"Allah has asked me to find the Holy Peach Tree of Texas," he says.

The scene dissolves quickly to Meridian Hill, right after a winter rain. All the walkways have vanished; there's nothing but dog tracks and potholes. Joe stands in the middle of the lawn with his arms wide open, waiting for the next available wind.

"I can't believe it," I say. "You're leaving me for a peach tree."

And then he shrugs and gives me his goofiest smile. "Come on, Snooks! It's Allah's will."

When the dream's over I do something I don't normally do. I wake Joe up to tell him about it. He listens with his eyes half-shut, and then he paws at my cheek.

"Texas," he mutters.

"What?"

"Don't think...peach trees..."

I know that, of course. I *know* Texas is not a big state for peach trees, but other states have them. Georgia, Florida. Virginia has them. There are peach trees everywhere, state after state, and chances are good there's a holy one somewhere, so what does it matter about Texas?

It must be a function of living together because Joe answers as though I've been talking out loud the whole time.

"Don't even like peaches," he says. "Too hairy."

On New Year's Day, Celia discovers that the restaurant once devoted to the Duchess of Windsor's memory has closed its doors indefinitely. The phone has been disconnected, the operator has no other listing, and Celia stands helpless in my parents' foyer with the cordless phone drooping in her hand.

"Where now?" she asks.

She means: Where are the Broome siblings going to have their annual lunch? It's really quite strange, because none of us (with the possible exception of Greg) has ever looked forward to this lunch—it became a ritual before we could stop it—and yet now that it's in danger of not happening, we're getting nervous.

"That can't be right," Greg says.

"They did such good business," Celia whines.

"We would've *heard*," I say. "We would've seen it on the news."

In the end, after much wavering, we settle on a Vietnamese restaurant off Wilson Boulevard in Arlington. Celia went there three years ago, and she remembers it as an elegant, mirrored room where the waitresses have ankle-length silk dresses and long, lacquered fingernails. This is, not surprisingly, the exact opposite of the place we find: a small, drafty room with cheap wainscoting and paper place mats and walls of mint stucco, laid on like meringue. A worried-looking woman in an untucked tuxedo shirt shouts to us from the kitchen door and points to the table nearest the bathroom.

"You sit!" she yells.

It's 10 minutes before a waiter approaches, which is just as well because we need a little time to adjust to our new surroundings: the coffered ceiling tile, the red-orange chopsticks, the smell of vinegar. We wriggle in our chairs, inspect the water glasses, and stare at the suspended globes of light in their woven cane baskets. I don't know whether we're appraising the place or being appraised by it.

I will say this though: The Broomes' annual lunch goes down easier than it used to. It helps, I suppose, that we order glasses of Singha beer and that Greg unconsciously mimics our grandfather by tucking his napkin into his sweater and that, for once, we have things to talk about. Greg, for instance, is stepping down from his current management position, which will subtract $10,000 from his salary and add 15 years to his life. Celia is getting a promotion, and Larry's dental practice is thriving. Hoy is doing quite well as receptionist although he has the bad habit of cruising female patients.

Even I have things to talk about. There's Joe Bryant, for instance, who has sprouted a white collar—he's become the reluctant office manager to a furniture supplier. And there's me too. After seven years I'm back in the job hunt: I'm looking for anything that doesn't involve the nation's business. And our apartment search is gathering steam—we've confined ourselves for now to the Hill, but we've reserved the right to swerve northwest.

Of course, the one subject I can't raise is the one that's still grafted in my brain.

Do you remember, guys?

I was supposed to be a father. I told you last year I was going to conceive a child. And it was supposed to happen by now, and it didn't. And I'd be more depressed than I already am if I thought either of you were keeping track. But I'm not sure you ever took me seriously enough to bother, and that's even more depressing in a way, and it makes me wish you *would* bring up the subject because it isn't the failures that kick the shit out of you, it's the failures no one talks about.

My brother, my sister, look how easily a dream dies! A year ago, I wanted a child; today I settle for the statistical possibility of a child. I tell myself that Greg and Sally are still in reproductive range, and Celia and Larry might someday make little vampires, and even Joe and I could get our act together, assuming Joe sticks around, and *anything* is possible, but is it plausible? Life wants to happen, but does it want to happen to us? Isn't it just as likely that the Broomes will still be meeting like this 20, 40, 50 years from now? The restaurants may change, but we won't—not in any outward way—and over time perhaps we'll take pride in the stability of our circumstances. We'll suppress the tiniest contractions of regret, crawl deeper into our caves.

And I can live with that.

That's the funny part. Today I can live with that—and a lot of other things. And they seem even a small price to pay for a Singha beer, a plate of five-spices pork, and the company of my brother and sister. Is it the new year? Is that what makes everything look freshly molded? Each of the people, each of the objects in this restaurant is exactly what it is, and when I turn halfway through the meal and find a 9-month-old girl staring back at me, I'm thrilled to see that she doesn't represent anything but herself. She has a grave, still, ancient face with Cupid's-bow lips and eyes of an indeterminate color—blue, maybe, passing into brown. She looks dazed, just roused from a nap maybe. Her hands move constantly, the fingers working independently of each other, searching for attachment points. She's only a few minutes into the meal, and the floor around her high chair is littered with Cheerios, a shredded napkin and place mat, a couple of chopsticks. Her blue bib towel is smeared with what looks to be lemongrass chicken.

Watching her, I feel my own appetite draining away, and I barely notice its absence. I watch the mother place a small cube of tofu in the young girl's hand. I watch the girl meditate over it for a few moments and then squeeze it hard enough to make a diamond out of it.

"Maybe it's early for the tofu," her mother tells her. She speaks very easily, matter-of-factly—they could be two girlfriends grabbing a workday lunch. "Maybe it's Cheerio time. Is it Cheerio time, Deborah?"

She takes a spill-proof container from her lap and pours a small mound of cereal into her daughter's flat palm. Deborah contemplates the food and then in an abrupt motion slaps it into her mouth. Her eyes take on a faraway cast as she chews: She seems to be reminiscing about herself. From the other side of the table comes the swift-running brook of her mother's conversation. "Done already, what an oink. OK, *two* more Cheerios because you took your nap. That's it—no more. Whoops, nice chin, let me wipe that for you. Very pretty."

And just as her mother reaches out to dab her face, Deborah sweeps her hand across the table, clearing everything in her path. Fortunately, there's nothing left to clear but her knife, which lands with a bright clatter next to my chair. Without a word, I grab it off the floor and return it to the table. Deborah's mother mouths a thank-you, and I nod back, and just as I'm pulling away, Deborah shoots out one of her hands and grabs my index finger.

Amazing how strong her grip is. She's holding on for dear life, and the only thing that keeps her from holding any tighter is the coat of saliva on her skin.

For a few seconds I freeze. I have absolutely no idea what to do. Do I let her keep the finger? Do I remove it, maybe with a little reprimand? What do parents do in these moments?

And then behind me I hear the most startling words come out of Greg's mouth. "Baby want a Nicky finger?"

And when I turn I find my brother actually leaning toward me, staring over my shoulder with greedy eyes. And then I see Celia, stretching her arm across the table, making the third link in our chain.

"Finger yummy," she coos.

And before long we've forgotten about English, and the air fills with nonsense syllables. *Ga ga goo ga. Hoomba humba. Tofu too too.* Even the mother abandons her worldly language and speaks in fragments: *Wittle wit wit. Wittle wit wit.* And Deborah in her high chair, presides over us, organizes our sound into chords. Her fists keep the beat, and her face opens into a small, secret smile. She is well pleased.